Palindor

D. R. EVANS

CHARIOT
FAMILY PUBLISHING

The Realm of
Palindor

GREAT SEA

Penmichael
Brea

Carn Toldwyn

Sunset
Islands

Perendeth

Machrenmoor

Beleron

N
W   E
S

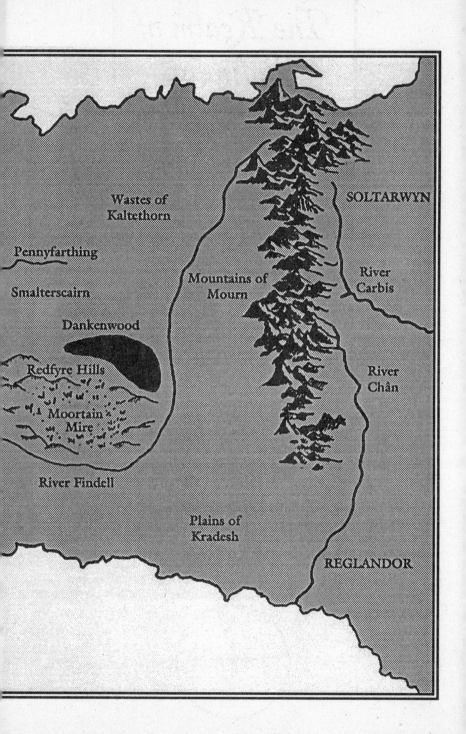

Chariot Family Publishing is a division of David C. Cook Publishing Co.
David C. Cook Publishing Co., Elgin, Illinois, 60120
David C. Cook Publishing Co., Weston, Ontario
Nova Distribution, Ltd., Newton Abbot, England

PALINDOR

Library of Congress Cataloging-in-Publication Data
Evans, D.R.
        Palindor/D.R. Evans.
        p.   cm.
Summary: While in the hospital after a serious car accident, a young girl is
visited by a mysterious figure who sends her on a quest to the ancient
kingdom of Palindor, where she plays a crucial role in the battle between the
forces of good and evil.
        ISBN 0-7814-0117-8
[1. Fantasy.]   I. Title
PZ7.E8745Pa1   1993
[Fic]—dc20   93-20220
                                                         CIP
                                                         AC

INTRODUCTION

MAJOR RACES OF PALINDOR
(Only the races important to our story are described here)

Dwarves

Originally underground dwellers, most of them now live above ground. Slightly taller than gnomes, somewhat shorter than humans, dwarves are the strongest and most belligerent fighters in Palindor. The pride of each dwarf is his (or her) battle-ax. Even though Palindor has been at peace for a long time, each dwarf still maintains his ax ready for use. The female dwarves are only slightly less strong than the males, and either would make short work of a human in combat.

Elves

There are many different types of elf, but only wood elves feature in our story. Wood elves are slightly shorter than gnomes, but are considerably leaner and more spry. They are sociable amongst others of their own kind, but considerably less so with other elves, and almost never interact with nonelf races. They live in the forest that covers much of Palindor, many of them in the town of Smalterscairn.

Goblins

A race of creatures that live underground and are rarely seen on the surface. Goblins can be quite startling at first sight, although most aboveground creatures go through their entire lives without seeing one. Goblins are distinguished by long, pointed noses and ears, large eyes, and dull green-black skin. Other races tell stories about goblins to scare their children, but there is nothing intrinsically evil about goblins—they merely care little for doings on the surface. It is rumored that the treasure of the goblins far exceeds that of all other races in Palindor.

Gnomes

The most bookish of the Palindoric races. Not of much use in battle, gnomes are slightly shorter than dwarves, but unlike the latter, who always go clean-shaven, male gnomes almost always grow long white beards. In the past, particularly intelligent and studious gnomes took an oath at a young age to become Holy Gnomes, the keepers of the ancient books.

Humans

The tallest of the common races in Palindor. In the earliest days of Palindor, the humans often led the other races in battle; and so in ancient times it was decreed that only a human could be king or queen.

Hunters

Not really a distinct race, the Hunters are humans who live in the forests. They are especially tall and strong, with keen senses. They are rarely seen, preferring to live solitary lives, but their skill with their longbows is unmatched in Palindor. They are sworn to come to the aid of the reigning monarch in times of need.

Wizards

A race not unlike humans in appearance and gnomes in inclination. They can command magic, but only of the common kind. No mortal race has power to control the kiríal[†]

Wizards vary widely in their prowess, depending on their individual talents and the length and depth of their studies.

[†]A Palindoric word with no good translation. Kiríal is the set of fundamental spiritual realities that underlies the Three Lands of Abuscân: Soltarwyn, Reglandor, and Palindor. (Palindor is the westernmost of the Three Lands.)

MAJOR CHARACTERS

Aramis
A Hunter who desires to protect Palindor from the evil of Malthazzar.

Catherine
The first High Queen of Palindor. A child from the world of humans whose task it is to save Palindor.

Cerebeth
A human, the Queen of Palindor, who has reigned for a thousand years at the time of our tale.

Drefynt
A Holy Gnome, particularly knowledgeable about the old times.

Entelred
The greatest living wizard in Palindor.

Gondalwyn
A dwarf, apprenticed to Entelred to become a wizard.

Harsforn
A great healer who lives with the seer Iadron.

Iadron
A seer who lives with Harsforn in a remote house in the Moortain Mire.

Malthazzar
The Lord of Evil. Banished from the realm of Olvensar, Malthazzar intends to take his revenge by subjugating Palindor under his own rule.
Olvensar
The High Lord of Palindor; at the start of our tale, it is long since he was last seen in that land.

Tarandron
A good, honest dwarf who does not always believe what he is told.

Trondwyth
An unusually practical Holy Gnome.

1

THE ACCIDENT

atrin Taylor was a week past her fifteenth birthday when the adventure began. She was tall, with long, dark hair that flowed around her shoulders, and dark eyes. She was a girl of strong opinions, was more than a little rebellious, and possessed a quick mind. It was a foregone conclusion that Katrin's name would be at the top of every list of test results—a fact that might have made her unpopular with her classmates, were it not for her mischievous smile and considerable athletic ability.

But schoolmates' opinions could be put aside, for it was summer vacation. The newfound freedom of the days in late May had become the long, torpid weeks of midsummer boredom. And to make the boredom worse, Katrin's best friend, Jane Newman, had moved away at the beginning of the vacation and now lived fifteen miles from Dayville.

Jane's parents had sold their tract home in a neighboring subdivision and moved to a house on ten acres in the country. Katrin and Jane, previously inseparable, now found themselves unable to see one another without careful planning and the explicit consent of parents, who were needed to drive one or the other of the girls to her friend's house. Next summer, the girls liked to remind one another, they would have learner's permits and no longer be dependent on others for transportation.

Katrin's was a pleasant family house toward the edge of Dayville, neither too large nor too small, and filled with a love that only occasionally felt stifling. While her home might have been more convenient for shops, church, and other amenities of the town, Jane's was closer to horses, streams, woods, and open fields—all the things that really mattered.

For several weeks, Jane and Katrin had been needling their parents to let them backpack and camp in the Springfield Hills, a long chain of forested and chiefly unpopulated hills that spread nearly fifty miles north and south from the Jane's house. Mr. and Mrs. Newman had eventually and with obvious reluctance given their permission, "providing it's all right with Katrin's parents."

But it was not all right with Katrin's parents. At least once a day for the past two weeks she had asked them, but always the same answer came back: a firm, unyielding no. As the days passed, Katrin became more and more sullen, until eventually her father proposed a compromise.

"Look, we just can't have you and Jane going out camping by yourselves in the hills. But if Jane will put up with you, how about if you go and stay with her for a week? You can go exploring during the day and camp out on the Newmans' property at night."

At first Katrin had been reluctant to accept, but at last she realized that it was the most she was likely to be offered. The girls agreed to the plan.

And so the day for the start of the trip had arrived. The

sun shone out of a clear blue sky and the thermometer rose steadily from its early morning 70° F to stand at 85° F by midmorning. By ten-thirty Katrin's backpack was filled with food and clothes and flung carelessly into the back of the Taylors' station wagon.

Shortly after eleven they arrived at the Newmans' sprawling property. Mrs. Taylor embraced Katrin and gave her an embarrassing peck on the cheek. "Take care of yourself, dear," she reminded her daughter for the hundredth time.

Katrin's gaze went heavenward. "Yes, Mom." She left the women to their coffee and conversation and went to find Jane, who was riding her horse in the meadow.

When the girls came in an hour later, flushed and breathless, Katrin's mother had gone. Mrs. Newman prepared a salad as the two friends discussed their plans for the coming week.

She set the heaped plates down on the table. "Katrin, you're looking very pale. And you've been letting Jane do all the talking." She smiled at Katrin. "Are you sure you feel all right?"

The reply was several seconds in coming. Katrin looked up at Jane's mother, then at the salad piled high on her plate. "I don't know." Then, in a single, hurried motion, she covered her mouth with her hand and raced for the bathroom.

She returned three minutes later, her face dotted with sweat and her steps unsteady. Reaching the table, she leaned against a chair for support. "Sorry about that," she said weakly. Then her legs promptly folded under her.

Katrin felt herself being moved and then lowered onto a couch. "What do you think, Mom?" she heard Jane ask.

"I don't know what to think. But you two certainly

aren't going anywhere with Katrin like this. Give Katrin's mother a call, will you, and I'll take her temperature."

Katrin opened her eyes and found herself in the living room, bright sunlight streaming into the room through French windows. She spoke weakly. "Do you think you could close the drapes?"

"Oh, of course." Jane's mother stepped across the room, and the heavy drapes swished almost noiselessly across the windows and darkened the room.

She came back to Katrin and slipped a thermometer between her lips. It seemed to take an age before there was a beeping sound. Jane's mother removed the thermometer. "A hundred and two."

Jane entered the room. "I told her mother. She wants to talk to you." Together, mother and daughter returned to the kitchen.

Katrin lay back, suddenly exhausted, the distant sound of conversation passing meaninglessly over her head. By the time they returned, she was asleep.

She slept fitfully all afternoon, finally awaking at nearly five o'clock.

Mrs. Newman came in with a glass of juice and the thermometer. She took Katrin's temperature and pronounced, "Ninety-nine. Much better. How are you feeling?"

Katrin paused while she took stock. "Weak, but a lot better."

"Your mother's coming over to fetch you. You can come back again tomorrow if you're feeling up to it, but we both think it's best for you to go home this evening."

Normally Katrin would have protested, but she had no energy for a fight. Besides, she really didn't feel like camping out. She sat up on the couch and drank the juice gratefully.

Jane began to talk again about the hills and the exploring that they would do as soon as Katrin felt better, but Katrin found it impossible to concentrate on her friend's torrent of words. Even the effort of an occasional nod of encouragement took too much effort. All she wanted to do was to lie down and go to sleep once more.

The doorbell rang, and Mrs. Newman left, returning moments later with Katrin's mother.

"Hello, darling. I'm awfully sorry you're feeling this way. Do you think you can make it to the car?"

"I'll try," replied Katrin. She finished the juice as her mother came to her side and helped her stand. The room swung unsteadily for a moment, but then became stable. "I'll be okay."

"Good. Just hold my hand, and we'll get you to the car."

Katrin and her mother made their way through the house and out to the car in the driveway, followed by Jane and her mother.

"Front seat or back?" Mrs. Taylor asked.

"I'm really tired, Mom," said Katrin. "Maybe I'd better lie down in the back."

"Okay," said Mrs. Taylor. "We won't be able to strap you in, but I'll drive carefully. I'm sure we'll be all right."

With some help from her mother and Mrs. Newman, Katrin maneuvered herself so that she was lying on the backseat. Vaguely she heard the sounds of good-byes being said and then felt the comforting throb as the engine started. The car was not a hundred yards down the road before she was asleep.

The journey between the two houses was nearly half over when Mrs. Taylor approached the narrow bridge over the river. Over the bridge came a car traveling toward her, moving slowly, on the opposite side of the road. Suddenly, out of nowhere, a car appeared from behind that car, moving out onto Mrs. Taylor's side of the road, trying to overtake the slower moving vehicle.

There was no time to think. Instinctively, Katrin's mother swung the wheel to one side, simultaneously pressing her foot down hard on the brake. The car spun and slipped off the road, bumping down the steep bank that led down toward the river. The car hit a tree and then a boulder, and Katrin and her mother were thrown first this way and then that. Still slipping, the car reached the very edge of the bank, the river running three feet below it. The car hesitated for only a fraction of a second as the wheels on the left side hung over the edge of the bank; then it toppled over on one side and splashed into the water.

The first rescuer was the driver of a passing car. He dived into the stream and, after two unsuccessful attempts, forced Mrs. Taylor's door open, pulled her free of her seat belt, and brought her to the surface. But he could not see far in the dirty water and didn't know that there was a second occupant in the car. Precious minutes passed before Mrs. Taylor regained consciousness and spoke her first words: "Where's Katrin?"

Her savior immediately realized the meaning behind her words and dived straight back into the swirling waters.

No one knew how long Katrin was without air, but the best guess was about eight minutes. The doctors were sure that her head was struck by the metal of the side of the car as the car rammed into the boulder before slipping into the murky waters of the rapidly moving river. Katrin's head had been thrust deep into the crack between the seat and its back. Air was unable to filter its way through the plastic of the rear seat as she lay, helpless and unconscious, while the water level rose in the car.

The doctors explained to Mr. and Mrs. Taylor that their daughter had sustained a serious head injury. That in itself might not have greatly affected their child. But she had been deprived of life-giving oxygen for at least several minutes. She had been brought in to the hospital, her body functions apparently intact, no broken bones apart from a fractured skull, but the electrical activity in her brain depressingly low.

After two weeks in a coma, a recording of the electrical activity in Katrin's brain was sent to a specialist in a nearby city hospital. It was his professional opinion that Katrin's brain activity was sufficiently impaired that she would never regain consciousness and, in the unlikely event that she did, there was no chance that she would ever be more than a vegetable, responding to only the most basic stimuli. Her centers of high-level thought displayed no activity whatsoever; she would never recognize friends or relatives, never speak, never walk again.

From a purely physical point of view, he informed her parents, Katrin was still alive and her body was fully functional; as long as they provided food through a hospital feeding tube and removed the wastes from her body, she would stay alive until some organ failed, probably many decades hence. But, for all practical purposes, their daughter was dead, and they should not permit themselves to hope that that prognosis would ever change.

At first, Katrin's parents could not accept what they were told. Every day they prayed and hoped desperately for a change. But days went by, and then weeks. Eventually three months had passed, and Katrin was in exactly the same state as she had been when she was first wheeled into the hospital, except that the bone in her skull which had been fractured in the accident was now almost completely healed. Mr. and Mrs. Taylor began to lose hope.

Then came the day when the doctor in charge of Katrin's care called them into his office and presented a shocking proposal to them.

"You must understand that the decision is yours. I would not exert any pressure over you, even if I could. But I feel that in order to fulfill my professional duty, I must point out the option to you. It is the opinion of all the specialists who have examined Katrin's case that it is impossible that there will ever be a change in her mental condition. As such, I think that you must consider the possibility of authorizing the hospital to remove the feeding tube."

Katrin's parents looked at one another, shock covering their faces. Mr. Taylor spoke. "You mean, let her die?"

The doctor nodded. "As I say, the decision is entirely yours. But I do think that you ought to consider it. I certainly would not advocate any hasty decision. It has only been three months. But I want to mention it as a possibility so that after, say, a year or so, if there is no change, you might want to think about it some more."

While they talked in the doctor's office, three floors higher in Katrin's room a strange thing was happening. A ripple passed through the room; a ripple as if one were observing not the hospital room itself but, rather, a reflection of the room in a pool. As if someone had dropped a pebble into the "pool" some distance away, a single ripple crossed the room, from window to door. As the ripple left it, the room was different in two ways. The second hand of the clock on the wall opposite Katrin's bed had ceased to move, and Katrin was no longer the only occupant of the room. Over near the closed door, as if he had entered by that way, although in fact the door had remained closed, an old man stood and looked in the direction of Katrin's bed.

The man carried a stick which looked even older than the man himself and, with the aid of the stick, he walked slowly towards the bed. It was hard to say just how old the man might be. Everything about him seemed indeterminately ancient. Even his clothes, which once might have been a cheery green, now appeared faded and not a little dirty, as if he had spent a hundred years working in full sun in a garden somewhere. His hair was gray-white and covered the top of his head. His face was hidden behind a full gray beard, which was long and unkempt. His eyes, however, were startlingly bright and alive for one so old.

The man's gait as he walked toward the bed was not so much infirm as slow and measured. Indeed, if one ignored the looks of the man and watched only the way in which he walked, one might conclude that this was a man of such supreme confidence and power that he knew nothing of importance could ever happen at a place until such time as he arrived there; therefore, he was never in a hurry to get anywhere.

Step by step he moved nearer the bed, although the clock on the wall betrayed that each slow step took no time at all. Eventually he was standing by Katrin's side. He could easily have stretched out his hand and touched her, but he did not do so. Instead he simply stared into her face. While the clock maintained its steadfast stillness, he looked at the face of the young woman, behind which the mind no longer functioned. His eyes betrayed no expression, although their twinkle seemed subdued.

At length he stretched out his hand toward Katrin. Her hands were above the bedclothes, in view. As his hand touched hers, the man spoke in a voice which seemed older than the earth itself, and yet that seemed to have seeds of new life sprinkled in the words.

"Come, my child," he said. "It is time."

A second ripple passed through the room, as silently and as unnoticed as the first. As it passed, the second hand on the clock on the wall began once more to move. The old man was gone; Katrin was once more alone.

For the first time in three months, her head moved slightly and a noise, a quiet, almost inaudible moan, came from her throat.

2

THE GARDENER

t was cold. No, not so much cold as merely cool; cool and dark. Katrin felt as if she were lying on something hard and surrounded by a cold blackness. How long she had been like this she had no idea; maybe she had been here for a second or two, maybe a couple of years. Without change, there was nothing by which to measure the passing of time. And there was no change. Just cool. And black. And the hardness against her back.

Then slowly at first, but with gathering speed, change came. At first it was just a feeling of movement. She felt as if, still horizontal, still on her back, she was moving upward. Then the color around her began to change. It was not so much black now as a very dark red. And she began to feel warmer. She was moving upward faster now and began to feel something, a response to her surroundings, that she could not place for a moment. Then a thought burst on her, and she quickly repressed it as being too silly. But the thought returned, stronger than ever. She was surrounded by warmth and something she could only describe to herself as liquid love. Katrin basked in it; she felt warm; she felt wanted; she felt important; she felt loved.

It was not that she had felt unloved before, but rather that this was a love that seemed greater than anything she had ever felt or even known existed. And she felt happy—no, not happy; positively joyful. This love was so deep, so vast, that it was tangible. Here and there she could see small, dark shapes rising more quickly than she, bubbles of some sort, rising to a surface high above her.

She lay back, the hardness against her back now gone, supported only by the love through which she was slowly rising, and feeling new strength enter her body. It went on and on. She felt as if it would never end and was not unhappy to think that she might spend eternity like this. Then suddenly, with a barely audible swoosh, it was over. She had a brief glimpse of color, mostly green, passing her by, as if she had broken through the surface of a liquid, and then she found herself, panting slightly, on the most luxurious, soft, cool surface that she had ever felt.

She opened her eyes, although she was sure that they had been open all along, and found herself in a small clearing in a wood. The surface she felt was a beautiful green grass, the like of which she had never seen before. She felt refreshed, which surprised her; somehow she had expected to be tired. She lifted herself to her feet and stood looking around. High above the clearing was the bluest sky she had ever seen, in which hung a large, yellow sun. She suddenly felt as though she had gone through life wearing dark glasses, seeing only shades of gray. This was color as it was meant to be experienced.

Katrin looked around her at the trees growing nearby and she walked over to the closest one. It was tall and luxuriant, and from its branches hung some kind of fruit, yellow-orange with a smooth skin, reminiscent of a nectarine, although the color was shaded more uniformly over its surface. She reached out and squeezed it slightly; it was soft, perfectly ripe. As she began to take her hand away from the fruit, it detached itself from the tree and stayed in her hand.

"Oh!" she said in surprise. She looked at it, feeling guilty, and then looked around to see if anyone had seen what she had done. She turned the fruit around in her hand. Having picked it, perhaps she might as well eat it. But maybe it was poisonous, though that seemed unlikely in such a beautiful place. In any case, someone must own this tree, indeed, the entire place, and she would hate to be caught eating fruit from the trees without the owner's permission. On the other hand, she now realized that she was awfully hungry and thirsty. She turned the fruit around once more in her hands.

"What's the matter? Aren't you going to eat it?"

Katrin was so startled that she dropped the fruit. She had heard no one sneak up on her. She looked around but saw no one.

"I say, now that you've picked it, you might as well eat it." The voice was coming from the ground, over there.

Looking carefully into the shadows under the trees, she saw a rabbit returning her gaze. *Surely not,* she thought.

"Excuse me?" she said, looking firmly at the animal.

The animal left the protection of the shadows and hopped up to the fruit that now lay on the ground next to her feet.

"I was just observing," said the rabbit, "that now that you've picked it, you might as well eat it."

Katrin bent down and retrieved the fruit, which

appeared to be completely undamaged by the fall. Perhaps the softness of the grass had cushioned the drop. Anyway, the rabbit seemed to think that it could do her no harm.

"But I can't do that," she said to the rabbit. "I don't know whose it is."

She had never seen a rabbit looked puzzled before, but there was no mistaking the look on this rabbit's face. It spoke once more.

"Whose it is? Whose it is? I don't know what you mean. If you mean, who planted it, well, who else could have planted it but the Gardener? But if you need it, then you can eat it, of course. You can always take anything that you need, can't you?"

"I . . . I don't know," said Katrin. "Can I?"

The rabbit looked at her some more, then shook its head in despair and was gone with a bound into the trees.

Katrin's gaze followed it for a moment, then dropped to the fruit in her hand. She lifted it to her mouth and took a bite, just a small one at first, so that she could spit it out if it proved to be sour. But, it was the most delicious thing that she had ever tasted. She let the fruit linger in her mouth. It was a nectarine, or at least a close relative. Like her experience with the colors surrounding her in the clearing, she now felt that for the first time she knew what food was supposed to taste like.

Finishing the fruit, she looked down at the stone in her hand, wondering what to do with it. She looked around. There was a little pool of water, perhaps three times her height across, a short distance away. She walked slowly toward the pool, enjoying the soft, springy grass on her bare feet.

Bare feet! she suddenly thought, and looked down at herself. She was wearing some sort of a brown dress; it felt as if it were made of leather, yet it was softer and more supple than even the finest chamois. She had never owned, nor even seen, a dress that looked like this.

Reaching the pool, she bent down and looked at her reflection, her long, dark hair nearly touching the still surface of the water. The face that looked up at her from its depths was definitely her own. She tossed the stone lightly into the middle of the pool, where it fell quickly out of sight as the ripples spread away from the splash toward the rim of the pool.

Then she knelt down and took a sip of the water. She was no longer surprised by the intensity of the taste; by now she had come to expect the things in this place to be more alive, more intense, more real somehow. The water was cool and sweet, perfect for quenching the thirst which suddenly grabbed at her throat. Three, four times she dipped her hand in the water and lifted it to her mouth, slaking her thirst.

She stood up and looked around, suddenly tired. Over there in the shadows looked like a good place for a nap, so she walked across, lay down, and in seconds was fast asleep.

She slept deeply, yet without dreams. When she awoke, the air was cooler and the sky was a little darker, with no trace of the sun which had warmed her before she slept. She sat up and looked across to the pool, then blinked. Rising out of the very center was a sapling, covered in green leaves and bearing a single small fruit. The fruit was exactly the same, although smaller, than the one that she had eaten earlier. She rose and stared at the tree. There was a rustle nearby, and she turned. Standing just a few yards away was a very old man.

The man looked at her and she looked at him. She could not take her eyes off him. There was something about him, something so old, something so serene, something so sure of itself, something so secure. Somehow she knew that he was the source of the power of this place, and that she was here because of him.

She noticed that he carried a stick to walk with, although whether he really needed it was not clear to her. She waited for him to speak.

"Good evening, my child. How do you feel?" he asked.

She knew that she had no need to answer the question. The man knew exactly how she felt without her having to find the words to tell him. Yet he had asked the question, and it would be rude not to reply.

"Oh, er, very well, sir." She wanted to ask so many questions, but something about the man warned her that now was not the time.

"Good. You are rested, and in no need of food or water, I trust?"

Katrin was once more surprised. Now that she thought about it, it was strange: since arriving at this place, which must surely have been at least several hours ago, she had eaten only one small fruit and drunk a few handfuls of water. Yet the man was right, she felt no need of further food or drink. Indeed, she had never felt more complete in her life. But the words seemed so weak, so inadequate, and in any case, she was sure that the man knew her feelings. So she simply said, "No, sir, I don't think that I need anything. I feel very well indeed."

"Good. Then let us take a little stroll together."

He turned slightly, and Katrin noticed for the first time a wide grass path heading off through the trees. The man motioned for her to join him and, trotting slightly to reach him, she found herself by his side as they began to walk down the path.

"Now, my child, time is of the essence. I cannot linger

with you, much though I might wish it otherwise. I shall permit you to ask one question, just one, which I shall do my best to answer. Then I am afraid you must put away your questions for the present."

Of all the day's events, perhaps this surprised Katrin as much as any other. This man seemed so much in control of himself—no, so much in control of everything—that she could not imagine how he might ever find himself short of time.

The man continued. "You may ask your question first, then I must ask you to be silent as we walk."

Katrin thought. There were so many questions. How had she got here? Where, indeed, was she? How long had she been here? How did the tree grow in the pool so quickly? And the rabbit: how had the rabbit been able to speak with her? All of these seemed like good questions, and it was hard to choose just one. But suddenly she realized what the one true question was, and she asked it without hesitation.

"Who are you, sir?"

The old man stopped and looked at her and smiled. Very quietly, so softly she could barely hear him, he said, "Good. She will do well." He looked deep into her eyes, into her very being, so that, even before his answer came, she was certain who he was. He looked away and began once more to walk, she keeping pace.

"The correct answer, my child, is I am who I am, just as you are who you are. But I doubt that that answer satisfies you. There are many names by which I am known. Even where you come from I am known, but one person will call me by one name, and another will call me by another. They are all useful; they all say something about me. Here"—the hand not using the stick waved around to encompass the green forest through which they were walking—"here I am usually known as the Gardener. Where you will shortly be going, my name is Olvensar, although there are few there that remember that name or, if they do, pay it much heed. Fewer still are the ones who will use it." He stopped, and Katrin stopped by his side. "Remember the name Olvensar, my child, for you will come to depend on it. It is a name older than any other in the land of Palindor, and it still has a power, part of the kirial of that world."

Katrin did not understand, but was afraid to interrupt. Instead she tried simply to remember what she was being told; understanding could come later. She was not happy at the idea of leaving this place so soon after arriving. But how long had she been here? She remembered the tree which had grown up while she slept. Surely she must have slept for an awfully long time for that to happen?

Olvensar began to move once more. Although he appeared old and frail and his motions were slow, Katrin found that she had to jog to keep up with him. "Come," he said. "There is little time left. You must be ready to leave."

"But . . . " said Katrin, trying to interrupt.

"No," the man said, not slowing his stride. "I am sorry, my child, there is no time now for further questions. I had to let you sleep to restore yourself, and now time is short. Ah, here we are."

Katrin nearly stumbled in her amazement. They had left the pool with the tree growing from its center well behind them now. Since leaving it, they had been walking down a wide, grassy path through the forest. Although the path had not been perfectly straight, she was sure they had made only a couple of slight turns. Looking back the way they had come, she could see perhaps a hundred and fifty feet to the closest bend. Yet here they were, back where they had started. In front of them was the pool with the tree growing from its center, the lone yellow-orange fruit still hanging from its branches.

Olvensar walked near the edge of the pool and looked back at her. She trotted forward and stood facing him. He placed a hand somewhere in the folds of his garment and withdrew an object, holding it out for her to see. It appeared to be a small gray pebble with a hole through it, threaded on a leather thong. Leaning his weight against the staff, he untied the thong with two hands and held it out toward Katrin.

She supposed that she was meant to wear the gift, and she bent her head slightly so that the old man could reach around it. He did so, retied the thong, and she could feel the slight weight of the pebble as he withdrew his hands.

She picked up the pebble that rested on her chest and turned it around in her hand. It looked perfectly ordinary, a small pear-shaped pebble such as one might find on a beach somewhere.

"Thank you," she said; she could think of nothing else appropriate.

Olvensar spoke in a voice which seemed graver than before. "That gift, my child, is older than the very foundations of the visible worlds. It is the Seeing Stone of Ganvestor. The source of its power is the kirial of the unseen worlds, and it cannot be misled by the wiles of the visible. Hold the stone in your hands."

Katrin did so; the pebble still felt just like an ordinary sea pebble.

"Now," continued Olvensar, "think of someone, someone whose features are familiar to you. Think on that person and speak his name out loud."

Katrin concentrated. She looked at the face of the old man in front of her and burned it deep into her mind.

Then quietly, almost whispering, she spoke the man's name: "Olvensar."

"Now look at the stone," the man said.

She opened her hands and looked in amazement. The stone was no longer a dull gray pebble. Instead, it shone with a deep, deep blue. Peering into the stone, she thought it seemed deeper than the deepest ocean. As she looked, flecks of other colors showed amongst the blue. She had the impression of steel, of battles, some long ago, some yet to come. Battles full of death, the very destruction of souls. She saw pain and loneliness, hope and despair; above all, she saw power: old, old power from days long gone. She thought that she glimpsed a brief flowering of the power, as if, ultimately, it was successful in its battles. And then suddenly she was holding a cold, gray pebble once more. She looked up at the man whose name she had spoken.

"The Stone sees deep into the heart of the spirit, my child. And what it sees, it tells. Hide the Stone underneath your clothing, for there are those who might recognize it and would kill to possess such a treasure. Keep it safe and use it sparingly, for kirial speaks to kirial, and it is well to disturb such things as little as possible." Olvensar raised his hand, holding his staff vertically in front of him. "Now, go, and do not be afraid. I will be with you." The hand came down, and the staff struck the ground in front of him.

There was no sound; the deep green grass absorbed any sound that there might have been. And yet, as the stick hit the earth, Katrin suddenly lost her balance. The ground seemed to swallow her up. She fell down toward, and then through, the ground. She let out a scream of fear, and then suddenly found herself standing upright, solid ground beneath her feet. It was no longer the soft, comforting green grass near the pool, but hard, brown earth. The sky was no longer hidden behind a canopy of green; a harsh yellow-white sun burned high in the cloudless sky. Around her was a wasteland of brown rocks and boulders. She shivered, not from cold but from fear.

3

PALINDOR

ANY YEARS AGO, long before anyone now living in the land first saw the light of day, the Kingdom of Palindor was known as a place of enlightenment, where each creature of the earth, be he human, dwarf, gnome, satyr, or any of the thousand and one races which then inhabited the world, could seek and find his true purpose in life. The kings of Palindor ruled with grace and love. They in turn were much loved by their subjects, who would willingly lay down their lives in battle when the kingdom was threatened by armies from the neighboring lands of Reglandor and Soltarwyn. No army carrying the flag of Palindor into battle had ever known defeat, no matter the might of the enemy.

The combined armies of Reglandor and Soltarwyn had been repelled, once and for all, in a final great battle, and had never again risen to strike at Palindor. That battle, on the Plains of Kradesh in the southeast corner of Palindor, near where it meets Reglandor, occurred in the final days of the reign of King Yndlarn V, a king hailed in his younger days for his great wisdom in ruling the country. But as he became older and near to death, some said that a change came over the king; he had become bitter, his mind had become small, and he died mourned as a king but not as a friend by his subjects.

But this was all many years ago. The young learned of these matters from their elders; they were imbued with a sense of how great Palindor once had been. But never did they question how great was the contrast between her past state and her present one.

King Yndlarn V was succeeded by his young daughter, Queen Cerebeth. At first, there was much joy in the land of Palindor at her accession to the throne. She was young and unafraid; she ruled the country, as had her father in his younger days, with wisdom and truth, seeking after justice, yet tempered always with understanding. But slowly, things in Palindor began to change.

By the time of our story, when Katrin arrived in Palindor from the world of humans, Queen Cerebeth had reigned for over a thousand years. She had grown older, it is true, but ever so slowly. She was now a small, old woman, bitter beyond measure, and preoccupied, it was said (although only quietly and in the most secure places) with a morbid anxiety about her own mortality.

Over the period of Queen Cerebeth's reign, learning gradually fell into disrepute. First the Holy Gnomes had their privileges revoked. Then reading and writing was taught less and less in the schools, until at the time of our story it was rare for a creature of any kind to be able to read beyond the most rudimentary texts. A single event some one hundred years earlier precipitated its decline more than any other: the burning of the Holy Barrows of Perendeth.

Although the citizens of Palindor had prided

themselves on their learning for many generations, the true caretakers of that wisdom were the Holy Gnomes. From their number, royalty had acquired its most sagacious advisers. The Holy Gnomes were responsible for the safekeeping of the accumulated knowledge of the ages. They were few in number, perhaps never more than a hundred, but they lived long and were industrious, and so their importance to the land was great in proportion to their small numbers. The Holy Gnomes wrote down all that they knew and maintained their library of knowledge in the Holy Barrows at Perendeth, not far from where the Great Sea pounds the cliffs in the west of Palindor.

In the library at Perendeth could be found any knowledge that man or beast could seek. Whole rooms were given over to books detailing the history of the world, the use of herbs in medicine, the battle campaigns of the great generals of all the known lands, the prophecies of Olvensar and their interpretations, or any one of a hundred different subjects. It was even said that there were books, although few in number and difficult to read, giving details of the kirial that undergirds the world.

All this knowledge was concentrated in the underground rooms of the Barrows at Perendeth. The books were guarded and tended by the Holy Gnomes who had turned away from the world, dedicating themselves to the accumulation and study of knowledge. The Holy Gnomes lived in chambers beneath the ground at Perendeth, always close to their precious libraries.

And then came that terrible night; a night of no moon; a night of confused tales, so that no one yet living could tell the truth behind what happened. All that was known was that in the gray light of the morning following, the three guards to the entrance of the tunnels of Perendeth were missing, never to be seen again, and the accumulated wisdom of the ages, as well as those called to its guardianship, were no more. Fire had swept through the library, feeding on the old, dry pages of the books with a devastating fury. The fire had spread so quickly that the gnomes had been trapped in their living quarters, unable to pass through the flames to safety, and all had perished.

In the early days following the fire, there had been a rumor that two Holy Gnomes had survived, a pair of brothers. But the queen's army searched for the survivors, and Queen Cerebeth herself issued a proclamation that if any Holy Gnomes would come forward, they need lack for nothing for the remainder of their lives, as she would keep them in grand style in exchange for their priceless advice in matters large and small. But the days turned into weeks, then into months and years, and it gradually became clear that none of the Holy Gnomes had survived.

The decline of Palindor, already accelerating under Queen Cerebeth, accelerated further after the end of the Holy Gnomes. Knowledge of the contents of the libraries contained in the Holy Barrows was lost; it was not long before this was followed by loss of knowledge of Olvensar.

Olvensar was the High Lord of Palindor, even, so some said, the creator of Palindor and of every man and beast therein. In the early days, long ago, it was said that Olvensar himself walked the land and spoke with his subjects. Then there followed a long period in which he spoke to only a chosen few; usually, although not always, to Holy Gnomes, who dutifully scribed his words even when they did not understand them. But now it was long since any claim of speech with Olvensar had occurred. At the time of the fire, some believed that Olvensar had spoken to the Holy Gnome Grantwith shortly before the death of King Yndlarn V, some nine hundred years before, but Grantwith had neither confirmed nor denied this to any creature, and he met with a mysterious death shortly after the accession of Queen Cerebeth.

Now the name of Olvensar, once proclaimed loudly as High Lord, was almost unknown in Palindor, especially in the towns and villages. Those who knew about Palindor's great past believed that it was due to the remarkable insight and wisdom of its great kings. Of the prophecies concerning Olvensar, none were now widely known.

But the reader should not believe that the general populace of Palindor was unhappy. Far from it; in their ignorance and apathy the residents of Palindor were, perhaps, happier than they had ever been before. There was no movement to reinstate learning, for they now knew that they could live without it. Providing only that food was in plentiful supply, as it had been continuously for at least the past several hundred years, there were no complaints and no deep-seated desire to upset the balance of their way of life.

Except, that is, in the hearts and minds of a very few. For beneath the veneer of contentment, there were a small number of creatures who knew how it had been in the old days from stories they had heard at the feet of their grandparents. And these few had, with the utmost caution and secrecy, passed on their thoughts and fears to their children. For if the queen should come to hear of it, death would be swift and sure; such had been demonstrated with devastating certainty many times through the years.

But there was one secret above all secrets that had not been told, because only two people were aware of it, and they knew that the time was not yet right for the knowledge to be spread.

The rumors following the great fire at the Holy

Barrows had not been false. Two Holy Gnomes had indeed escaped with their lives: two brothers, who had been but youngsters of less than a hundred years when the fire came, and were now little over two hundred years old, in the prime of their lives. Trondwyth and Drefynt were their names, the great-great-grandchildren of the Holy Gnome Grantwith, who had been killed by Queen Cerebeth when he refused to disclose the nature of his discussions with Olvensar as Cerebeth's father lay on his deathbed.

For twenty years following the fire at Perendeth, Trondwyth and Drefynt had lived secretly in the forest in the north of Palindor. One day, hearing a noise, they had found another gnome exploring the forest, and had joined up with him, saying that they too were explorers, but from a land far away. They had returned with him to the capital of Palindor, Carn Toldwyn, and settled there to become part of the community.

Drefynt had quickly established a reputation for being a wise gnome although, all agreed, not of the caliber of the old Holy Gnomes. He even demonstrated an ability to read simple writing, although he could not write himself. Trondwyth, his brother, displayed no such talents but, unlike most gnomes, he was handy with his hands and was much sought after as a maker and repairer of wooden furniture.

After many years, Queen Cerebeth came to hear of Drefynt and the high regard in which he was held in the small gnome community on the eastern edge of Carn Toldwyn, and she requested that he visit her. With some trepidation he did so and was pleasantly surprised when, after a short interview, the queen asked if he would accept a position as one of her ministers. So Drefynt became installed in the queen's castle, Dynas Carn

Toldwyn.[†]

Drefynt was the only gnome among the queen's five chief ministers, the others being a pair of dwarves, a human and a minor wizard. Drefynt soon discovered that the queen had little use for her ministers; rather than requiring advice of them, the queen chiefly used them to act as judges to resolve disputes as they arose between her subjects. In fact, he found that he rarely saw the queen, who spent her days locked away in her private quarters in the northern tower of her castle, only occasionally venturing out into the remainder of the castle, and almost never moving outside the castle walls.

When he first saw the queen, she looked old and shrunken. But, Drefynt reflected, after living for a thousand years, that was to be expected. No one could remember any human living more than a tenth as long before. Even gnomes and dwarves, the most long-lived of the inhabitants of Palindor, rarely lived to see their six-hundredth birthdays. There were two common explanations for the queen's longevity: either she was only part human, and part something else which lived for considerably longer, or she was in command of some kind of magic that gave her such a long life. Drefynt did not subscribe, exactly, to either of these theories; and once he had met the queen for the first time and had a chance to look into her face at close quarters, he was sure that his explanation was the correct one. The first of the popular explanations he dismissed out of hand for, if true, it would have meant that she had no standing to rule the country. As far back as even the oldest holy writings had been scribed, Palindor had been ruled by humans, and rule had passed from generation to generation unceasingly. If Queen Cerebeth were only part human, then the chain must have been broken

---

[†] 'Dynas' is the Palindoric word for 'castle'

somewhere, and that would violate the rule of kingship laid down in the Book of Origins, said to have been dictated by Olvensar himself.

As for magic, there was no recorded magic capable of sustaining life beyond its allotted time. Although no expert himself in such matters, he had, when a youth, consulted Entelred, the oldest and greatest living wizard, and Entelred had assured him that the holy books were correct on that score. No, the wizard had told the young gnome, the source of any power that lengthened one's days could only be kiríal, that truest and deepest of realities, beyond the reach of even the wisest and most capable of wizards—the power of Olvensar himself.

But, though untrained in matters of kiríal, as a Holy Gnome, Drefynt and, for that matter, his brother Trondwyth, were adept at spotting kiríal at work. For the holy writings of Perendeth had been full of tales of the power of kiríal, especially the oldest writings that spoke of Olvensar and Malthazzar† of potions, of stones, of rings and shoes, indeed of all kinds of deep kiríal. They told not of how such power worked, but of what it could do, what it had done to those who lived in the earliest days; there were even descriptions of the war of kiríal that had occurred before the beginning of the foundation of Palindor, when Olvensar fought Malthazzar and banished him from his world.

When Drefynt first looked into the face of the queen, all doubt was removed from his mind; he was looking into a face built by the forces of kiríal. Only deep forces could construct a face so lifeless, so vacant of original thought or emotion. Queen Cerebeth, human at birth, had long ago had her humanity sapped from her; now she was merely a shell, driven by the thoughts that kiríal placed in her head. Casting his mind back to the holy books, he felt sure that,

† The name `Malthazzar' is pronounced as if the letter `h' were absent.

somehow, the queen had stumbled upon the Elixir of Life and, not knowing its nature, had held on to life while losing Life.

Many years had passed since Drefynt and Trondwyth had reappeared in Carn Toldwyn, but little had changed there or elsewhere in the realm. The population was still happy in its ignorance of the great and important mysteries of life. Drefynt had been a minister of the court for some fifty years now, dispensing justice as best he felt able, using the precepts he had read in the holy writings of Perendeth when a mere youngster. His name had become well known in the kingdom; some said, indeed, that he was wiser than the wisest wizard, perhaps even as wise as the old Holy Gnomes themselves. Fortunately, such words had not yet reached the ears of the queen, but Drefynt was becoming anxious at the thought of what might happen to him were they to do so.

Trondwyth, meanwhile, had buried himself in the small gnome enclave on the edge of town, where it nestled against the great Forest of Palindor, which covered much of the realm. He had gained a small reputation as a gnome of hard work although, perhaps, a little strange in his use of language. Most gnomes felt that Trondwyth's speech was a little too correct, almost, one might think, as if he had spent time amongst the Holy Gnomes. For had they not spoken in a similar manner, using long words and thinking deeply before they made known their thoughts? Not that anyone seriously considered this, of course; who had ever heard of a Holy Gnome who was good with his hands? Still, Trondwyth was a little strange. . . .

Generally, however, Trondwyth was accepted merely as a hard working, talented gnome with one or two minor eccentricities. He and Drefynt took tea together once a week but, apart from that, they led lives with almost nothing in common. Those who asked about the weekly teas had to be reminded that the two gnomes had travelled from a distant country together and had arrived as the best of friends, despite their differing talents and ways.

It was during their weekly tea in Trondwyth's cottage that the strange thing happened. Drefynt had just been sharing his anxiety about his growing reputation and the unwelcome comparisons with Holy Gnomes, when there was a single sharp knock on the door. This was a surprise, for Trondwyth had few visitors. For all his popularity, few gnomes would actively seek Trondwyth's company; his eccentricities were just a little too pronounced, and all the gnomes in the town knew that this was the afternoon in which Drefynt came to visit. Gnomes being the polite creatures that they are, none would knowingly interrupt the tea and conversation of the two old friends.

But a knock at the door there most certainly was. Trondwyth arose and crossed to the door. Opening it, he was surprised to see what appeared to be a human, although he could not be sure; possibly it was a wizard. In any case, it looked to be an old, old man with a scruffy gray beard that just reached his chest. He was dressed in what once had been a green suit of some kind, but was now old and soiled almost beyond recognition. *A wizard,* Trondwyth concluded, although reserving the right to change his mind.

The wizard, if such he was, stayed on the doorstep waiting for Trondwyth to speak. At last, Trondwyth realized that he was being rude and greeted the stranger.

"Good afternoon, good, er, wizard. May this humble gnome be of assistance?"

"Wizard, eh?" The old man's face wrinkled and his

eyes shone, and something seemed to pass through the very air between the man and the gnome. All those years reading the holy books flashed through Trondwyth's mind and suddenly he knew, with awesome certainty, just who it was standing outside on his doorstep. Before he could speak, the stranger continued.

"Well, maybe 'wizard' is not such a bad description of me after all, although I confess that no one has called me that in many years. Still, I have come to speak with you and your brother."

At this, Trondwyth's heart almost ceased beating. No one, but *no one* had been told that he and Drefynt were brothers since they had returned to Palindor nearly eighty years earlier.

"I have come to speak with you and your brother about a matter of the utmost"—the stranger's voice became quieter and more grave—"yes, the utmost importance. I request entrance to your abode, that I might tarry and discuss these matters with you."

Trondwyth noticed that the man's speech had quite changed character, becoming the polite but exact speech of the Holy Gnomes of Perendeth.

Trondwyth stood to one side; glancing past his doorway, he could see no others in sight, and so he too risked the form of speech of his youth. "Stranger and yet most holy and exalted one, this gnome would be indebted if you were to spare your thoughts with him and his kin." Trondwyth bowed low while Drefynt, startled to hear this flowery speech coming from the doorway, looked up from his tea in time to see the low bow and the entrance into the room of Olvensar, High Lord of Palindor.

There was no doubt in Drefynt's mind, not for a second. The light was dim in the room and all he could see was the silhouette of the stranger in the doorway, yet he had no need of sight. He knew, but did not know how he knew, the identity of the one who was entering the house. He arose and, as the man with the tall staff walked into the center of the room, Drefynt, too, lowered his head in a deep bow of respect.

Trondwyth raised himself from his bow, hurriedly closed the door, and reentered the room.

"You would do this humble gnome a great favor if you were to partake of his hospitality," he said. "Do please be seated." He gestured toward the chair in which he had been seated, the gnome way of demonstrating that all he had was in the service and at the disposal of the newcomer.

"Well met, young gnome. I thank you for your hospitality." Olvensar's eyes roamed the room and settled on a comfortable looking chair "I believe that that chair will do me perfectly." He crossed the room and sat down slowly.

"Good gnomes, Trondwyth and Drefynt, do please be seated. I must not stay for long, for no doubt my presence in the kingdom is already known. It will, I am afraid, inconvenience you greatly should the forces of your queen find me here. So, for the sakes of your own lives and for the sakes of the lives of all in Palindor, I must request that you let me tell you my story. Interrupt if you must, but only if you must, for every moment that I spend here the danger to the kingdom is increased."

Neither gnome was greatly worried about Olvensar's words of introduction. They had known almost all their lives—since their childhood when grandfather Godolphin, great grandchild of the Holy Gnome Grantwith, had taken them aside and spent many hours instructing them privately about their ancestor's conversation with Olvensar many years before—that this moment would one day come. So they were prepared for it. Now that the real work of their lives was to begin, it was almost with a sense of relief that they settled themselves into their chairs to hear Olvensar tell his story.

4

OLVENSAR'S VISIT

S YOU HAVE already ascertained, I am the person you know by the name of Olvensar," began the white-haired visitor. "You read about me at length in your youth, though as to the veracity of all the tales told concerning me, I have my doubts. Still, enough of them are true that I believe you two good gnomes have formed a reasonably correct opinion as to who I am and what part I have played in the history of this realm.

"It is long since I have walked in your country; the reasons for my absence are unimportant. What matters is that the nature of this country has changed much in recent centuries. Palindor was once a jewel in my crown, but it has fallen into decay. Its ways are no longer my ways, and I cannot permit this decline to go unchallenged any longer." His voice changed abruptly as he focused his gaze upon Drefynt. "Your queen, good Drefynt. What think you of your queen?"

Drefynt was torn for a moment. If he spoke his mind, he would be guilty of treason, punishable by exile in the catacombs. But one look into the eyes of the visitor calmly seated in his brother's living room, and all doubts left his mind. "The good Queen Cerebeth is no more," he said. "When she left us I cannot say, but the creature who now rules this country is no queen of mine."

"A good answer, young Drefynt," said Olvensar. "And how do you suppose that this came about?"

"Well, sir," replied Drefynt, "I cannot be sure, but it is my opinion that she is in the hold of the powers of kiríal, possibly through the Elixir of Life, and that potion has robbed her of the very thing she thought it would bestow."

"Excellent, my good gnome. Your guesses, if such they are, are remarkably accurate. The Elixir of Life, sought by many and at great cost, was discovered in the Mountains of Mourn shortly before your queen ascended her throne. Not knowing what he had found, but suspecting its value, the young dwarf Staubyn the Courageous sent it to the wizard Geevonred, who oversaw that region for King Yndlarn V. On his next visit to Carn Toldwyn, Geevonred presented it as a gift to the king. The ancient Yndlarn had no wish to prolong the pains of this life, and so the elixir lay amongst his personal items until after his death.

"The potion was discovered by Queen Cerebeth a few months after her coronation and has never left her presence since. She wears the vial on a thong around her neck, and every evening for nearly a thousand years she has opened the vial and drained it of its contents. Every morning it is full once again, for that is part of its wonder.

"But the queen knew not the true nature of the Elixir of Life. Even kiríal cannot prolong life indefinitely for those beings who do not possess unnumbered days. She has aged, although more slowly than other humans, and is now nearing the end of her span. This she has suspected for some time, and now knows with a certainty that terrifies her. She once thought to outlive all other life, and the knowledge that many of her subjects will live beyond her own span of days fills her with hatred and bitterness.

"But a deeper part of the kiríal she still does not understand. As you say, young Drefynt, the Elixir of Life both gives life and takes it away. The queen's very being, her own life force, has been sucked out of her by the elixir. The queen's body still exists, old and soon to die, as does her mind—a little enfeebled, perhaps, but still active. But her spirit is gone lo these many years. In its place resides the spirit of darkness: the spirit of Malthazzar. It is that spirit which has laid waste to your land; it is that spirit which has destroyed learning and caused the deaths of the Holy Gnomes; it is that spirit which is stirring and threatening once more to move abroad. It is the spirit of Malthazzar that must be defeated before Palindor can regain the greatness that I mean her to have." Olvensar stopped and tilted his head, as if listening to a faraway sound.

Drefynt shivered, momentarily cold.

Olvensar turned back to the gnomes, his voice full of a new concern. "We must hurry; I have less time than I had hoped for. Malthazzar knows that I am in this land, and the queen will summon her soldiers to go forth and search for me. For your sakes, my friend, we cannot afford to let her find me here—for your sakes and that of Palindor. For the task of the saving this country has fallen onto your shoulders. You will not carry the burden alone; I will help whenever I am able. Indeed, if it will comfort you to know it, the greatest burden will lie not on your shoulders, but on those of another who has yet to come to Palindor. But your tasks will be difficult, and your successes are necessary to the defeat of Malthazzar. I cannot linger to provide you with all the details you would like, but must send you on your separate ways.

"Trondwyth, bravest of gnomes, you must prepare yourself immediately for the long journey to the Wastes of Kaltethorn. Take as much food and water as you can carry. You will know what to do when you get there.

"Drefynt, wisest of gnomes, you must leave here and return unseen to the queen's castle, where you will continue your work as you have done before. Be not anxious about the risk to yourself; render your judgments as you have in the past, trusting to your training in Perendeth." Olvensar arose. "Drefynt, do not think that your way will be easy; it will not. Now I place my trust in the two of you, that you will stay true to the tasks before you."

The two gnomes stood. Trondwyth bowed low, and Drefynt spoke. "Yes, Exalted One, I understand."

Olvensar looked at him. "No, my young friend, you do not understand. But remember your task, and worry not about other things." Olvensar strode to the door and opened it. "You must hurry. Your lives are in danger. When the queen's soldiers arrive here, they must find you gone." He closed the door behind him and was gone.

The brothers looked at one another. Trondwyth was the first to speak. "Bravest of gnomes?" he said. "Why is it, then, that I feel absolute terror?"

Drefynt managed a wry smile of understanding. "We have no time to wonder. The High Lord made it clear that we must leave at once. I will help you pack your things, and then we must leave."

"Yes," said Trondwyth, still doubtful. "Let me get my largest pack to carry food. I have a little money stored away in that jar." He gestured toward a small crock standing atop the mantelpiece. "If you would be so good as to fetch it, I will put it into my pouch and pray that it is sufficient for my needs."

Trondwyth hurried into his bedroom and returned moments later with a large, dusty pack, which the two gnomes hurriedly filled with food. Drefynt handed Trondwyth the jar from the mantle, and Trondwyth carefully decanted its pitifully small contents into a small leather pouch. This he also stuffed deep into the pack. On top of all he placed a large canteen of water.

It was only minutes since Olvensar had taken his leave, but the two gnomes shared a dangerous sense of foreboding. With help from Drefynt, Trondwyth hoisted the pack on to his back and shifted it to make it a little more comfortable.

The brothers looked into one another's eyes. They embraced, briefly and somewhat awkwardly, for Trondwyth's pack made it difficult.

"May the High Lord Olvensar look over you," said Drefynt, his voice as serious as it had ever been.

"And may he also look over you," responded Trondwyth, completing the ritual.

The two stepped apart, cast their eyes briefly around the room, and made their way to the front door. They left the house. Drefynt walked down the path toward a cluster of houses belonging to other gnomes, for all the world as if he were strolling back to Dynas Carn Toldwyn. Trondwyth, with a brief glance about to ensure that he was not observed, plunged into the wood that lay behind his house.

Their departure came not a moment too soon.

It was the spirit of Olvensar. Malthazzar remembered that spirit well. For the first time in a thousand years,

Malthazzar felt that spirit moving abroad in Palindor; it was nearby, perhaps even in Carn Toldwyn. He had felt the spirit in the realm before, but always in the periphery, sufficiently distant that there was no way he could confront the coward Olvensar before he vanished. But this time it was different. With no warning, Olvensar was present here, somewhere near the castle itself. That Malthazzar could not permit.

Although the spirit of Malthazzar inhabited the body of Queen Cerebeth, it refrained from making itself known directly to the people of Palindor. There was no point in taking unnecessary chances. Even though he had relegated the name of Malthazzar, like that of Olvensar, to bedtime stories told to young children, there was always the possibility that, if he were to make himself known, the people of the kingdom would recollect the great stories from their past, and the kingdom would be lost to him for another age. No, it was much better to move slowly, invisibly, planting first this idea and then that one in the mind of the queen and thus, ever so slowly, working his wishes on the once-great country of Palindor.

None of this, of course, was known by the queen. On the day of Olvensar's visit to the gnomes, Queen Cerebeth felt a vague uneasiness that she could not place. As the minutes went by, she grew more and more troubled until at last, her mind made up, she called for her page.

The page, a young gnome, entered the room and bowed low. "You desired to see me, Your Majesty?"

"I wish to leave the castle this afternoon. Prepare a carriage. We will leave within the quarter hour."

The page stood in shocked silence. In the two years in which he had been in her service, the queen had *never* desired to leave the castle. Indeed, it was rare that she saw another living creature other than her personal servants. She even dined alone, admitting others into her presence merely for the purpose of delivering food and retrieving the dishes.

The queen spoke again. "Did you not hear my command? Am I in need of a new page? One with ears to hear the demands of his queen?"

"No, no, Your Majesty. I will see to it immediately." With an extra-low bow, he was gone to make the preparations.

The page's announcement met with great confusion around the castle. At first the horsemen didn't believe him, but as they saw him growing more and more agitated, their disbelief was replaced by a concern for what the queen might do to them if the carriage were not ready in time. They rushed around this way and that, preparing the horses and dusting off the old royal carriage. All was barely presentable when the queen strode out into the courtyard and, without a word, climbed into the carriage.

The poor dwarf who held the post of Royal Carriage Driver climbed into his seat atop the carriage, wondering what would happen next. He leaned over the side of the carriage so far that his cap nearly fell off his head and nervously called out, "Your Majesty, where would you like me to take you?"

Inside the carriage, hidden in the shadows where none could see her, the queen was confused. She did not know where she wanted to go; indeed, she did not even know why she was embarking on this unheard-of trip. In frustration she replied, "I know not. Just drive. Take me away from this castle." She leaned back wearily into the soft, dusty fabric of the seat as the carriage moved out of the courtyard.

The carriage driver headed down the hill on which the castle stood, the hill whose name the town of Carn[†]

† The word "carn," which originally meant "a rocky outcrop," has come to mean "hill" or, occasionally, "view."

Toldwyn had assumed. He drove aimlessly through the roads of the town, eventually reaching the easternmost part near the edge of the forest, wondering how long the queen would want to be driven about like this. He had just decided that he had taken Her Majesty far enough from her abode, and was slowing the horses preparatory to turning, when he heard a shout from inside the carriage.

"Stop! Wait here!" The queen did not wait for her page, who was seated alongside the driver, to attend her, but flung open the carriage door and stepped out.

Some distance away, a small cluster of gnomes had gathered to watch the progress of the royal carriage. The queen looked vaguely about for a few moments, ignoring the onlookers. She walked slowly around the carriage, looking in all directions, her nose high in the air as if she were sniffing for something. Suddenly she stopped in front of a small track which led away from the main roadway. Without a word she began to stride purposefully up the path. Her page, who had been seated alongside the driver for the afternoon's jaunt, quickly disembarked and followed her, racing to catch up.

The path wound past several small houses and then made a sharp right turn toward the direction of the forest. It stopped suddenly in front of a small, immaculately kept gnome house that sat right on the edge of the trees. The front door was closed, but the queen strode straight up to it and, without knocking, opened the door and walked in.

The page, thoroughly confused, walked into the house a couple of steps behind her, hoping that the occupant of the house would forgive the terrible rudeness of the monarch.

He need not have worried. Once his eyes adjusted to the light, he saw that there was no one in the house but the queen, who stood in the center of the large front room looking about and once more appearing to sniff the air. Two cups and saucers had been carefully placed on tables, and a small summer fire still burned low in the grate. It looked as though the occupants of the room had left hurriedly a short time ago and would presumably soon return. The page could hear the queen talking, almost arguing with herself, in the center of the room.

"Three of them, not just him and the gnome," he thought he heard her say. Then she continued, "But who can the third one be? And why come to the house of a gnome? What good are gnomes? They don't feature in the prophecies, do they? But it was him all right. Yes! He was here, without a doubt. How dare he invade my kingdom this way! He will pay for this. I will have his little friends found and executed. Yes! That's what I'll do."

Suddenly the queen ceased her talking; she looked up toward the front door. Without another word she brushed past the poor bewildered page and out once more into the late afternoon sun.

Down the path a short but respectful distance stood the cluster of gnomes who had watched the queen's arrival. They had been talking amongst themselves, but all speech stopped at the queen's sudden appearance.

She pointed a finger toward one of the group and called loudly, "You there! The gnome in the yellow hat! I want to speak with you."

The poor gnome wished that he had not tried to gain such a good view of the proceedings. He looked around, hoping that perhaps there was some other gnome in the group wearing a yellow hat, but that hope was quickly dashed. Fearfully he stepped forward and bowed low. "Good afternoon, Your Majesty. Gelerant, gnome of Carn Toldwyn, at your service."

"Gnome!" the queen said. "Do you live nearby?"

"Yes, Your Majesty," he replied, turning to point back down the path. "I live in a house just down this path. You walked right past it just now when you came here."

"Then no doubt you can tell me the name of the gnome who lives in this house," she said, indicating the house behind her.

The gnome was glad for such an easy question. "Oh, yes, Your Majesty. That house belongs to Trondwyth."

Trondwyth . . . Trondwyth . . . The spirit inside the queen could not remember hearing the name before.

"Trondwyth?" said the queen. "I do not think that I know the gnome Trondwyth. Pray tell us about him."

The gnome gulped and tried to gather his wits. He knew Trondwyth only slightly, but had always been impressed by his quick intelligence and willingness to help a gnome in distress. What sort of trouble might Trondwyth be in? "Well, Your Majesty, I know him only slightly. He is a good gnome; at least, we all think so, although I believe that he is not originally of Palindor. He and his friend came here many years ago now, in the company of a third gnome whom they had met wandering in the northern forests. The three journeyed here together. Trondwyth and the other gnome, Drefynt—" He hesitated as the queen sucked in her breath, but she said nothing, so he continued. "They liked the look of Carn Toldwyn and stayed here. Trondwyth is a great help around the area, and Drefynt, well, Your Majesty knows about Drefynt. He is now one of your own ministers," Gelerant finished.

"Is that all?" the queen asked. "What more do you know?"

"Nothing, Your Majesty. Trondwyth keeps to himself. I don't think that anyone, apart from Drefynt, knows him very well."

"And this afternoon," said the queen. "Have you seen the gnome Trondwyth this afternoon?"

Gelerant thought for a moment and then replied: "No, Your Majesty, I don't believe I have."

Throughout this conversation, the little knot of gnomes had been creeping slowly closer, the better to hear. Now one of them spoke up.

"Your Majesty, today is the day of the week when Drefynt always takes tea at Trondwyth's house. I saw Drefynt arrive as usual this afternoon, as he walked past my house on his way. And he left not half an hour since, making once more for the castle, I would judge. But of Trondwyth I have seen nothing."

"And a man? Or a creature that looked like a man, dressed in grubby green clothes, carrying a tall stick? An old man with a gray beard? Did you see him as he passed your house earlier?" the queen asked the gnome who had spoken out.

A man? Here in the gnome village? Now that would attract some attention.

"No, indeed, Your Majesty," the gnome replied, and all the others rushed to add their assurances. There had been no man in their village that day, nor for many a year.

The queen stood quietly after receiving this information. She seemed confused, hesitant. Finally she muttered, "Drefynt. Drefynt. I must think about this." Without a word of thanks or leavetaking, she strode down the path in the direction of her carriage.

5

SMALTERSCAIRN

LTHOUGH IT MUST not be forgotten that both Drefynt and Trondwyth were Holy Gnomes, and therefore of high intelligence and steeped in learning, there could be no doubt that Drefynt was the more gifted thinker of the two. Trondwyth, on the other hand, was remarkably practical considering the bookish training he had received at the hands of his teachers at Perendeth. And so, if a long journey on limited resources were to be made, there was no doubt as to which was the better equipped to undertake it.

Trondwyth walked into the trees behind his little house on the edge of Carn Toldwyn without a backward glance. As a young gnome, he had sworn allegiance to the High Lord Olvensar. Through conversations with their grandfather, the Holy Gnome Godolphin, he and Drefynt had known that a day would come when they would be called on to play their parts in the history of Palindor. And so, while his mind might question the wisdom of departing on a journey of such magnitude without adequate preparation, his heart told him that if Olvensar insisted on speed, there must be good reason for it. He only hoped that he would, as Olvensar had promised, know what to do when he reached the Wastes of Kaltethorn.

For the remainder of the afternoon Trondwyth walked eastward, away from the area that had been his home for the last eighty years. He had never visited the Wastes before, although he and Drefynt had passed nearby in their wanderings in northern Palindor. But there was no reason for any living thing to enter the Wastes themselves. They were some three days slow travel from one side to the other. Three days in which the sun always beat down, no matter what the time of year . . . three days of endless clambering over and around red-tinted boulders without even a blade of grass for relief. Even the birds of the air rarely ventured into the Wastes, preferring to take the longer routes around the desolation.

But it would be at least four days before he would reach the westernmost border of the Wastes. If one traveled along the major tracks and highways of Palindor, they could be reached in two days of determined walking from Carn Toldwyn. But Trondwyth was determined to keep his journeying a secret until he was well away from the capital, and making his way through the forest would slow him considerably.

He wondered again if he had sufficient provisions. There was probably enough food, but he would have to purchase a larger flask in which to store water before too long. While he stayed in the forest, streams would be common, but after that he knew water would be harder to come by unless he made himself known in the hamlets and villages along the way. He would walk for three days and then try to buy a water flask at the next village he came to, unless there seemed a good reason to avoid being seen.

Having thus decided his course of action, he set himself to the serious task of picking a path through the trees.

For three days he walked, keeping off any footpaths or tracks that crossed his way, stopping at night in deep parts of the forest, eating berries when they were available and filling his flask at every stream. His progress was good; on two occasions he had to detour for an hour or so to find bridges over streams, but he moved steadily closer to his destination. There were few travelers abroad these days in Palindor, so it was no surprise that he passed the entire three days without once having to hide from fellow travelers. He passed close by four settlements, but easily avoided detection.

How different from the old days, Trondwyth thought. His reading of history told him that in those days the country was full of wandering explorers and discoverers. Now the spirit of adventure seemed absent from the land.

Toward the late afternoon of the third day, he arrived at the outskirts of a small town. He had seen no trace of a stream all day until he came nearly within sight of the town, when he espied a small river flowing through the forest to his right. Though small, the river was too large to cross without a bridge, and he was forced to follow it for a short distance until a bridge came into view. A few houses could be seen on the opposite bank of the river, half hidden amongst the trees. The houses were small and distinctly elvish in appearance.

This must be Smalterscairn, he thought, as he looked into the village across the river. He studied the ground around him, but not finding what he was looking for, he retraced his steps, going back into the forest until at last he found a small pebble lying on the ground, just the right size to fit in the palm of his hand. He picked it up, placed it in his pocket, and returned once more to the riverbank near the bridge.

Smalterscairn was built deep in the heart of the Palindor forest, on the eastern bank of the Pennyfarthing River. The river wound its way through the trees, eventually passing south of Carn Toldwyn, merging with the River Findell, and disgorging into the Great Sea. The village was populated predominantly by wood elves who, though sociable enough with their own kind, were markedly reticent even with other elves and almost hostile to other races. But the insularity of the wood elves was a boon to Trondwyth; here the sway of Queen Cerebeth was weak, and he was not likely to be given away provided he minded his manners. So he casually strode forward out of the forest onto the path before him, crossing the bridge into the village itself.

He had not gone far before he was aware of eyes watching him from behind the windows of the small cottages that were built between the trees. He passed a few elves on the street, smiled at them, and said "Good afternoon" courteously, but none returned his greeting. The most he won was a brief nod of the head to acknowledge his presence as the elves hurried on their way.

Turning a corner, he found himself in the small village square. In front of him, in the very center of the square, was a pile of small round pebbles, perhaps half as high again as himself: the cairn that had given the village its name. He walked up to the cairn, slowing as he neared it, and then stood quietly before it. He knew he was being watched from countless windows around the square and self-consciously pulled the pebble from his pocket. He looked down at the stone and rolled it around in his hands.

It was the custom of the elves in Smalterscairn, when fortunes were going well, to seek out a stone and add it to the pile in the village square, to thank Olvensar for his many blessings. Conversely, when needing assistance, custom dictated that one could approach the pile and remove a stone, indicating to those watching a need for aid.

Trondwyth stood a full five minutes in silence, turning the pebble in his hands, so that those watching would know this was no empty gesture. Then slowly he stretched out his hand and dropped the pebble onto the side of the pile.

Shifting the weight of his pack slightly, he walked around the cairn to the other side of the pile of stones. For another five minutes he stared at the pebbles, as if he were somehow drawing strength from them. Then once more he put out his hand and slowly picked up a stone from the pile, looking at it as he turned it in his hands. Finally he placed it into the same pocket from which he had taken his original pebble.

A sound caused Trondwyth to look up. Trotting toward him across the grass was a young wood elf.

"Caldorn, wood elf of Smalterscairn and humble page of Ederagorn the Wise, at your service, sir," said the elf with a low bow. "If you would follow me, please." Without waiting for an answer, the elf turned and walked rapidly back the way he had come.

Without a word, Trondwyth followed. They walked straight across the clearing toward what was, even in wood-elf terms, a poor abode. Its appearance was particularly noticeable, standing as it did next to what was, for a wood-elf, a magnificent residence (although, if truth be told, even this house was considerably less grand than Trondwyth's little cottage back in Carn Toldwyn). Without stopping, the young elf opened the front door of the smaller house and led the way into the dwelling. He stood to one side to let Trondwyth pass.

Inside, was dark and smelled musty. As Trondwyth's eyes slowly accommodated themselves to the darkness, the young elf spoke from behind him. "The gnome, Your Honor."

Trondwyth heard the sound of the door being closed. Looking in front of him, Trondwyth could make out the person of an elf seated in an old armchair. There was an empty chair opposite the first, and the seated elf gestured toward it.

"Pray be seated, good gnome," he said in a tired, cracked voice.

Trondwyth walked across to the empty chair and removed his pack from his back. He seated himself in the proffered chair with some difficulty, gnomes being somewhat larger than the elves for whom the chair had been made. The chair was threadbare and old. Casting his eyes around the room, Trondwyth could see that everything in the room was ancient. The room looked like it had been untouched for decades, perhaps centuries. The elf before him spoke, and Trondwyth dragged his eyes back toward him.

He was indeed an extremely old elf. His face was wizened, his movements slight and slow. But around the elf's neck was a narrow gold chain which Trondwyth recognized at once. It was the Chain of Smalatern, handed down from the wisest elf of each generation to the wisest one of the next on the deathbed of the elder.

"Welcome, my good gnome, to Smalterscairn and to

the dwelling of Ederagorn," the old elf said. "Please forgive the surroundings. I need little to live. My eyes are not what they used to be, and I find it difficult and unnecessary to travel much. But my young page here tells me all that I need to know about the world outside. And just now he told me of something that I do not believe has been seen before in this good village. Tell, me, gnome, what is thy name?"

Trondwyth spoke. "My name is Trondwyth. I am a gnome, come from the town of Carn Toldwyn."

"Oh, ho!" The old elf almost chuckled. "Ah yes, that much is true. But how much truth did you leave unspoken, young gnome? That is the question. Perendeth looks to be your true home, I judge, but that is neither here nor there. My page tells me that you visited the cairn and there both laid a stone and removed one. Is this true?"

Trondwyth bowed his head slightly, although he was far from sure that the old elf would be able to see this mark of respect. "Yes, sir. I knew of your customs, and since I feel both blessed and in need of blessing, it seemed to me the right thing to do."

"Well said, young gnome. And so I ask you first: what was the reason for the stone you placed on the cairn?"

Trondwyth raised his head once more. This was the first risk he would be taking in his journey, the first time that he would tell his secret, and he wanted to watch carefully to see if Ederagorn's face would register the news. "You are right, sir, about my home. My present journey began at Carn Toldwyn, but in my youth, my home was at Perendeth. I am, as you surmised, a Holy Gnome. But more than that, I have been greatly blessed. But three days since, I was honored to speak face-to-face with the High Lord Olvensar himself."

He waited for the elf to urge him on, but all Ederagorn

said was, "The High Lord Olvensar? A high honor for a young gnome. A high honor indeed, even for an old elf. And what of the second stone, the one that you removed? Of what do you have need?"

"The need comes from the blessing, as is so often the case. Olvensar has sent me upon a journey to the east, and I am in need of food and water. I must stay away from towns and villages, and yet I fear that I have insufficient food and my canteen will hold too little water for the journey."

Ederagorn sat without speaking. There was no sound at all in the room; all Trondwyth could hear was the sound of the blood in his ears. He began to feel uncomfortable. At last, just when he was thinking of speaking once more to break the heavy silence, the elf spoke.

"Good gnome, your requests shall be granted, as much as it is in my power to do so." He looked toward the page, who was still seated in the corner of the room behind Trondwyth. "Caldorn, take the gnome's pack and fill it with the items that you gathered yesterday."

"Yes, Your Honor. It will take but a few minutes."

The old elf continued. "When it is filled, place it by the cairn where the good gnome can retrieve it for his journey onward."

"Yes, Your Honor," Caldorn said. He moved forward and with considerable effort raised the pack onto his own back. Refusing all offers of help from Trondwyth, he retreated out the door through which he and Trondwyth had originally entered the room.

A confused Trondwyth looked back at the old elf. "Yesterday?" he said. "Did you already know of my arrival?"

Ederagorn smiled. "Did you not think that Olvensar

would help you on your journey? Two days ago, the High Lord spoke with me from the very chair in which you now sit."

Trondwyth found it hard to imagine the tall High Lord squeezing into the small chair, but he said nothing.

"He told me of many things, some past and some yet to be. I shall die within the week, to be with Olvensar always, but I shall die happy, knowing that I have spoken with the High Lord while still on this earth. But you—" said Ederagorn, for the first time looking Trondwyth directly in the eye—"you have a hard task ahead. I do not envy you. All I can offer you is this advice: remember that nothing is hidden from Olvensar and, no matter how bleak things appear, he will always have gone before you to prepare the way. It is only when you stray from his way that trouble, difficulty, and darkness will come upon you."

The two creatures, gnome and elf, sat and talked of Olvensar, of life in the old days, of Perendeth, of troubles they had seen and troubles yet to come, for a considerable part of the afternoon. At last Trondwyth glanced out the one small window and saw that the light was fading. Although he wished he could tarry, he knew that he must walk long into the darkness this night to make up for the time he had lost.

"I am afraid I must be going," he said, rising from his chair, "or I will be neglecting the task that the High Lord has given me."

The old elf seemed sad. "Yes, I understand. Your time has come, as has mine. You will find your pack out by the cairn, and there should be sufficient provisions and water for your journey. May the blessings of Olvensar be with you, my good gnome," he said, raising his hand in benediction.

"Thank you," said Trondwyth, "and also with you." He saw the elf's arm suddenly fall to his side, the exertion too great.

In a barely audible voice Ederagorn said, "Thank you. Now go."

Trondwyth turned and went out the door without looking back. The light was even less than he had thought; he could barely distinguish the shape of his pack from the pile of stones near which it lay. He hurried across the clearing and lifted the pack. It was not heavy, he found, somewhat to his dismay. In fact, it seemed lighter than when he had arrived in Smalterscairn. He suppressed the urge to open the pack right there to discover what it contained; hoisting it on his back, he looked around the clearing one last time to get his bearings, then set off with determined stride toward the east.

6

THE HIGH QUEEN'S ARRIVAL

RONDWYTH MARCHED AS best he could through the woods at night. The forest thinned somewhat to the north and east of Smalterscairn, for which he was thankful. Had the forest been as dense as between Smalterscairn and Carn Toldwyn, he would have had to surrender to the difficulties of the journey and pitch camp shortly after nightfall. As it was, going was slow but continuous.

By morning he found himself on the easternmost edge of the forest, peering into the rising sun above a mist-filled valley of green meadowland. Exhausted, he dropped his pack among the trees and curled up on the ground. He awoke at lunchtime, hungry and thirsty. Looking out over the valley, he could discern no sign of habitation; indeed, the vista was motionless, except for a pair of birds wheeling high in the sky.

He pulled his pack toward him. Rummaging around inside it, he found that it was half full of small, round whitish loaves. Lying beneath them was a canteen no larger than his own (which, he observed, was no longer in the pack). A few personal items, including his money, lay untouched at the bottom of the pack.

He lifted the canteen to find that it felt light, even empty. Unscrewing the stopper, he saw no trace of water inside. Instead, just visible over the neck of the flask, was a small piece of paper. Trondwyth pulled it out and looked at the writing on one side. It was writing from the old times, an elvish writing that he could not read well. However, one thing clearly stood out: the note concluded with the Holy Mark, the sign of Olvensar himself.

Slowly Trondwyth made out the words, trying to remember the lessons of his youth. He wished that Drefynt were there, for his brother would make light work of such a task. The sun was noticeably lower in the sky before Trondwyth was satisfied with his translation.

My dear gnome Trondwyth,

Greetings! I apologize for requiring you to remember the lessons of your youth to understand this writing, but I had to be sure that it would not be read by others. I have tarried awhile with the good elf Ederagorn and explained to him some of your mission. He is to be trusted, although there are many other elves about which the same cannot be said. Ederagorn has arranged for you to receive a goodly supply of elven bread; this should be sufficient for your journeys.

Journeys? Not journey? Trondwyth hoped, with no real expectation, that it was a simple mistake on the part of the High Lord.

As for water, so long as you keep this canteen with you, you will not be thirsty. Every time you open the stopper, the canteen will be filled anew

with fresh water, until such time as the moon next
becomes full. At that time the spell will be broken.
Until we meet again, you have my blessings.

Thirstily, the gnome replaced the stopper on the canteen. As he did so, it at once became heavy. Opening the stopper once more, he put the canteen to his lips and drank deeply of the coolest, freshest water he had ever tasted. From the corner of his eye he caught sight of Olvensar's note; suddenly it burst into flame and was consumed.

His thirst quenched, Trondwyth pulled an elf loaf from the pack and ate it. Although the loaf was small, it was satisfying, and he had no need of a second. Once again he lifted the pack to his back—noticing that it felt heavier now because of the canteen of water—and started down into the valley.

He trudged eastward in this way for the remainder of the daylight left to him, crossing the meadow and then dropping into a shallow valley. He passed through a narrow wood on the far side. And so, on the evening of the fourth day since leaving Carn Toldwyn, he arrived at the western edge of the Wastes of Kaltethorn.

He stepped out of the narrow wood, and without warning, the soft earth on which he had trudged for four days was no more. In its place was a coarse sand strewn with reddish-brown boulders. Away in the distance, on the far side of the Wastes, he could see the snowcapped Mountains of Mourn. Although the Kingdom of Palindor laid claim to the Wastes of Kaltethorn and the western side of the Mountains of Mourn, there were no settlements there—apart from the small elvish village of Penclaw—and travelers were almost unknown.

With a dark foreboding hanging over him, Trondwyth camped the night under the trees of the little wood. He slept uneasily and awoke early, before the sun had risen over the mountains on the horizon. He ate half a loaf of elf bread and drank only a few sips from the canteen before pulling on his pack and making his way out into the Wastes.

Before the morning was half over, he had stopped to slake his thirst three times. The sun was hotter than he had ever known it, blazing out of a fierce white sky. Looking back toward the west, he could see the wood, a bank of cooling cloud hanging above it; in the Wastes themselves, there was no respite. He could hear no sound, see no moving creature. There was no wind, nothing except the burning sun, sand, and boulders. When the sun reached the highest point in the sky, Trondwyth stopped behind a particularly large boulder to take some more water and a little food. The rock offered little in the way of protection from the sun, and he hurriedly finished the remainder of the loaf that he had started for breakfast. He took several long gulps of the water from the canteen and had just finished tying up his pack when, with no warning, a thunderclap burst upon his senses, nearly causing him to lose his footing. It was immediately followed by a sound from the other side of the boulder.

Leaving his pack, Trondwyth cautiously peered around the boulder. To his astonishment, he saw a creature, a human girl no less, standing not ten paces distant. She was looking around and, before he could recover from his surprise, turned to face him. She wore a leather tunic and skirt and a wide belt around her waist and practical leather boots on her feet. Her long, dark hair flowed down her back. This alone, even without the spectacular mode of arrival, would have held Trondwyth's attention. Such had been the style in the days of old, but for many generations female humans in Palindor had worn their hair short. Looking carefully at the girl in front of him, he saw that, though she was barely a woman, she had the look of a warrior, a queen of the olden times, rather than the feeble look of the humans who were scattered around the kingdom in these days.

It was futile to try to hide; the girl had seen him. Trying not to betray his fear, he slowly stepped out from behind the rock.

The girl looked around her with a puzzled air, as if she were lost and were trying to place herself.

Trondwyth took a deep breath and spoke. "Good afternoon. Trondwyth, gnome of Carn Toldwyn, at your service."

Eventually, but with obvious hesitation, she said: "Good afternoon, Mr. Trondwyth. My name is . . . er . . ." She looked confused. "My name is . . . er . . . Ka . . . Ka . . . Ka . . ." She stopped in exasperation.

But Trondwyth had stepped forward three paces while she spoke, and his eyes were no longer on her face. He was gazing at the belt buckle at her waist. It was oblong, with some simple raised characters around the perimeter and a single dull white stone set in the very middle. He had never seen such a buckle before, but he had seen a drawing of such a design long, long ago, he was almost sure. He took another step forward. There could be no doubt. It was a design he had seen in the First Book of Prophecies as a young gnome. He tried to remember the prophesy that went with it. . . . Of this he was sure: a belt with such a buckle could be worn only by a High Monarch of Palindor. The color of the stone would tell him which one. How did that prophecy go?

A white stone for Catherine,
First Queen of Palindor;
A red stone for Michael,

The High King of War.

He could remember no more, but he had no need. The stone was white; a grubby white, it was true, and not the kind of gem that he would have expected in a monarch's belt, but it was white nonetheless. He bowed deeply in front of the girl. "High Queen Catherine," he said, rising slowly from the bow.

The High Queen was mumbling to herself. "Catherine? Catherine?" he thought he heard her say. "That doesn't sound quite right. And yet. . . ." Then she spoke aloud.

"What did you call me?" Gesturing to include the expanse of the Wastes around them, she asked, "What is this place? And what kind of creature are you?"

"I called you High Queen Catherine; is that not your name? The tales of the Old Times tell of humans who will be called High Monarchs of Palindor—humans sent directly by the High Lord, not crowned in the way of ordinary kings and queens. Unless I am mistaken, you are the first of the High Queens, whose name has been foretold to be Catherine. As to this place; these are the Wastes of Kaltethorn, in the northeastern corner of the Kingdom of Palindor. And I? Why, I am a gnome, of course." Trondwyth wondered if the human was some kind of simpleton. Who would not recognize a gnome when she saw one?

The girl still looked confused. "Look," she said, "perhaps you can explain some more. I was sent by an old man who goes by the name of Olvensar, but he explained very little of my purpose here."

"Perhaps," said Trondwyth, "you would care to sit with me and partake of a little food, while we try to determine more precisely our situation. For the High Lord Olvensar sent me also, and with little explanation. But now that you are here, I have little doubt that his purpose was that I should meet you and accompany you in our land. I have food and water aplenty in my pack on the other side of this boulder."

The High Queen looked up into the sky. "It is so hot here. Can't we find some shade? We could eat and talk while we walk, and in that way accomplish three objectives at once."

"Certainly we might, Queen Catherine, but it is a half day's walk to the nearest shade—back the way that I have already come this day," said Trondwyth, gesturing in the direction of the woods.

"No, that doesn't seem right," said Catherine. She looked around, and her eyes settled in exactly the opposite direction, on the peaks of the Mountains of Mourn. "That is the way forward," she said, pointing toward the mountains. "I feel sure of it."

Trondwyth debated with himself whether to argue with the newly arrived (and obviously confused) queen. "In that direction," he said, "there is nothing but the Wastes for some two and a half days' hard journeying. And then there are the Mountains of Mourn, hardly a pleasant introduction to the realm."

"Well, that's the way I'm going," the girl insisted.

Reluctantly Trondwyth gathered his pack. Conversing uneasily, the two began their long march toward the distant mountains.

7

THE TESTING OF
DREFYNT

EREBETH, QUEEN OF Palindor, hurried up
a flight of stone steps near the top of the
north tower of her castle atop a hill on the
northern edge of Carn Toldwyn. Reaching
the top of the steps, she located a key ring
hidden deep in the folds of her garb and unlocked a
massive oaken door. She opened the door, stepped into a
small room, and locked the door behind her.

The room occupied nearly the entire diameter of the
tower. In it stood a single unadorned table and chair.
Sunlight streamed through a north window, adding to the
quiet openness of the room. A window at the southern
end overlooked Carn Toldwyn, providing a magnificent
view of the capital. Indeed, the town had received its
name from the hill that overlooked it and on which the
royal castle had been built by King Yndlarn I. Off in the
distance to the southwest, had the queen cared to look,
were the hills of Perendeth, and beyond them the sunlight
glistened on the cliffs leading down to the Great Sea.

But the queen wasted no time admiring the view. Her

mind was confused, and she had come here to try to dispel her confusion and her feelings of being used. Or so she thought.

Malthazzar knew better. He had driven the body of the queen to this room not because *she* needed to think, but because *he* needed to do so. Now his spirit retreated from the body it occupied while he tried to clarify his thoughts.

For nearly two hours the two creatures, one seen and one unseen, considered carefully their respective positions. At last, Malthazzar concluded, the time had come. Olvensar was coming too close; it was obvious that, after a thousand years in which he had paid little heed to doings in Palindor, he had returned and intended to release the country from the quiet stranglehold in which Malthazzar was placing it. Gone was the time for subtlety and skulking; the time for action was come.

The queen, too, had come to a conclusion. Her mind unfettered by the spirit of Malthazzar, she realized that she needed help in trying to understand what was happening to her. She must seek advice, but from whom? How she wished that the Holy Gnomes had not been destroyed; they surely would have been able to help. . . .

Drefynt! He seemed to be the wisest of her ministers. He would have to do, and she hoped he could tell her what was clouding her mind.

She rose from the chair, her decision made. She crossed the room and fitted the key in the lock, but the door would not open. She strained at it, but no matter how hard she pulled, it would not move. Out of the corner of her eye, she suddenly saw movement in the room. She turned and her hand flew to her mouth to stifle a scream.

In front of her was a dark creature, so dark that she could distinguish no features. Indeed, it appeared more as a black shadow than as a living being. It was doubly black against the sunshine that streamed in through the window, and yet for all its brooding blackness it cast no shadow. Her mind flew back a thousand years to when she was a little girl and her father would frighten her with stories of Malthazzar, the Lord of Evil, who had once battled the High Lord Olvensar himself and who had been dispatched from Olvensar's kingdom to roam the world of material beings. There was no doubt that this was he of whom she had been told all those years ago.

In the almost formless face of the creature before her, she saw open eyes; dark eyes, black on black, they rested upon the queen. Her hand fell away from her mouth and she started to scream, but the sound was never fully formed. Under the gaze of the lord of demons, the old, frail body disintegrated; he made no motion as she turned to dust before him.

A grin spread over his visage and his form began to change. Slowly he became smaller, and color began to flow into him; a shadow began to form until once more there appeared to be only Cerebeth, Queen of Palindor, in the room.

The queen walked across the room, her feet stirring up the pile of dust near the door. She took the key out of the door lock, opened the door effortlessly, left the room, and locked the door once more behind her.

Their lessons over for the day, two young dwarves were playing as usual in the remains of the Barrows at Perendeth, not far from their homes west of Carn Toldwyn. A hundred years ago, they knew, this had been a special place, a place of such learning as was now unknown in the land. But for the two young dwarves it was simply a wonderful, vast playground. They knew all the tunnels by heart and played hide-and-seek in the labyrinth by the hour.

It was Dargant's turn to hide, and Smilthron's to search for him. Dargant scuttled through the maze of tunnels, leaving Smilthron to count slowly to ten for the first of ten times, using his fingers to keep track.

Suddenly Dargant's rushing ceased. He nearly fell over in his haste to stop. He retraced his steps. There it was, no doubt about it: a hole in the wall where none had existed before.

"Smilthron! Smilthron! Come quickly! A new tunnel!" he shouted.

Smilthron stopped his counting and turned his head this way and that, judging the direction from which the shouting had come. Then he began to hurry down a nearby tunnel, calling, "I'm coming! I'm coming!"

Breathless, Smilthron drew up to his friend. Dargant was right. There, where yesterday there had been nothing but smooth tunnel wall, was now a hole. Without another word, the two friends set to work widening the opening until it was large enough to allow a young dwarf through without too much difficulty. Smilthron stood back to let Dargant go first. After all, his friend had discovered the tunnel; it was only right that he should be the first to explore it.

Dargant squeezed through, followed by Smilthron. They rushed down the tunnel, one behind the other. But they were disappointed to see that no other tunnels branched off this one; no great new maze of passages was theirs for the exploring. This tunnel just went straight, sloping gently downwards for a couple hundred paces before it widened into a little chamber with no other exits. The two ran into the chamber and stopped, disappointment showing on their faces. They were about to leave the little room when Smilthron's foot kicked against something hard buried in the lightly packed ground. He knelt down and scraped around in the dirt with his hands. Dargant knelt to help, and together they carefully removed from the earth an object they knew at once to be a book, though neither of them had seen one before this day.

Smilthron opened it gingerly. There were marks on the paper. He closed the book.

"What shall we do with it?" asked Dargant.

"I don't know. Maybe we should take it home and ask our parents. My house is closest, and, in any case, I found it, so why don't we see if my father is home? He'll know what to do."

Dargant refrained from pointing out that Smilthron would not have found the book if *he* had not first found the tunnel. If there was one book here, maybe there were others, and he could come back later without Smilthron and see if he could find them. So all he said was, "All right. Let's do that."

Back out on the surface, unimpeded by the twisting passages, the two friends ran as quickly as they could toward Smilthron's home.

Behind them, in the chamber in which their prize had so recently lain, there was a small movement, as if a breath of wind had somehow penetrated to the depths of the Perendeth tunnels. A dark shadow slowly moved across the chamber. It gave an evil chuckle in the silence and was gone.

The following day, Drefynt looked up from his desk at a sight he had never expected to see again in his lifetime. Three dwarves stood in his doorway, and one, a youngster, held an old, beaten-up leather object—a book!

And by the looks of it, an old book—a Holy Book.

The dwarves stepped inside the room, waiting for the queen's minister to speak. For a few moments, Drefynt was speechless, and then, at last, he spoke to them. "Yes?" he queried. "What can I do for you?"

The elder dwarf spoke, pushing forward the one holding the book. "Tarandron, dwarf of Carn Toldwyn, at your service, good sir. My son and his friend were playing in the tunnels beneath the barrows at Perendeth, and they found this in a chamber."

The young dwarf without the book interjected, "It was in a chamber at the end of a tunnel that we had never seen before. But when we went back later, there was no sign of the tunnel or chamber. We dug and dug where it had been, but it had disappeared!"

"Now, now, Dargent," said Tarandron. "I am sure that the minister doesn't care to hear about how you couldn't find your way back to the chamber again." Then to the other he said, "Smilthron, give the book to Master Drefynt."

The young dwarf reluctantly walked up to Drefynt's desk and laid the book on its surface.

Drefynt was silent for a moment while he stared at the object in front of him. The book was old, battered, and soiled. On the front was the title, written in one of the very oldest scripts: *Prophecies Concerning the Most Holy Gnome*.

He wanted so much to stretch out his hand and look through the book, but he knew that was something he must do in private. It would not do to let it be understood by anyone, even these innocent dwarves, that there still existed in the realm a Holy Gnome, one who could read the old writings of long ago.

"It is a book from the Old Times," he said. "You did

well to bring it to me. I shall bring it to the queen's attention, and she will no doubt reward you handsomely." He peered at the two younger dwarves. "How did you come to find it?"

Both the youngsters began to speak at once, and in the commotion he could understand neither.

"Wait! Wait! One at a time." He pointed to the one who had not carried the book. "You first," he commanded.

Young Dargant told Drefynt the whole story, except for the part that Smilthron did not know—that he, Dargant, had gone back alone in search of more books and found the tunnel gone and only feigned surprise when he and Smilthron could not find the tunnel the next day.

"I see," said Drefynt, although in truth there was much that he did not understand. "Well, if you would return in a couple of days, I am sure that the queen will have a reward for you. Thank you again."

With that he dismissed the dwarves, then closed and locked the door of his study. He felt somehow uneasy about the whole thing. In the first place, there was the tunnel which appeared and then disappeared. That smacked of magic. Worse yet, it sounded like magic for the sake of magic. And while magic was not unheard of amongst the gnomes at Perendeth, it was used as little as possible and only for the good of others, such as when the magic of healing was called for. He could not remember any case in which magic had been used in this way before. And then there was the book itself.

He returned to his desk and fingered it, turning it over in his hands, but carefully refraining from opening it. It certainly looked just like a Holy Book should look. He had never seen this book before, but there were many books in Perendeth that he had never seen. But one with such a title? He would have expected to have seen such a book during his training if its existence had been known.

Prophecies Concerning the Most Holy Gnome. There was no tradition in the Barrows that there would one day be any particular Holy Gnome any greater than the others. If anything, the reverse. The traditions of the Holy Gnomes had it that they were to understand, to learn, to scribe, but hardly ever to participate in the happenings of which they wrote. That a particular Holy Gnome warranted prophecies worthy of note—an entire book of them, no less—was a strange notion.

He turned the cover of the book to the title page, placed a finger under the ancient letter forms and began stumblingly to read. "Prophecies Concerning the Most Holy Gnome"—then the subtitle, "Being Prophecies of the High Lord Concerning the Holy Gnome Drefynt."

He pushed the book away from him. Surely this could not be true! There had been others far more deserving. And yet here it was undeniable, on the desk before him. A set of prophecies about *him*. *He* was the "Most Holy Gnome" of the book title.

He paced around the room for fully five minutes before returning to his seat. Part of him wanted to open the book and read it cover to cover, but another, more cautious part spoke to him that it was not well for a gnome, even a Most Holy Gnome, to know too much about the future. Inwardly he struggled and then finally, wearily, came to a bargain with himself. He would read the first two pages only. After that, no matter what he read, he would hide the book away for at least a year before reopening it.

At peace with his decision, he turned the first leaf of the book and began to read.

In the final year of the reign of the queen who rules for a thousand years, the gnome Drefynt, last of the Holy

Gnomes,—last of the Holy Gnomes? Did this mean Trondwyth was dead?—*will speak with the High Lord in the burned-out Barrows of Perendeth. And such will be the beginning of that period in the history of Palindor which will come to be known as the Age of Drefynt.*

Drefynt will travel in daylight to the Holy Barrows and enter them. He will travel to the very deepest part of the tunnels and there invoke the name of the High Lord, and the High Lord will come, and the High Lord will speak to Drefynt of many things: some things long past, and some things yet to come, and Drefynt's eyes will be opened.

Drefynt struggled with himself whether to turn over on to the third page. But no, he had made a promise. He closed the book, arose, and looked out of the window of his little room in the lower portions of the great castle. It was yet only midafternoon; there was ample time, if he hurried, to reach Perendeth before nightfall. He pulled his coat from the stand in the corner and left the room, carefully locking the heavy entrance door behind him, and hurried down the passageway to the stairs which led down to the courtyard two stories below.

Those who saw him leave the castle were surprised; they had never seen Drefynt the gnome in such a purposeful hurry before. Without comment to any, Drefynt headed out of the town and began the trek up the hill to Perendeth.

He looked across the narrow strip of land separating the mounds from the ocean below as he stood at the entrance to the Holy Barrows. The sun was still above the horizon, but would not be so for many more minutes; he had underestimated the amount of time that it took to reach Perendeth.

I must be getting older, he thought wryly.

With one last look at the sun, he plunged into the Barrows for the first time in a hundred years. After a few seconds' hesitation at the first two or three junctions, he found that he could recall precisely where he was. He journeyed deeper into the tunnels and saw that the passageways were in a remarkably good state of preservation. The kobolds who had dug these tunnels in the early days of Palindor had done their job well.

It took nearly ten minutes of scurrying through the twisty passages before he found himself in what was once the meeting room of the Holy Gnomes, the deepest and largest of the chambers underneath the Barrows. He hurried to one corner of the chamber and there, just as he remembered it, was a small tunnel which led to a tiny chamber just large enough to hold three, or perhaps four, gnomes. It was a study chamber, where those preparing to speak at a meeting of the gnomes could invoke Olvensar's guidance on their speech. He looked around, then paused to listen. Had that been a footstep in the passageway behind him?

Impossible, he decided. Apart from children such as the young dwarves Dargant and Smilthron, it seemed unlikely that the Barrows saw much use these days. He was just a little uneasy, alone in the Barrows after so many years.

But he had a task to perform, and perform it he would. He began to speak out loud, as if to the chamber itself.

"I am come to this place," he intoned, "to seek wisdom, to seek knowledge, from the mouth of the High Lord Olvensar himself."

That was as far as he got. A cackle from the doorway interrupted him, and he spun around to see Queen Cerebeth standing behind him.

"Much too late for that, my dear," she said. "So I was

right! You are a Holy Gnome! And one who has been well trained, I see, for it did not take you long to understand the oldest writing of the gnomes. So tell me, Drefynt, how many Holy Gnomes are still alive?"

Drefynt was momentarily terrified. Long, long ago, in the very meeting room through which he had so recently passed, he had sworn an oath to uphold the truth, so that Olvensar would uphold him in his time of need. Yet where was Olvensar now, when he needed him most?

He looked long and hard at the queen. She was old and frail, he thought, although she looked younger and fitter than he remembered seeing her before.

A gnome in his prime should be able to escape past such a human, he thought.

"Do not even think of escaping," Queen Cerebeth added. "In the passageway without are ten foot soldiers in full armor, swords in hand and bows and arrows on their backs. One gnome—even a Holy Gnome—does not stand much chance against my Royal Guard."

Drawing himself to his full height, which was not substantially less than that of the old human herself, Drefynt answered her question. "There are two of us. That is all."

The queen seemed pleased. "I am glad to see that you have not forgotten your oath, so-called Holy One. And now, pray tell me, on what journey has Olvensar sent your friend Trondwyth?"

Drefynt was stunned. How could she know about this? Was this the danger of which Olvensar had spoken but four days before in Trondwyth's little cottage?

"Journey? What journey?" he said, and immediately felt ashamed of himself. While not exactly an untruth, he felt that a Holy Gnome should not have tried to mask the truth so obviously.

"You know very well what journey," snarled the queen. "The journey on which Olvensar sent him four days ago; the journey that has taken him through the Palindor forest and through Smalterscairn. The journey that seems to be taking him to the very Wastes of Kaltethorn themselves. What is the purpose of that journey?"

"Your Majesty," said Drefynt. "We were told not the purpose of the journey, only that he was to take a pack full of provisions and travel northeast, toward the Wastes. Olvensar said that Trondwyth would know what to do once he was there." Silently Drefynt blessed and thanked Olvensar that his brother had apparently been unharmed thus far. He realized now that the book which had led him here was no more than an elaborate ploy. He had never heard of such a book before simply because there *was* no such book. He realized also, a little crestfallen, that he was indeed not worthy of the title "Most Holy Gnome."

Queen Cerebeth was looking at him intently. "All right. You are a Holy Gnome, and therefore bound to the truth. I believe you. Come! Follow me!" Turning on her heel, she walked up the short corridor to the meeting chamber.

Seeing nothing else for it, Drefynt obediently followed her. He emerged into the chamber to find it seemingly filled with humans: the queen's Royal Guard.

The queen was already striding out across the chamber, no longer looking even remotely like a human a thousand years old. Without glancing behind her, she called out to her troops, "Bring him back to the castle and throw him in the deepest dungeon. Give him food and drink sufficient to keep him alive, but no more."

8

A RIVER CROSSING

T WAS TOWARD the close of Trondwyth's third full day of travel across the Wastes of Kaltethorn that he and the High Queen finally reached their easternmost edge. Together human and gnome had braved the searing heat of the day, the bitter cold of the night, and the unrelentingly difficult passage over and around the boulders. Neither of them was exactly sure what to make of the other.

For Trondwyth's part, he was amazed that the High Lord had sent someone who knew so little of Palindor. Why, this so-called High Queen did not even seem to understand what a gnome was . . . or a dwarf . . . or an elf. Telling her of his journey from Carn Toldwyn, he described the pile of stones in Smalterscairn, and her reaction had been to say "Strange custom" under her breath; she seemed to have no understanding of the long history behind the custom. If it weren't for the fact that Olvensar was the High Lord, Trondwyth would have wondered if perhaps a mistake had been made.

If Trondwyth was unsure what to make of his companion, Catherine was even less sure of what to make of hers. She had spent most of the last two days confused, disbelieving, and not a little scared. What scared her most was that she seemed to have lost her memory. Again and again she tried to remember beyond the time that she had arrived in the Wastes. She had a recollection of a garden and an old man who called himself Olvensar and a vague, uneasy feeling that whatever it was she was doing here, it was frightfully important. But beyond that, absolutely nothing.

And what was she supposed to make of this strange creature by her side? He looked like an old man, with a long white beard that came down to his waist—which, actually, was not so very far from his chin, since even if he were to draw himself to his full height, the top of his head would fall well short of her own shoulders. He called himself a gnome, and he talked casually of other creatures—dwarves, elves, and the like—as if such beings really existed. And this continual pretense that she was a queen of some kind. Even though she could not remember who she was or where she had come from, she was as sure that she was not a queen as she was that there were no such things as gnomes, or dwarves, or elves.

Ahead of them they could at last see arising, seemingly out of the Wastes themselves, the green of a forest and, beyond that, much closer now, the snowcapped peaks of the Mountains of Mourn.

The eastern edge of the Wastes was as sharply delineated as the western. One moment the uneasy companions were walking past hot, dry, dusty rocks. The next, their feet landed on soft brown soil. They entered the shade of trees and all was cool, green moisture.

The two collapsed on the ground, and Trondwyth immediately pulled his pack off his back and sought out two more of the elvish loaves and the canteen of water. Catherine and he ate their loaves hungrily and drank deeply from the canteen.

Trondwyth had been keeping a careful eye on the state of the moon. It was growing larger by the day, but he judged that the canteen would be useful for several days further. He hoped—but doubtfully—that the adventure would be over by then and with it the need for the canteen.

They made camp that night amidst the cool greenness of the forest and awoke refreshed the following morning. They breakfasted again on elvish bread and water.

While the belt around her waist confirmed that the girl was the High Queen Catherine, she still seemed unsure of her role. Twice on their journey Trondwyth had asked her what they would do once they reached the far side of the Wastes. On both occasions Catherine had ignored him. But now the question had to be answered, so he asked it a third time: "Where do we go from here?"

Catherine rose and looked around, although it was impossible to see more than a few paces into the dense forest around them. Twice, and then thrice, she turned slowly in a circle, then shrugged. "I don't know. This way?" She pointed towards the mountains.

Wearily Trondwyth lifted his pack onto his shoulders, and they began to trudge through the forest in the direction in which Catherine had pointed.

They traveled slowly and with difficulty. About midmorning they heard above the sounds of the creaking trees and singing birds a sound as of continuous thunder. Simultaneously, Trondwyth noticed that the ground was shaking slightly. They continued on their way with the noise growing louder and louder until it overcame all else and the trembling of the ground underneath their feet was unmistakable. Without warning they found themselves on the edge of the forest, looking down on a foaming white torrent, narrow but impassable.

Catherine looked across the white waters. Here and there a rock could be seen, but all detail was lost in a flurry of spray as the waters passed over the rapids before them. On the other bank, through a haze of spray, she could see once more the trees of the forest and, brooding ominously over them, the mountains that she sought.

"Look, down there," said Trondwyth, shouting to be heard over the noise of the rapids and pointing a little way downstream.

Catherine's eyes followed the pointing arm, and she saw a little wooden bridge that crossed the river at its narrowest, yet most violent, point.

Together, gnome in front, girl behind, they walked carefully along the narrow strip of green grass by the side of the thunderous waters. The forest rose tall on their right side, while the foaming whiteness raged to their left.

They reached the bridge with no misadventure, then Trondwyth suddenly halted. Catherine was about to walk past him, when his arm came out and held her back.

"I don't like this," said the gnome. "If only there weren't so much foam flying about in the air, I am sure that I would be smelling troll."

Catherine gave a sigh of exasperation. "Next you'll be telling me to watch out for giants or witches on broomsticks. Come on, old man. I don't see any sign of a troll."

"Hmmm . . . no. But then again, one never does until it is too late," murmured the gnome, mostly to himself. "Well, we should just be careful, that's all." He hurried forward until he was a pace or two in front of Catherine, and they made their way out onto the wooden slats of the bridge.

The bridge was in surprisingly good repair, it seemed to Catherine. It must take quite a battering from the continuous spray rising around it, yet it looked almost as if it were brand new. She was pondering this as they neared the opposite shore, when with no warning there came a roar so loud that it could be heard distinctly even over the rushing waters beneath their feet. Out of nowhere, an enormous three-headed troll blocked their path. Catherine let out a horrified scream, and turned to run back across the bridge, but her hand was grasped firmly by Trondwyth, who tugged at her to stop her flight. As she looked back the way they had come, she saw that it was a good thing he had held on to her securely. Where moments before they had been treading safely on bright shiny new boards such as those that they now stood on and which led to the further shore, she saw that the boards they had already crossed were now old and rotting. To set foot on one of those boards would bring instant death, for the boards would surely give way and she would fall to the mighty rapids beneath.

She ceased pulling on Trondwyth and turned back to face their foe. The troll stood nearly twice Catherine's height. Out of the top of its body grew three necks, each as wide as Catherine's waist, and atop each neck was a head. Each head and face was different, and each seemed uglier than the other two.

She realized that the troll's heads were having a conversation amongst themselves. Probably it was supposed to be a private conversation, but the troll seemed incapable of speaking in a normal voice and, if she concentrated through the sound of the roaring water,

Catherine could make out the words clearly enough.

"So, what have we here?" said the leftmost head; Head Number One, Catherine dubbed it.

"Ah! It be breakfast by the looks of it," said the rightmost head, Number Three.

"No, they look valuable to me. I bet they're carrying treasure," said Head Number Two.

"Treasure?" scoffed Three. "If'n they do 'ave treasure then let us first be killing them, and then we can be taking the treasure as well."

"Now, now," said One. "You know the rules. If they give us a treasure, then we must let them pass by. We don't want to be turned to stone again, do we?"

"Ohh, ahh, no. I be remembering last time. And it was cold. And all those people using the bridge wivout our say-so. No. I don't wanna be turned to stone again, fank you very much," said Three.

"Ah," said Two. "But there are two of them. That means one treasure each. That means, let me see, yes, two treasures."

Catherine was beginning to form a not-very-complimentary opinion of the intelligence of at least two of the troll's three heads, but she wisely kept her opinion to herself.

The first head spoke to Catherine and Trondwyth. "You may pass only if you give us two treasures."

"What if we refuse?" shouted Catherine above the roar of the water.

This seemed to confuse the troll. The first head fell silent, but then the second one spoke. "Then we will eat you for lunch."

Catherine and Trondwyth exchanged glances. "But we don't have any treasure," said Catherine to the gnome.

"You do, but I don't, unless the troll will take a magic

canteen, which I doubt," replied Trondwyth. "Take off your belt and give it to him."

Catherine looked down. She had quite forgotten about the belt that had appeared around her waist when she had arrived in Palindor. Yes, that should pass for a treasure. At least it had some kind of a stone inlaid in the buckle, albeit not a very impressive one. She did as the gnome had suggested and held out the belt towards the troll.

The troll beckoned her to come closer. Nervously, and reaching her arm out in front of her, she approached the troll until it held out one of its large, fat hands and took the belt from her. The troll turned it over in his hands, looking at it.

"It isn't much," said Head Number Two to no one in particular.

"Well, I think it's enough. Look at the poor dear. She doesn't have anything else. But the gnome has a pack that is probably stuffed with treasure." Then the first head spoke once more to Catherine. "You may pass. Do come this way again." And the troll stood to one side to let Catherine pass.

Catherine glanced back at Trondwyth. "Go on," he urged, waving her forward.

Reluctantly she edged her way past the troll to the ground on the other side of the bridge. She took a few steps along the side of the river to distance herself further from the troll, which was standing right at the very edge of the bridge, nearly on the bank on which she now stood.

"Now, young gnome," she heard the troll say, "what present do you have for me?"

Trondwyth tried not to look nervous. "Oh, great troll, defender of this most marvelous bridge. I have a treasure the like of which you have never seen before, here in my pack," he said, pulling the pack off his back and placing it on the ground in front of him. As he rummaged around in the pack, he looked up at the troll, whose third head appeared to be fully occupied in examining the belt. "You should try the belt on," said Trondwyth. "It would make you even more impressive."

The troll, clasping the belt which had fit Catherine so perfectly, tried to wrap it around his own huge waist, but there was no way that he could make it come even close to reaching around his girth.

"Perhaps it would fit around one of your necks?" suggested Trondwyth.

At this the heads nodded in agreement.

"I was the one who asked her for a treasure," said the first head.

"But it would look better on me, because I am in the middle," said the second.

"But she was most scared of me," roared the third, and brooking no further debate, the hands lifted the belt and placed it firmly around the neck belonging to the third head.

All three heads swung back toward the gnome. "Now—" began the third head, but then it fell silent.

Catherine watched in horror as the troll began to change color. Spreading outward, up and down from where the belt was now firmly affixed around the third neck, the troll was turning gray. The other two heads swung around just as the gray reached the top of the third head and simultaneously began to travel across the troll's body.

"No!" screamed the first head, and the troll raised its arms desperately to try to remove the belt. It was too late. The line of gray spread rapidly across its body, down its arms to its hands, which suddenly ceased moving. In seconds it was over, and the troll stood there, turned to stone.

For a few seconds longer there was no motion on the bridge. Trondwyth began to tie up his pack once more. But then, as Catherine looked on in horror, the remaining good timbers on the bridge began to change from yellow to dirty brown. With a mighty crash, the stone troll fell through the bridge to the bank below, causing the rest of the bridge to collapse along its length. Trondwyth grabbed desperately at his pack, holding on to it tightly as he fell into the rushing waters. He was swept downstream, and Catherine saw his body rise up only twice, disappearing under the white water each time before it was swept out of sight around a curve two hundred feet away.

She looked back at the bridge, to see that there was no longer any trace of it; it was as if the way across the river had never existed. But against the bank on which she stood lay a statue of a three-headed troll. The leather belt with its white jewel, which seemed to glitter more brightly than it had done just a few minutes before, was strapped around one of the statue's three necks. She looked back down the river, but knew with a sinking feeling that there was no point in trying to follow Trondwyth.

She walked back up the riverbank a few steps to where the troll leaned against the bank. Although the water swirled around the new obstruction, it was clear to Catherine that the weight of the statue would keep it from moving. She held out a hand and found that she could easily reach the belt which she had so recently given up. She clambered up onto the troll and undid the belt buckle, half afraid that the troll would come back to life, but the gray stone gave no sign of changing back to flesh and clothing. Grasping her prize firmly, she jumped back down onto the riverbank.

She looked the belt over; there was no doubt that the white jewel appeared brighter than it had been before. She wondered if it was safe to put the belt back on. She did not want to be turned to stone like the troll. But, she reasoned, she had worn the belt without incident for three days already, so she grasped the ends of the belt firmly and buckled it around her waist. She looked down and, after a few seconds, gave a sigh of relief.

Then, wearily, she sat down on the bank, her emotions and thoughts colliding haphazardly. Thus far she had given no credence to Trondwyth's claim to be a gnome. But the happenings of the past few minutes changed all that. Undeniably, the statue a few yards from her had until moments ago been a living, breathing three-headed troll. And if that were so, perhaps Trondwyth really was a gnome. And perhaps those stories he had been telling for the past tree days were not just stories.

But it was too late; even if he were still alive, Trondwyth must be far away by now. What was she to do? She was a stranger in this land, all the food was with the gnome. Looking about, she observed a little track leading into the forest from where the bridge had stood. There was nothing for it but to follow the track.

She went to the river edge and, lying out on her stomach, scooped handfuls of water up from the river and quenched her thirst. Then resolutely she stood, looked around once more, and set out along the track.

9

UNDER THE
MOUNTAINS

T WAS FOUR HOURS since Catherine had left the river behind her; for nearly half a day she had followed the little track from where it left the riverbank. It had almost immediately wound around to the south and continued in that direction for the remainder of the day. But as she had trekked, the path had risen steeply up the mountains that rose ominously to her left. At first the going had been easy, surrounded as she was by the coolness of the forest. But for the past hour the forest had thinned out, and the sun in the north shone down on her back, making her sweat with the exertion of the continual climb. For some time now, she had been seeing small patches of dirty snow by the sides of the track, in the shadows of the pines to her right.

Now, as midafternoon passed into late afternoon, a new worry began to surface: what about the night ahead? If she had not been walking hard all day she would already be chilly. As soon as the sun set, the air would become cold, and she had no way of keeping warm. All she could do was to press on and hope that the track which had so singlemindedly wound uphill all day would soon take a turn downwards.

She trekked on desperately for another half hour, the sun no longer behind her, but now below the line of trees to her right. Still the track wound up the side of the mountains, the snow patches becoming larger and larger with each passing minute. She stopped, gasping for breath. There was nothing for it, she decided, but to leave the track and strike back to the west down the mountainside in search of a warm spot to spend the night. She stopped at a patch of snow and scrabbled away the dirty layer on the surface. Then she took handfuls of the exposed clean snow and let them melt in her mouth. It was not pleasant, but it would do her good, so she forced herself to the task. After several handfuls of snow, she continued on her way down the mountainside.

Just as the sun began to set through the trees, she found a little hollow up against a large boulder in which there were several inches of soft, old pine needles. She set to moving the needles around so as to make a big pile into which she intended to thrust herself and sleep as snugly as possible for the night. For perhaps fifteen minutes she toiled away, until she was satisfied that she could do no more. She leaned against the boulder next to the pile she had formed, resting her aching body.

Suddenly her right foot, which was in a little dip in the ground buried under the pine needles, slipped sideways. The movement was too fast for her to prevent what followed. Deeper and deeper her foot and then her leg slipped, and in no time she found her entire body sliding downward. She slipped and bumped for a couple of seconds, and then all motion ceased. She stood up, blinking her eyes to see where she had landed. She was covered in pine needles from the fall, and she tried to brush them off and tidy herself while looking around.

It was too dark to see anything clearly. The sun had set, and almost no light reached into wherever she was. Above her, three times her own height, she could make out a light patch of sky, as if she had fallen down into a small subterranean cave. She put her arm out and felt a soft wall to her left. It felt and smelled earthy, loamy. Feeling around on the floor, which appeared to be of the same substance as the walls, she decided that she was unlikely to find a better place in which to spend the night than this. In any case, she had no choice, because she could not climb out of the hole without more light.

So as darkness settled on the forest outside, Catherine, First High Queen of Palindor, covered herself with a layer of pine needles and rested her weary body for the night. Her sleep was interrupted only once when she woke up, her heart beating wildly, from a dream in which she saw Trondwyth swept away out of her sight by the white river. She had no idea whether gnomes could swim, nor even if Trondwyth had remained conscious as he was swept away. As tears of remorse wetted her bed of needles, she cried herself back to sleep.

The following morning she awoke to the sound of the dawn chorus as the forest birds greeted the new day. She raised herself up from her bed and stretched herself thoroughly to rid her body of the aches of sleeping in such a place. She looked up to where the previous night she had seen the small gray patch of sky. Now the sky was blue, but it was no larger, just a patch of bright blue against the otherwise black sky of a small underground chamber. She had not been mistaken last night; the entrance to the chamber was ten feet or more over her head, and she could see no obvious way to reach the hole in the ceiling. She looked away from the bright light above and closed her eyes tightly, counting slowly to one hundred. Her eyes cast to the ground, she reopened them and tried to see around her in the gloom of the chamber. It appeared to be almost a room, with what passed for corners about every ten feet around the side. The walls and the floor were made of soft, crumbly brown earth, the sort of soil in which almost anything can be made to grow. All except the middle of one wall. There, a few feet from her, there appeared to be a hole in the wall. She walked over the pine needles piled up on the ground across to the hole. Leading away from the chamber was a small passage, just large enough that she could stand upright in it.

What else could she do? Hungry and thirsty once again, she took a step forward into the tunnel, then another and another. Within a few steps, Catherine realized that, despite appearances, the chamber which she had just left was not at all dark; this tunnel was *truly* dark. She could barely see anything ahead of her as she continued to walk, her hands stretched out, one in front of her so that she might not walk into anything, and one held in front and slightly above her, running along the ceiling, so that she would not bump her head if the tunnel were suddenly to become lower. But from some way in front of her she could see a dim glow.

The tunnel angled downward into the ground with walls, floor, and ceiling of the same brown earth as the chamber behind her. She walked slowly onward; after a couple of minutes, the glow ahead was definitely brighter and closer. Suddenly—and she was glad that she still had her hands outstretched—the corridor turned a corner sharply to the right. Another few steps, and the nature of the tunnel changed completely. No more was it passing through dark brown earth. Instead the tunnel was hewn from a gray rock the like of which Catherine had never seen before. It was this rock that was shining dimly, lighting up the corridor.

Catherine lowered her arms, for now she could see clearly enough around her. The tunnel was just as she had surmised it would be: about five and a half feet high and maybe two feet across, hewn roughly out of the rock. The height looked sufficiently constant that she would not have to worry about bumping her head, as long as she proceeded slowly and carefully. Running in the tunnel would be difficult, she thought.

The tunnel appeared to continue onward, traveling downward at about the same angle as it had done before. The leather boots which had appeared on Catherine's feet with her arrival in the Wastes echoed unnervingly as the stone amplified the small sound of each footstep.

She continued in this way for perhaps half an hour when suddenly the tunnel opened into a little chamber. She saw that it contained a total of four entrances: the one through which she had entered and three others, each angling downwards but otherwise identical to the one through which she had been traveling.

Arbitrarily she chose the leftmost tunnel and followed it for a while. First on one side and then on the other, tunnels led off from the one along which she was progressing. Then suddenly there seemed to be tunnels everywhere. She couldn't travel more than a hundred feet without another tunnel branching off or crossing hers. And every few hundred feet there would be a chamber in which several tunnels met. By now, Catherine realized, the tunnels sloped (although never steeply) in all directions, some upward, some downward.

She was now thoroughly lost and confused. She

entered yet another chamber—her tenth? she had lost count some time ago—and sank to the ground in the middle of the floor, too tired and lost to continue.

As she sat there mulling over her situation, she heard a scurrying sound nearby. Looking up, she saw a small, furry creature staring at her from a tunnel. It was only a couple of feet high, golden haired, and looked not unlike a giant dormouse. Its whiskers flicked nervously as it stared at her from steady, dark eyes. Then it spoke, but quietly, so that its voice did not carry through the tunnels.

"Hello," the creature greeted her. "What kind of animal is this, I wonder? Can you speak?"

"Well, yes, I can speak," said Catherine. Her voice was barely more than a whisper, but it still seemed to echo around the room dismayingly more than had the other creature's.

"Shh. . . ." said the animal, "or they'll find us. Nice belt you have there."

"Who will fi—?" Catherine started to ask.

"Shush!" the creature spat out, tilting its head to one side.

Catherine listened, but could hear nothing.

"They're coming. I will talk to you later. In the meantime, whatever you do, don't tell them who you are. Remember that—it's most important." With a flick of its tail, the creature disappeared down the passageway.

Catherine wanted to call out after it, but stifled her shout. She listened intently. Yes, there were sounds: voices and feet. She could make them out now, and they seemed to be getting louder, coming this way. Should she hide? As quietly as she could, she crawled over to the passageway through which she thought she had entered the chamber, although she was by now so thoroughly lost that she had no way of knowing for sure. She pressed herself down against the gray stone. To her surprise, it was warm to her touch.

From her hiding place she saw the first of the repulsive creatures. Large headed, with a greenish tinge to its skin and ugly, pointed ears, it marched into the middle of the chamber, followed by another three identically ugly creatures. They almost filled the little room, and Catherine slid quietly backwards a few more inches into the shadows.

Goblins! she decided. *They must be goblins.*

The three attendant creatures waited while their leader sniffed the air, his beaklike nose waving to and fro.

"The dablik was here," announced the leader, "but there is another smell."

Catherine was amazed that the goblin could sense anything over the stench that had accompanied his party into the chamber. It reminded her of nothing so much as partially rotted seaweed.

Suspiciously the goblin turned, and his oversized eyes looked straight up the tunnel in which Catherine was hiding, directly into her own eyes. "There!" he said in a loud voice. "A human! Grab it!"

Almost before she could move, the goblins were upon her. They pulled her unceremoniously along the ground, out into the chamber which now, with the one human and four goblins, was truly a tight fit.

"Stand up!" barked the leader.

As best she could, Catherine did so.

"You will come with us," he said to her, adding under his breath, "This will be a surprise for the king."

Catherine was marched out of the chamber, the leader and one goblin in front of her and the remaining two behind. Each goblin carried a stick that reached nearly to the roof and was tipped with a ferocious-looking metal point. She was hurried along the winding passage. Soon the passage became broader and taller and the chambers similarly became larger. She noticed other goblins hurrying this way and that through the tunnels. Many stopped to let them by, gazing at her in amazement. "A human!" she heard a couple of them say incredulously.

After several minutes of this, by which time Catherine had adjusted to the smell which now must surely surround her, they arrived at a particularly large chamber. The leader instructed the others to remain there and guard Catherine. He disappeared down a little tunnel, to reappear a minute or so later.

"You may leave her to me," he said. "The king will see her now." The other goblins stepped back, and the leader lowered his stick to point threateningly at Catherine. "You! That way!" he commanded her, pointing his stick in the direction of the tunnel through which he had just emerged.

Followed by her captor, Catherine walked down the tunnel until it opened out into a small, bright room. The light appeared to come both from the rock, which seemed to be brighter than in the other places she had been, and from the gold and bejeweled trappings of the room. Everywhere she looked, she could see precious stones reflecting the light in a kaleidoscope of colors. All about her were magnificent golden tables and chairs decorated with the finest royal purple cloth, which seemed to shimmer with a life of its own. At the end of the room farthest away from the entrance was an elevated portion on which sat a golden throne covered with bright red stones. On the throne, a small crown of purest gold on his head, sat the goblin king, his gray-green skin shining slimily in the reflected light.

Catherine was unsure what she should do, but the

king soon informed her.

"Is it not usual to bow in the presence of a king, human?"

Catherine nearly forgot the dablik's warning and blurted out that if anyone should be doing the bowing it was the goblin. Remembering just in time, she merely lowered her head. Raising it again, she apologized. "I am sorry, great goblin king. I was so awed by the magnificent decorations of the room that I forgot my manners."

The king looked somewhat mollified. "Well, never mind," he said. "The question is, are you indeed a human? You smell like a human, although it is many, many years since I have breathed the rank odor of humankind. But you have a different look to you. I remember them as being lumbering creatures of little intelligence."

"Your Majesty," said Catherine, "I am indeed human. Catherine is my name. I am but a visitor to Palindor."

"I see. But how come you to be wandering in our tunnels? We have never in my memory—and I have a very long memory—had a human visitor before."

"I am sorry if I have intruded upon Your Highness," said Catherine, "but I came here by accident. I was wandering in the forest on the surface and fell into a chamber from which the only escape was into these tunnels."

The king considered this for a moment. "But what was a human doing wandering in the Mountains of Mourn?" he asked. "Humans are a rare sight even on the surface in these parts, unless things overhead are greatly changed indeed."

Catherine decided that honesty, at least up to a point, might prove the best policy. So she said, "Your Majesty, I was sent on an errand to the Mountains of Mourn by Olvensar—"

The king immediately interrupted her. "Olvensar, Malthazzar, what care we for the likes of them down here? They are creatures of the surface and have no power here in the very bowels of the mountains. You there," he said to the goblin who had brought Catherine into the room, "give her such food and water as she needs and let her roam the tunnels as she will. We will consider her future once we have captured that dablik."

It did not escape Catherine's notice that at the mention of Olvensar's name the goblin king had hurried to rid himself of her presence. She wondered if it were true that Olvensar could not reach her here.

"Yes, Your Majesty," her captor said, bowing so low that his head nearly scraped the rock of the ground. He lowered his spear toward Catherine once more, and Catherine knew that the audience was over. He led her away down the tunnel once again and repeated the king's command to the other three goblins. One of them stepped forward and volunteered to look after Catherine while the others resumed their search for the little creature.

The volunteer led Catherine away through the tunnels. He was chatty and seemed a pleasant enough sort, for a goblin. Catherine learned that the guard's name was Kalingroth, and the king, who ruled over all the goblins in these parts, was King Goldarth. Kalingroth was a middle-aged goblin, 175 years old, and he had never seen a human before, although he had been out on the surface many times in his younger days. He confessed that he knew little of Olvensar and his enemy, Malthazzar, saying, like the king, that they were of the surface and unimportant to the goblins who ruled their own kingdom here, deep in the rocks.

Catherine asked him about the tunnels and passageways, and her guide informed her that they had been built long, long ago. There was little need for new passageways these days, he said, although occasionally they would dig some new tunnels in search of jewels or other treasure. He also confessed that most of the tunnels in the area where she had been found were now unused, and that many of the goblins were frightened to venture so far from the more spacious tunnels of the deeper, populated portion of their system. No goblin knew more than a tiny fraction of the entire system and it was a rare week that passed without some poor goblin getting lost in the fringes of the system, never to be seen again.

After a few more minutes of trudging through the corridors, they arrived at a small chamber at the end of a long, narrow tunnel. Two other tunnels led away from the chamber. On the floor was a generous supply of some soft material.

"This is where you stay until the king decides what to do with you," the guard said. "You're free to roam around the tunnels as much as you like. Food will be brought when you need it." Without another word, the friendly guard turned on his heels and was gone.

Catherine looked around and collapsed onto the soft floor. For the first time since she had arrived in Palindor, she felt completely alone and uncared for. Wondering if she would ever see Trondwyth again, she could no longer suppress her tears. They dripped down her face and onto the floor against which she was huddled until, eventually, sleep came upon her.

When she awoke, there were two bowls by her side. One held water and one a substance which she supposed to be food. It looked like some sort of cold porridge and smelled like nothing she could describe, but to her surprise, it tasted remarkably pleasant. She devoured the porridge and then drank from the water bowl. She wished

Kalingroth would come back so she could ask for more food. Although she could hear the sound of many scurryings in the tunnels around her, there was no sign of anyone coming into her chamber.

Feeling better for her tears, sleep, and food, she decided to do a little exploring. She learned that she could find her way around as long as she kept within a couple of hundred paces of her chamber, and she tried to memorize the layout of the nearby tunnels and chambers. If she once lost track of where she was, Catherine knew she would never find her way back. Goblins stared at her in the tunnels, but never spoke to her; they seemed almost afraid of this strange creature from the overworld.

Engaged in her small explorations, she completely lost track of time. At intervals of what seemed like about three hours, food and water were brought for her. She soon realized that the goblins made do completely without night and day. There was roughly the same amount of activity going on in the surrounding tunnels whatever time of day it might be up on the surface far above her head. She was told simply to sleep when she was tired.

She had no idea how long she was in this state. At the time it seemed like a week, although later, when she calculated it properly, she found that it was probably no more than two full days. In any case she was surprised one morning—she called it morning simply because she had only just concluded a meal following a period of sleep—to hear a quiet shushing noise coming from one of the tunnels which joined her little chamber. She looked toward the hole in the wall, and there was the little furry creature—the dablik—that she had seen just before she had been captured.

It popped its head out into the chamber and looked around cautiously, then it scurried across the ground until it was standing next to her. The resemblance to a giant dormouse was even more striking than it had been before.

"Good day," said the creature. "I trust that you have not told these friendly folk who you are?"

"No. I told them my name, but that was all," whispered Catherine. "But who do you think I am, and who are you, and why are they chasing you? You shouldn't be here, you know. They might capture you."

"Not much fear of that," said the creature. "But let me introduce myself properly. It is not every day that one stumbles across a High Queen seated in a goblin's chamber." With that, the creature raised itself up onto its hind legs, and bowed low. "I am known as the dablik, and I am at your service, Queen Catherine."

"How do you know my name?"

"Even if I had not heard you give it to the king the other day, your belt gives you away. Only the High Queen Catherine can wear that belt without being turned to stone. And in any case, after a thousand years of that woman ruling the land up above, Palindor is just about in need of the first High Monarch."

Catherine did not pretend to understand much of this speech, but she realized that this was not the time for further questions.

"I am trapped here, you know," she said.

"Trapped?" said the dablik, surprised. "You don't look very trapped to me. And in any case, that is not the usual goblin way. Usually they give their guests the run of the system."

"Well, yes, they did say that I could go anywhere that I liked," admitted Catherine. "But I would get lost quickly if I went very far from this place. I might as well be trapped." She looked over at the creature, who did not respond. Catherine plucked up her courage. "I hope that you don't think me rude, but what kind of creature are you? I can't say that I have seen anything exactly like you before."

"I am sorry. I thought I told you," said the dablik. "I am a dablik. Well, actually, *the* dablik. I don't think there is more than one like me. One of Olvensar's little experiments, my friend Glandryth always says, although that's more than I know, I am sure."

"I see," said Catherine. "Well, good dablik, you never told me why the goblins were trying to find you."

"Jealousy, simple jealousy. They have probably told you all about how vast their system of tunnels is and that no one knows more than the tiniest portion of it."

Catherine nodded.

"Well, that's a load of poppycock. In the first place, their part of the system—that is, the part which the goblins of Mourn claim as their own—is only a tiny fraction of the whole thing. Why, you can go from here to Carn Toldwyn without ever seeing the light of day should the urge take you. And while it may be true that the goblins don't know very much of it, the same certainly can't be said for the dablik. They have been trying to capture me, off and on, for oooh, ever such a long time now, but it doesn't seem likely that they'll succeed. They don't like the idea of someone else using their tunnels, you see, especially when that someone uses them so much more efficiently than they themselves."

The dablik's tone of voice suddenly changed. "Well," he said, "time is moving along, and we had better be going. Follow me." He turned toward one of the tunnels which joined the chamber—not, Catherine was fairly sure, the one through which he had entered.

Catherine rose to her feet and followed; anything was better than sitting in her chamber indefinitely. The dablik had dropped to all fours and was hurrying along. It was difficult for Catherine to move as quickly while remaining quiet, especially as she had to run slightly stooped to keep from hitting her head against the stone roof of the tunnel the dablik had selected.

The dablik quickly saw Catherine's problem and began to move more slowly. She had to admire his skills at navigating. Even the goblins who had first captured her had moved slowly through the tunnels, continually checking that they indeed knew where they were. But the dablik didn't hesitate once. He would enter a chamber and leave it again by one of the numerous possible exits without any hint of indecision. Every now and then, he would suddenly dive off into a side tunnel, as if he knew exactly where he was going and which was the most efficient route.

At first Catherine was wary of meeting goblins. But within a few minutes it became evident, as the tunnels began to resemble the narrower and rougher ones down which she had traveled to reach the domain of the goblins, that they were leaving the goblins behind. The passages began to angle upward and there were no longer any chambers. Only occasionally was there a joining of tunnels. Mostly the dablik no longer took side tunnels, and only rarely changed the general direction of his upward travel.

Without warning, they turned a corner, and suddenly it was pitch black ahead. Catherine stopped, taken aback by the blackness into which the dablik had fearlessly walked. She put out her hand and felt warm, soft earth. Oh, how relief spread through her body! The earthy smell overwhelmed her; the stench of goblins was far behind. She had not realized until this moment how deep were her fears that she might never feel such ground again.

"Come on. Nearly there!" called out the voice of the dablik ahead of her.

"I'm coming," she said, "but it's so dark."

"Oh, I'm sorry. I forgot about that. Wait there a minute."

She stood still, her hands still grasping the beautifully soft earth when, some distance ahead, a light appeared. Not a dull, artificial, constricted light such as a candle gives off, but the gloriously glowing natural light of sunshine. She hurried toward the light and, not ten seconds later, stepped into a small room into which sunlight was streaming through a window.

10

THE WIZARD AND
HIS APPRENTICE

RONDWYTH'S FIRST THOUGHT as he saw the shiny new boards beneath his feet turning to decayed, rotting wood was annoyance at his own stupidity. He had known, if the words about the High Monarchs of Palindor in the *First Book of Prophecies* were to be trusted, that no one except the High Queen Catherine would be permitted to wear the belt that his companion wore so negligently around her waist. The prophecies were very clear: each High Monarch would have his or her own belt, the buckle carrying a similar engraving whose meaning was now lost to all, but each with a unique stone, a different color for each monarch. Anyone other than the rightful owner who attempted to wear such a belt would be turned to stone for a hundred years.

But it was the first time that the gnome had seen a fellow living creature turned to stone by the power of kir´al, and he had been spellbound as he watched the change take place. But then the boards changed color, and he knew in a flash what he should have realized before—the bridge was part of the troll's enchantment, which dissolved as its master turned to stone. Trondwyth crashed through the boards, holding tightly to his pack.

The pack absorbed the shock of impact, but it could do nothing to help him against the rapidly moving waters. The water had only recently been snow and ice high above in the Mountains of Mourn, and there was nothing to protect him from the icy chill as the river swept him away. He tried to keep his head above water, but the current was too strong, and time and time again his head was dragged under. It was all he could do to hold on to the pack and grab a breath of air each time his head surfaced.

He had no idea how long he was swept downstream in this way. His whole body was in pain as he was buffeted along, hitting rocks and bouncing off them, only to have the water pick him up and throw him at yet more rocks. His arms were getting tired gripping the pack, as were his lungs as they fought to take breaths at irregular intervals.

At last the rocks were no more and he was simply being swept along by the river. He was barely conscious and, even had he known how to swim, he was far too overcome by fatigue and pain to exert himself. Eventually the river took a sharp turn to the right and he was carried up against the left bank. It was shallow here at the outermost edge of the river's meander; he tried to pull himself up onto the shore, but he was in too much pain and was simply too tired. He collapsed on top of his pack, half in and half out of the water, and there lost consciousness.

Trondwyth remembered nothing of how he traveled from the riverbank to the little house half buried in the side of the hill. He had a vague recollection of being pulled and carried, but nothing more than shadowy impressions, and he could not be sure if they were real or the remnants of uncomfortable dreams.

The last thing he remembered clearly was reaching the riverbank; the next was waking to find himself in a warm bed encased in clean linen, in a bright and airy room with the sun streaming in at the open window. He tried to sit up in the bed, but found that he ached all over, and fell back from the pain and effort. He must have made a noise because, without warning, a dwarf stuck his head around the open doorway.

"Oh, good," he heard the dwarf say to himself, and then the creature was disappeared.

He heard voices, too far away to be understood, and then, a couple of minutes later, the dwarf reentered the room, accompanied this time by an old, unkempt man. Trondwyth had no need to look twice to be aware of the air of magic around the man; there could be no doubt that he was a wizard.

"Ah, good morning," said the wizard, bowing slightly so that the tall green hat he wore appeared in danger of falling off. "I am so glad to see you recovering. You have slept for more than a day. How do you feel?"

Trondwyth was surprised to hear how weak his own voice sounded. "Tired and sore."

"But no great pain, only soreness?" asked the wizard.

"Yes, I think that is all," said the gnome. "I tried to sit up, but it was too hard."

"Yes, yes, it would be. Maybe this afternoon." The wizard turned to the dwarf. "Gondalwyn, would you be so good as to bring us the bowl of broth from the stove? I think that it will help our guest to feel considerably better."

The dwarf bowed slightly and was gone. The wizard

turned back to see Trondwyth trying to raise himself once more. "No, no," said the wizard, "time enough for that later. For now you need to get something inside you and then rest some more."

But Trondwyth had just remembered the events that had occurred immediately before his fall into the river. "But my companion . . ." he said.

"A companion?" said the wizard, betraying interest but no surprise. "Could you please describe this companion?"

Trondwyth gave up the struggle to sit and reserved his strength for speech. "A young human woman, little more than a child really, with long hair. . . ." He was interrupted by the sight of Gondalwyn reentering the room carrying a small bowl from which the most peculiar scent arose. One second it smelled like strawberries in season and the next more like potato soup.

"No more talking," said the wizard. He took the bowl of steaming liquid from the dwarf. Between the two of them, they raised Trondwyth's head so that he could taste of the broth inside the bowl. The flavor came as much of a surprise as the ever-changing smell. It tasted of herb and plant, of root and stem, of wildness and strength. Trondwyth, for all his two hundred years, had never tasted anything like it. He wolfed it down with the help of the wizard and the dwarf, and the liquid went into his stomach, leaving him feeling pleasantly satiated and warm all over. Then the wizard and the dwarf let his head rest back on the pillow.

Trondwyth opened his mouth to speak, but found that he was battling closing eyelids. He could not utter a complete word before he was once more fast asleep.

"Good," said the wizard. "He should awake again by teatime. He will be considerably stronger by then."

As the wizard had predicted, Trondwyth slept deeply

and well until the smell of freshly made tea came curling into the room and found his nostrils. He awoke, hungry and thirsty and feeling, if not exactly perfect, certainly strengthened. He sat up in bed without difficulty and noticed for the first time that he was wearing pajamas a little too large for him. Presumably they belonged to the dwarf who, although roughly the same height as the gnome, was of a considerably more sturdy build.

Trondwyth found that he could stand and walk as long as he was careful. Motion that was too rapid made him feel dizzy and forced him to close his eyes, but as long as he took things gently he could get around quite nicely. He walked out of the bedroom and entered a cozy front room into which the sun now shone as brightly as it had done in the bedroom earlier in the day.

There were four large armchairs spaced around a central wooden table. Two of the armchairs were occupied by the wizard and the dwarf. The dwarf was just in the act of pouring a cup of tea for the wizard as Trondwyth entered the room.

The wizard looked up. "Ah, good. I'm so glad that you are feeling better. Do please join us for tea." He waved toward one of the empty armchairs, and Trondwyth slowly walked across the room and gently sat down.

"Thank you," he said to the wizard.

"Now," said the wizard, "not another word until you have some tea and a slice of cake inside you."

The dwarf dutifully poured a cup of tea into the cup which, to Trondwyth's surprise, was already waiting for him, and passed over a slice of fruitcake. Trondwyth realized how hungry and thirsty he was. But the cake was deceptive; he found that he was feeling full once more even before he had finished eating the slice.

Suddenly there was a swishing noise to Trondwyth's

right. He looked across the room to where the noise had originated, and saw that a curtain had been pulled away. He could not see clearly what lay beyond the curtain; it looked dark, almost as if it were nothing more than a hole in the wall. And seeing as how the little house appeared to be at least partway underground on the side of a hill, that meant the hole would lead straight into the earth.

But he caught only a quick glimpse of what lay beyond the curtains before a creature walked out and pulled the curtain closed behind it. In all his readings as a Holy Gnome, Trondwyth had never encountered a creature whose description matched the animal that he now saw before him. It looked like some sort of large mouse, golden in color. It was standing on its rear paws, but soon dropped onto all fours to cross the room. It looked friendly enough as it padded across the room and took its place at the fourth armchair. Trondwyth saw that the dwarf had poured a cup of steaming tea which the animal hurriedly grasped and began to drink.

"Glad you could make it," said the wizard to the creature. Then he turned back once more to Trondwyth. "Forgive me," he said. "You must think me rude. Allow me to perform the introductions. My name is Entelred. This," he said, gesturing toward the dwarf, "is Gondalwyn, my courteous and worthwhile apprentice. And this," indicating the newly arrived mouse-like creature, "this is the dablik. And now," he continued, giving Trondwyth time to do no more than nod at each of the three in turn, "you must tell us how you came to be washed up by the side of the river. And please, tell us a little of your companion also." Perhaps it was Trondwyth's imagination, but he was sure that he saw the wizard look meaningfully at the dablik as he said this last sentence.

But at least the wizard's speech had clarified one

puzzle. He was in the home of Entelred, the oldest and most famous of living wizards. The wizard had lived not far from Carn Toldwyn until about twenty years ago when, without warning, he had disappeared one day.

"Your Magnificence," Trondwyth said, employing the courteous greeting of gnome to wizard, "I wish to thank you for saving me."

"Pooh. It was a little-enough thing. You should thank Gondalwyn. He did most of the work of getting you here, strapping you to the cart and pulling it up the road to my humble abode."

Trondwyth bowed his head toward the dwarf and thanked him. Then he proceeded to tell his story, leaving out only the parts in which Olvensar featured and the fact that his companion who was now, he feared, wandering lost through the woods nearby was actually a High Queen of Palindor.

He told his tale through to the end without ceasing. Then the wizard spoke. "A nice story, as far as it goes, young Trondwyth. But I fear that it does not go far enough. Pray tell me, what interest does the queen have in you? That is a question on which your tale sheds no light."

"The queen? Interest in me?" queried the gnome. "I know not of what you speak."

"Hmmm. . . . Perhaps you speak the truth," said Entelred. "Then it is just as well that I should warn you. Gondalwyn and I saw a hawk of the night watching over you when we found you. And no sooner had we reached you than it turned and made its way west—to report to the queen, unless I am very much mistaken. Still, no matter, at least for now. You are still weak. Perhaps in a couple of days you will be sufficiently recovered to leave and go in search of your companion. There is little danger in these parts, even though we are remote from the civilization of Carn Toldwyn—indeed, perhaps the danger is less because we are so removed from civilization—and I doubt that she will come to much harm."

This time Trondwyth was in no doubt. A look had passed between Entelred and the dablik.

Suddenly, the dablik rose out of his chair. "I must be going. It's been a pleasure to meet you," he said, bowing low to Trondwyth. He turned toward the wizard. "Tomorrow, do you think?"

"Yes," said the wizard. "That would be fine. I am worried about what might happen if we leave it longer."

Without any words of explanation, the creature bowed low toward his host and then dropped onto all fours and scurried away across the room. Once more Trondwyth caught a glimpse of darkness as the curtain was drawn aside to let the creature pass.

For the next twenty-four hours Trondwyth felt a peace that he had forgotten existed. It reminded him in some ways of his youth. Here in the home of Entelred there was no pressure to do anything. The wizard and the dwarf made good company, talking of this and that, nothing in particular. The wizard was particularly interested to be told, over a late night cup of cocoa, that Trondwyth knew Drefynt: "that most intelligent of gnomes," as Entelred described him. Although Trondwyth did not tell the wizard of their relationship, he could not escape the feeling that Entelred knew far more about Trondwyth and Drefynt and, in particular, Catherine than he ever let on.

Trondwyth slept deeply that night, and by the next morning, as he lay stretched out in the warm sunshine, he was feeling as well as he had ever done. The only worry that infiltrated his peaceful state of mind was concern over Catherine's fate. He wondered what had become of her and, after an aimless morning during which he became increasingly guilty about his inactivity, he went looking for Entelred. He intended to tell the old wizard that he would be leaving the following day to look for his lost companion.

He found the wizard sitting on a log a short distance from the house in a glade into which the sunshine poured. Looking at Entelred from the edge of the clearing, he realized with some surprise how old he must be. The wizard was leaning on a staff, a frown giving his face an appearance even more lined and careworn than usual. He did not glance up as Trondwyth approached. Trondwyth sat on the cool grass in front of the wizard, awaiting the latter's recognition of his presence before he spoke. For perhaps five minutes they sat like this, during which time Trondwyth saw Entelred's frown deepen.

Without looking up, the wizard suddenly spoke quietly to the gnome at his feet. "It is bad," he said. "I had feared that I would live to see this day. And now I fear that the day is upon us and I will not live to see it through. She is calling on powers that are not hers to command, and yet they obey her. There is a deep mystery here. You must leave here before the day is finished, blessed gnome. Tonight the forces of darkness will come, and they must not find her here." The wizard's frown lifted a little, ever so slightly, and he looked deep into Trondwyth's eyes.

Trondwyth held the gaze as long as he could, but then looked away. He did not understand what was troubling the old wizard, but it was clear that he was deeply moved and that the gnome's desire to move on in search of Catherine would be of no consequence to the wizard.

The gnome raised himself to his feet, and the wizard put out his staff toward Trondwyth. Trondwyth grabbed at the staff and helped Entelred to his feet. Together they walked in silence back to the house buried in the hill. The sun still shone down on the hillside; the house's beautiful little windows with bright yellow curtains fluttering lightly in the breeze were no less homely than they had been just a few minutes before when Trondwyth had gone in search of his host. But somehow, in a way that Trondwyth could not explain, everything seemed different, more sinister, now.

The two retired to the front room and sat silently in armchairs, each with his own thoughts, until Gondalwyn popped his head in and said "Teatime" in a cheery voice. The cares lifted themselves from the wizard's face as if by one of his enchantments.

"Ah, good," he said, and settled back more comfortably in his chair.

Gondalwyn busied himself bringing in the tea things. Trondwyth noticed that this time he brought five slices of cake and five cups and saucers. Also, he saw that the dwarf pulled up a small stool next to Entelred.

The gnome's thoughts went back to that teatime, not so very long ago, when an unexpected visitor had dropped in and changed his life. He wondered how his brother was faring back in Carn Toldwyn.

Gondalwyn poured the tea, filling each of the five cups. Suddenly they heard again the swishing noise over to Trondwyth's right, and he saw the dablik enter the room. This time, however, the dablik remained standing, leaving the curtain pulled to one side as he peered back down the tunnel. Trondwyth looked into the darkness but could see nothing. Then he heard the sound of footsteps. He knew immediately that these were not the footsteps of gnome or dwarf, and his heart leapt as he realized that there was only one person it could be. Into the room stepped Catherine, High Queen of Palindor.

11

THE DARK KNIGHTS

ATHERINE STOOD STILL, blinking in the unaccustomed light and breathing deeply of the air in the room. As her eyes grew more capable of seeing, she saw that the little room was filled with people. But she had eyes for only one of them. She ran forward, her head still ducking instinctively to avoid hitting against the now absent stone roof, and flung her arms around Trondwyth.

"Oh, Trondwyth, Trondwyth. I'm so sorry. I thought I'd never see you again, and it's all been my fault. I didn't believe you, but you were telling the truth all the time, weren't you? And I was so worried about you," she said, her thoughts tumbling over one another.

"Oh, and I was worried about you, too," said the gnome, standing and embracing the young High Queen as firmly as she embraced him.

"Which only goes to show," said an old voice in a nearby armchair, "that it never pays to worry about that which one cannot change. Permit me to introduce myself, Your Highness. Entelred the Wizard at your command."

Catherine turned around and saw an old man seated in the armchair, inclining his head in her direction. A dwarf, seated next to him, bowed his head respectfully toward her. "And Gondalwyn, Apprentice Wizard Dwarf," said the dwarf, an unmistakable note of pride in his voice.

"Do join us for tea," said the wizard, and he patted the small seat next to his armchair. Catherine gave Trondwyth one last hug and sat herself by the side of the wizard.

Tea was a joyous affair, all smiles and laughter. Even the dablik, so quiet the previous day, joined in the stories and news telling. Gradually the bright sun, which had been shining in through the window, began to dim as it dipped behind the trees outside, heading toward its resting place for the night.

Entelred leaned forward in his chair, and silence fell across the room. He pushed his cup sideways across the table until it stood in front of Catherine.

Trondwyth noticed that the tea in the cup was untouched.

"Tell me," said the wizard to Catherine, "what do you see?"

Catherine looked down at the cup of tea. At first, she saw only a milky brown liquid, still slopping sideways from the movement across the table. But as she looked longer she began to see more. Slowly, in the depths of the liquid, she saw a shadow beginning to form. She watched it, unable to remove her eyes from it as she tried to make sense of the outline that was forming beneath them. The shadow seemed to grow and grow. Bigger than the teacup, it continued to grow until it seemed to tower over her. A knight it was, all black in the blackest armor, astride a black horse and carrying a black lance. Only one thing in the image before her was not black, and that was the blood drip-dripping red from the end of the lance.

Catherine stifled a scream and looked away, burying her head in her hands, her eyes tightly closed against the apparition. But she could not close her heart to the cold terror that gripped it momentarily.

"It's all right. You can look now," said the wizard.

Slowly she turned to see the eyes of the others on her, wondering. "Didn't you see it?" she asked, looking around the room. But one look at their eyes showed that no one else, apart possibly from the impassive wizard, was aware of the story that the innocent cup had told. She looked at Entelred questioningly.

"It was a Dark Knight, Your Highness, a pawn of the Lord of Evil and one of three who left Carn Toldwyn late in the evening two days ago. He and his companions are at this very moment nearing the foothills of the Mountains of Mourn and will be here shortly after nightfall. They will not rest, Your Majesty, until you are dead."

Catherine's gaze remained fixed on the wizard, and she knew that he spoke the truth. She cast her mind back to the journey across the Wastes of Kaltethorn with Trondwyth and the prophecies of which he had told her, foretelling the arrival one day of the High Queen Catherine who would face Malthazzar, the Lord of Evil, in combat to free the Land of Palindor from his evil grip.

But the vision that had just appeared had terrified her. If a mere underling of Malthazzar could affect her so, she knew that she was unequal to the task which lay ahead of her. She was sure that there must have been a mistake.

"But why me? People keep calling me High Queen, but I am no queen. I think there's been a dreadful mistake."

"No, Queen Catherine. There is no mistake. You have been sent by Olvensar to save the land of Palindor from a threat that it does not even recognize. Queen Cerebeth is more powerful than I would have imagined possible for a human. Indeed, I sometimes wonder if she is human at all. But she is held tightly in a grip of evil; in her actions the hand of Malthazzar is plain. Cerebeth must be killed. Otherwise she, and then Malthazzar, will hold all of Palindor under her sway. And if that were to come about, it would mean the doom of this once great and noble land.

"Queen Catherine, it has been foretold since before you were born that with the first true test that faced the land of Palindor would arrive the first High Queen; a queen of humble birth and little more than a child, but who would wear a belt of queenship with a white stone at the center of the buckle." He pointed, and she followed the direction of his finger toward the belt buckle in which the white stone seemed almost to be glowing.

The wizard turned to Gondalwyn. "It is time, my apprentice and friend. You must lead our guests away from here quickly, before the Knights are upon us."

The dwarf and the old wizard stood and embraced. Catherine noticed that there were tears in Gondalwyn's eyes, though he tried to hide them. The two parted, and the dwarf disappeared through a doorway, calling for Trondwyth to follow. The dablik slid out of the armchair in which he had been sitting, bowed deeply to Catherine and the wizard, moved across the room to the curtain which covered the entrance to his tunnels and was gone. Entelred took Catherine's hand and led her outside to where the cool air already spoke of the coming evening.

Catherine looked at the wizard, who did not speak, but merely returned her gaze until she could stand it no longer and was forced to look away.

Gondalwyn and Trondwyth returned, each carrying a pack on his back. Trondwyth carried a third pack in his hands, which he held out to Catherine. "Take this," he said. "It is for our journeying. It is best if we each carry provisions, so that if we become separated once more we will neither starve nor thirst."

Catherine took the pack and managed with some difficulty—for it was clearly not designed for humans—to strap it to her back. The three took their leave of the wizard, Gondalwyn once more fighting back tears. Setting his face, Gondalwyn turned away from the wizard and led the other two down the track away from the small house in the hillside.

As they disappeared around the first bend in the track, Catherine took a quick look behind her. She saw Entelred sitting peacefully on a log beside his front door, absorbing the rays of the setting sun, his head nodding slightly as if in light sleep.

They walked, wordless and grim, for about an hour. Catherine wondered where they were bound, but since Gondalwyn seemed to know where he was going, she let him lead the way and refrained from breaking the silence. The sun had set and the first stars were begin to glimmer in the sky when without warning Gondalwyn stopped and looked around him. For the first time since their parting from the wizard, Catherine saw a slight smile playing over the dwarf's features.

"Do you see it?" the dwarf asked.

Catherine and Trondwyth looked around them. It was gloomy here at the edge of the forest. Only twenty feet away the closest of the mountains reared up steeply out of the ground, reaching high above them in a wall of rock. Neither the human nor the gnome saw anything remarkable.

"Close your eyes and count to five," commanded Gondalwyn.

Both did so, and they heard a rustle as the dwarf moved on the count of one. When they opened their eyes, their companion was gone. They peered into the gathering darkness but could see no trace of him. Suddenly they heard laughter, seeming to come from the base of the mountain. Out popped Gondalwyn from nowhere. "Here, come with me," he said.

They walked off the path toward him and found, as they ducked down to avoid the branches of a pine tree, that they were in a little hollow hidden from the track along which they had been traveling. Near the rear of the dell was a crack between two boulders. The two squeezed through without too much difficulty, climbed a few steps higher, and found themselves at a vantage point from which they could easily look out upon the track without being seen and where, if they ducked down, they were hidden in a grassy depression, invisible from all sides.

The little bowl in which they found themselves was hard against the mountainside, and there appeared to be a large fold in the rock of the mountain at this point. Gondalwyn walked the few paces across the grass, took a sudden step sideways, and was once more lost to view. Catherine followed, with Trondwyth behind her. Stepping around the fold in the rock, she found herself in a cave of the same dimly shining rock as the tunnels in which she had so recently been held a prisoner. The cave was large and easily accommodated the three companions.

Gondalwyn removed his pack and the others did likewise. "I used to come here to play when I was a young dwarf," he said. "When I was older, I used it as a place of solitude, a place to think, safely hidden from the rest of the world. Then one day I came here and found signs that someone else had been here. I was most upset and determined to see who it was who had come across my secret. I spent every spare minute here, waiting for the intruder to reappear. When he did, imagine my surprise at discovering that it was none other than Entelred, the most famous, wisest wizard alive. He said that this was a special place, a place from long, long ago, and that he had been drawn here to find an apprentice wizard. It was some time before I realized that he was talking about me. In the whole history of Palindor, there has never been a dwarf wizard before." It was hard for him to keep the pride out of his voice.

Then he hastened to qualify himself. "Not that I'm always a very good wizard. But Entelred has been good to me and so patient. I think that I have learned a few things from him. Yes, I think so. . . ." His voice trailed off, his mind obviously elsewhere.

Catherine looked around at the rocky walls that disappeared into shadow at the far end of the cave. "How far back does the cave go?" she asked.

"Quite a long way, but there are no passages out of it," replied Gondalwyn.

Nevertheless, Catherine was curious to see for herself. Leaving her pack behind, she made her way deeper into the cave. It twisted and turned so that she quickly lost view of the others, but as there were no side tunnels she was confident of being able to retrace her steps. After a little while, she saw that the walls and ceiling were closing in on her. No doubt the end of the cave, she thought. But just before the ceiling dropped to the point where it would be impossible to go any further, she saw off to the left a little passage that looked older than the rest of the cave. She followed it for a short distance and then, without warning, found herself in a small chamber.

Inside the chamber, leaning against an ancient staff, was an old, old man dressed in dirty once-green clothes.

Olvensar looked up at her, unsmiling, as she entered the chamber.

Trondwyth and Gondalwyn were left alone with their thoughts once Catherine had gone exploring. Neither felt much like speech. To Trondwyth, as to Catherine, it was clear that Gondalwyn's heart was heavy, and his mind went back to the conversation he had had with Entelred earlier in the afternoon, when the old wizard had seemed to prophesy his own impending death. Such dark thoughts tempered his joy at being reunited with the High Queen.

For some time, gnome and dwarf sat in silence, each with his own thoughts. Suddenly they were jerked back to reality by sounds coming from outside the cave. Gondalwyn motioned Trondwyth to stay still while he crept slowly to the cave entrance to peer outside. He soon reappeared, looking frightened, and placed his finger to his lips.

Placing his lips close to the gnome's ear, he whispered, "Dark Knights. Two of them. We should be safe in here as long as we are silent." In the dim light of the walls of the cave the two sat, waiting for the noises of movement and subdued speech outside to cease.

Then Trondwyth heard a sound from behind them, the sound of leather on stone. He looked back to warn Catherine of the new danger, and was astonished to see Catherine, certainly, but not the Catherine who had left them just a short time before. This was quite a different Catherine from the one who had wandered to the rear of the cave. She seemed taller, although they realized later that it was her stride and bearing that had changed rather than her height. Even in this gloom, there was no mistaking the fire that burned in her eyes.

Trondwyth took one look at her, and any remaining

doubts concerning the High Queen flew away. He bowed his head to the ground and said, "Your Majesty."

Gondalwyn was not so affected, nor did he seem surprised by the transformation that Catherine had undergone. He merely placed his fingers to his lips and said, "Dark Knights outside. We must stay quiet."

Without a word, but nodding in acknowledgment toward the dwarf, Catherine continued by without breaking her stride. She stepped outside into the little bowl overlooking the track, her companions following as far as the mouth of the cave. Although the sun was now set, the moon, gloriously full, was well risen, and it was not difficult to see as she peered over the rocks. On the track beneath were two black shadows on horseback. Where the moonlight struck them, it seemed to be swallowed whole.

The two knights were not speaking. Their mounts stood quietly, and the air of the pair was one of expectation. Then Catherine heard the sound of a horse galloping along the trail, and into view came a third horseman, just as black as the first two. He drew up to the others and reined in his horse. The newcomer carried a long, dark object: a lance, from the end of which dripped red drops.

The picture was that which had appeared in the teacup earlier and had so frightened Catherine. Now she merely pressed her lips firmly together and continued watching the scene before her.

The new arrival spoke. "He would not talk. In the end he gave his life, but I told him that it was to no avail. We will find them and kill them."

"They are around here somewhere," said one of the other horsemen. "The horses can smell them. They left the trail here, and not long since."

The first horseman looked around, and his gaze settled exactly upon the place where Catherine, not visible through the branches of the intervening trees, was staring back at him. The horseman raised his spear and pointed it directly at her. "They are there somewhere. Let us go forward."

The three horsemen formed a line, the one with the spear in the lead, and left the track. As they made their way into the little dell, Catherine purposefully stepped back behind the fold in the rock, awaiting her moment.

Realizing that they could never hope to pull their mounts through the tiny crack in the rock, the three Knights dismounted. Two of them drew their swords, which shone with a dark blackness in the moonlight. One after another they squeezed with difficulty through the crack in the rock, until all three were standing in the little grassy bowl in front of the fold in the mountain.

Then Catherine stepped out from her hiding place. The jewel in her belt flashed brightly, more brightly than daylight itself, and the Knights stepped backward at the sight of it. Then it faded so that its brightness was no greater than that of the moon that shone down on them all. The Knights recovered themselves and stepped forward once more. They were no more than a sword's length from Catherine now, as she raised her hand.

"Halt!" she called. "Who dares disturb the peace of a High Queen of Palindor?"

The leader of the Knights spoke out. "We have been sent on a mission by Cerebeth, crowned Queen of Palindor. The queen requests your presence at her castle in Carn Toldwyn. We are not to return without you."

"Begone! I will make my way to Cerebeth in my own time. You may tell the one who sent you that it will be all too soon for her liking."

The leader of the Knights stepped to one side and one of the others, carrying his drawn sword, took his place. "You do not understand. We are commanded to bring you back to the queen, and we will not leave here without your body. Whether it has life in it or not is of little matter to the queen and of less concern to us. You would do well to come without resistance." He drew back his sword menacingly.

"You dare threaten me?" Catherine roared, standing her ground. "Your queen will have much to answer for when I face her."

The leader of the Knights stepped once more to the fore. Letting his lance fall to the ground, he drew his own sword, which somehow seemed blacker and more menacing than the others' drawn swords. He stepped forward, drew the sword back further, and then, in a mighty horizontal sweep, drew it across in front of him so that it would slice his opponent in two.

But the sword never made contact with Catherine's body. As it accelerated toward her, the light from her belt once more shone forth brightly, steadily this time, and, as the sword drew nearer, it became heavier and heavier in the hands of the Dark Knight. As he turned his eyes away from the bright light enveloping Catherine, the sword fell harmlessly at her feet.

"Go before I lose my patience," commanded Catherine. "Tell your queen that she shall have her wish: I am coming to Carn Toldwyn to meet her, and she will answer to me for the wrongs that she has done."

The light from around Catherine's waist remained steady, so that it was as bright as noonday in the little clearing. Still the Knights were as black as black. But now their leader fell back and said to the others, "Come. We must tell the queen of this." He picked up his lance from the ground, turned, and led the way back through the crack.

Suddenly the jewel flared into brilliance and the Knights' mounts, disturbed by the great light, could be heard whinnying and neighing on the track. There was a sound of noisy galloping as the horses fled in fear. As the light from the jewel began to fade, Catherine heard the sounds of the Knights chasing after their mounts as they fled back the way that they had come.

She turned and saw Gondalwyn and Trondwyth emerging from the cave. In Trondwyth's eyes was a mixture of amazement, awe, and gratitude, but it was Gondalwyn who spoke.

"That will not keep them away for long, Your Majesty. You took them by surprise this time. But once they report back to the queen, she will show them how to stand fast against the power of the jewel. Next time they will not be so easily discouraged."

Catherine said nothing, but looked down at her feet at the discarded sword of the Dark Knight. She stooped and picked it up by the handle. She felt a strange prickling in her arm as she held the cold, hard object. It was heavy, as if made of metal. Yet, like the Knights themselves, it appeared to swallow any light which touched it. She held out the thumb of her other hand to test the blade's sharpness.

"No!" shouted Trondwyth and Gondalwyn together.

But it was too late. Catherine's thumb touched the dark blade, and she remembered no more.

12

OUT FROM UNDER
THE CASTLE

REFYNT WAS CONFINED to a dungeon deep below Dynas Carn Toldwyn. Three times a day a guard brought food and removed the empty bowls from his previous meal. He was provided sufficient food and water to keep him from dying, but far from enough to maintain his strength.

For the first time in his two centuries of life, Drefynt understood the meaning of the word despair. As each day went by, he found himself feeling weaker. The dungeon in which he was held had no windows and only one small wooden door through which the guard came in.

The dungeon smelled bad when Drefynt first entered it, and the stench became worse with each passing day. He shared his space with rats that scurried about in the dirty straw, eking out a living on soiled scraps. The only light came from a small crack under the door, which admitted a glow from flaming torches attached to the walls of the corridor outside.

Drefynt spent much of his first few days trying to find

a way of escape. He knew that many of the dungeons beneath the castle had secret exits, placed there so that the early kings of Palindor could always escape, should they ever be imprisoned in their own dungeons. But all such exits were hidden by magic, and eventually he gave up trying to uncover any secrets. With no sun to guide him, he soon lost track of time, although he decided that if he reckoned on three meals per day he would not go far wrong.

By this reckoning, it was on the seventh day of his captivity that hope reappeared. Outside, although he did not know it, it was night. A full moon shone brightly off the towers of the castle. Inside his dungeon, Drefynt had just been awakened from sleep by a particularly forward rat chewing on his matted, filth-encrusted hair. He brushed the rat away and sat up.

For some reason, he felt particularly sorry for himself this night. Never before had he suffered personal privation; now that he had learned what it was like to be completely helpless in the face of an enemy, he wished that Olvensar would come to rescue him. Not for the first time, he began to cry, but this time the tears flooded from his eyes as never before. Eventually, there were no more tears in him.

"Oh, Olvensar, Olvensar," he said, "why don't you come to help me now? How can I be of any use locked up in here like this?"

The only answer was the sound of the rats scurrying about in the dim light.

But then, over the sound of his own sniffling, Drefynt heard a new sound. It was the deep, low rumble of large rocks moving, sliding, grating against one another. It appeared to be coming from the corner farthest from the doorway. Stiffly he stood up and wiped his sleeve across his face, drying his eyes.

Was it his imagination? No, it could not be. Over in the corner, a small hole, black against the darkness of the wall, had appeared. He walked across the floor and examined what he found there as best he could in the dim light which filtered under the door. In the wall was a hole of perhaps half his height. It took but a moment for the realization to dawn that he had somehow triggered the escape route out of this particular dungeon.

He thought back. It must have been Olvensar's name, although it certainly was not the first time that he had spoken it out loud since his arrival. Well, whatever it was that he had done, it hardly mattered now. He stooped down and entered the dark hole.

At once he heard again the grating sound of rock on rock. He turned and saw the doorway closing behind him. Now he had no choice. Turning again, he could see that the walls of the passageway shone dimly. He was standing on a steep downward incline. He took a couple of tentative steps forward, testing his footing. The ground was dry and, despite the slope, he seemed in little danger of falling. He found that the ceiling rose up quickly, so that in the space of a couple more steps, he could stand with no difficulty.

Naturally, he realized, the escape route had been fashioned for humans, so a gnome should have no difficulty in using it, unless it required extensive climbing at some point further on.

He walked forward. He was weak and slow from his imprisonment and afraid of making noise and drawing attention to his passage. For perhaps five minutes he walked in this way. The passageway was relatively straight, with only the occasional turn to right or left.

Suddenly he was brought to a halt. In front of him appeared a flight of stone steps, apparently leading up to the ceiling above. Slowly, hesitantly, he climbed the steps, until his head was brushing against the rock of the ceiling. Raising his hands, and using all the feeble energy that he could muster, he pressed hard against the rock above his head.

The rock seemed to return his push. As he let go, unsure of his next move, the rock slowly descended. It slid silently across to one side, revealing a square hole above which loomed a star-studded sky. Drefynt felt a breath of wind against his face. It was magnificent! He had forgotten how good it felt to be free, to breathe fresh air.

He wasted no time in clambering out into the open. Once more, no sooner had he passed through the opening than the stone slipped sideways again and rose to take its usual place. Looking down, he saw that the moving stone was completely indistinguishable from the others which composed the ground on which he stood.

He looked around. High in the sky, a bright silver moon shone down, lighting up the scene. Of course! It was the combination of the full moon and the spoken name of Olvensar which had opened the passageway for him. Perhaps there were other ways of opening the door as well, but he was grateful to have stumbled on one accidentally.

Looking around, it took him a few moments to realize where he was. Behind him and running around to his left was a tall wall. Immediately to his right was a building, a wing of the castle. The wall to his left turned across in front of him some distance ahead, but there was a gap between where the building ended and the wall began. Slowly he crawled along the side of the castle wall and stuck his head around the corner.

He stood aghast at the sight that met his eyes. Although it was the middle of the night, lined up in the courtyard was a group marching under the command of a tall human. It was too dark to recognize individuals in the crowd—there must have been over a hundred people—but he could see well enough that the group contained mostly dwarves and gnomes with the occasional human or faun thrown in. All were in some way armed. The dwarves swung battle-axes and the gnomes carried hunting knives. The humans held vicious-looking metal spears, and the fauns bows and arrows.

He withdrew into the little yard into which he had emerged from the tunnel. Palindor was preparing itself for war. But why, and against whom? Much must have happened in the few days since he had last smelled fresh air.

He wondered what to do. It would only be a matter of time, and not much time at that, before his escape was discovered, but he was too weak to travel. He needed food and water and rest. Besides which, he must discover the cause of the marching in the courtyard. He walked slowly across to where the wall behind him joined the castle. Yes, if he were careful, he felt that he could probably climb the wall, which he judged to be some ten feet high.

There seemed nothing else for it. He could not hope to pass unnoticed through the courtyard; he would be spotted in a moment. Tentatively he stretched out his hands, found a good hold, and began to climb.

For one who was so recently feeling weak and dizzy, he did remarkably well. By climbing slowly and cautiously, he was able to reach the very top of the castle wall. He leaned forward and pulled himself up so that he was sitting astride the wall. Looking down, he could see that on the far side the ground was grass, and the distance to the grass on the outside of the wall was perhaps only half the distance to the flagstones of the castle yard from which he had just climbed. Sliding around so that his legs dangled over the outside wall, with only his hands holding on to the top, he let go. With a quiet thud, he landed on the soft ground outside the castle.

Drefynt had already decided on a place to spend the next couple of days. He looked around to get his bearings and then, stooping so that he was harder to see in the moonlit night, he made off as quickly as he could down the hill toward the woods. He did not look back. If he had done so, he would have seen a large bird, which had been perched on a tower overlooking the castle wall he had just scaled, suddenly take to the air. With lazy flaps of its wings, the bird circled once and then settled on a window ledge high in the tallest tower of the castle. Without hesitation, the bird marched through the slit of the window and into the room beyond.

Drefynt quickly reached the forest that surrounded the northern and eastern sides of Carn Toldwyn and began to follow its edge from the north end where the castle stood around to the eastern edge of town. It was much harder going than he had expected; the days of bad food and water and lack of exercise were catching up with him. It was nearly an hour later that he walked out of the shadows at the edge of the forest and into a little house which backed up against the forest on the very edge of the town.

The back door to Trondwyth's little house was closed but unlocked. Drefynt opened it and entered the cottage as quietly as he knew how. He spent the first five minutes peering into every room in the house to make sure that it was unoccupied. By now the moon was dipping low in the sky and the sky to the east was growing light with the coming dawn. Fatigued from his exertions, Drefynt made his way to the spare bedroom, threw himself on the covers of the bed, and fell asleep.

The spare bedroom was at the back of the house, facing the woods, so he was not awakened by the bright sunlight of the new day. Instead he slept on until shortly past noon. When he awoke, he was immediately aware of a pungent, particularly unpleasant smell. It would have made him sick had there been sufficient food in his stomach to warrant bringing it up. He sat up on the bed, sniffing the air, wondering what could possibly be causing such a disgusting smell. The window to the little room was stoutly closed. A thought dawned on him and, cautiously, he placed his nose closer to his tunic. He coughed as the odor caught the back of his throat. Of course! Well, the first order of the day would be a long, lazy, hot bath. The bath did Drefynt at least as much good as the hours of restful sleep that had preceded it. Once it was over, he sought out some traveling clothes from his brother's wardrobe and put them on, feeling like a new gnome. Then he turned his attention to the kitchen.

It had been well over a week now since Trondwyth had occupied the cottage, and on that occasion much of the food in the larder had been removed and placed in Trondwyth's pack. But, like many gnomes, Trondwyth had a fondness for fruit, and his larder still contained several small hampers of edible apples and oranges, as well as numerous jams and jellies. Drefynt made himself a breakfast of two oranges, three crackers piled high with rhubarb jam, and a large glass of fresh water. This unorthodox meal was the most delicious food he could remember eating in a long, long time.

He spent the remainder of the day eating and resting. He saw occasional gnomes wandering by the cottage, but he made sure to keep his head down so that no one would know he was there. Although he needed more rest, he knew that it could not be long before the queen thought to search Trondwyth's cottage for her escaped prisoner.

Late in the afternoon, he spent an hour or so packing

a shoulder bag with fruit and a small water canteen, the only one that he could find in the house. It was not really suitable for long travel, and the food was sufficient for two days at most, but it would be enough to get him well into the forest and out of the immediate reach of the queen. As evening fell, he slung the bag over his shoulder and went outside. As he was making his way across the few paces of open space between the back door and the forest, he was stopped by a quiet greeting.

"Ho! Well met, gnome Drefynt," said a voice.

Drefynt stopped and looked around in shock. Leaning against the corner of the cottage was a dwarf whom he judged to be somewhat older than himself. For a second he did not recognize the face, and then he remembered. It was Tarandron, the dwarf who had brought in the youngsters with the book from the tunnels at Perendeth.

"Good day to you, Tarandron. You gave me a surprise standing there like that."

"Not nearly as much of a surprise as you gave the good queen, I hear," said the dwarf.

Drefynt felt uncomfortable. He wondered how much Tarandron knew, and whether he was in the service of Cerebeth. He could think of nothing to say, so he remained silent.

The dwarf continued. "It could not have been very pleasant, being a guest of Her Majesty in her visitors' quarters under the castle."

"No," agreed Drefynt, "it was thoroughly unpleasant."

"Pray tell me. I have wondered ever since the news was spread abroad, was your imprisonment anything to do with that book that my son found?"

"Well, yes, it was," admitted Drefynt. "Although you could not have known that she was merely using you to entrap me."

"Well, now, I am glad to hear you say that. I was brought up the same way that I try to bring up young Smilthron. If a body is not honest and open in his dealings with people, then he is nothing at all. I wanted to be sure that you knew I had nothing to do with that book. I merely thought that it would be best in the hands of a creature known throughout the land for his wisdom."

Drefynt bowed slightly. "I am honored that you consider me so. Alas, I feel that those days are behind me now. I shall be leaving Carn Toldwyn forthwith, and I doubt that I shall ever return, at least while Cerebeth reigns."

The dwarf moved closer to Drefynt. With some alarm, Drefynt observed that the dwarf carried his battle-ax stuck into his belt, within easy reach. The gnome also realized that here in the shadows between cottage and forest, out of sight of the path which passed by the front of the house, the dwarf could sever Drefynt's head from his body in the blink of an eye and nobody would be the wiser.

But Tarandron's hand rested only lightly on his ax, more as a support for his hand's weight than as if he had any intentions of drawing it. He spoke further, his voice lower now, conspiratorial in tone.

"She'll kill you now, you know, if you let yourself get caught again."

"I know," said Drefynt, unhappily. He hesitated a moment, wondering how much more he should say. In the end, he decided against speaking against the queen. He merely added: "I plan to leave this place forever."

"Good luck to you," said Tarandron. "But don't think it will be easy to escape or to find shelter. How much do you know of what has transpired in the past week?"

"Nothing," said Drefynt, almost eagerly. "When I escaped, I saw the beginnings of an army parading, as if making ready for war. And I see that you, a dwarf of peace, are walking around openly carrying a battle-ax. What has become of Palindor in the last seven days?"

"What has become of Palindor is that we are about to be attacked," said Tarandron, a note of grimness in his voice. "The queen has had news that invaders are stirring along our borders with Reglandor to the east, on the far side of the Mountains of Mourn. We expect to be attacked within the month. Between you and me, I don't like the sound of it at all. There are rumors that the Dark Lord Malthazzar will be leading the invaders, and against that kind of power a few arrows and battle-axes will be useless."

Drefynt recalled his meeting with Olvensar in the cottage behind which he and Tarandron now stood; Olvensar had said that the spirit of the Dark Lord lay in the queen's body. Perhaps that spirit had now fled and the Lord of Evil, having weakened Palindor from the inside, was preparing to lead an army against the kingdom.

"Malthazzar!" exclaimed Drefynt. "So that mighty power has risen once more against Palindor. Yes, indeed, it will be difficult to match his prowess this time. Without a trained army or Holy Gnomes skilled in the understanding of the ways of kirial, and wizards mighty in the forces of kirial, we shall be no match for him."

"Aye, so I think, although I would not be so bold as to say so out loud. But, in that case, I wonder why they need such as you to act as spies for their cause?"

Drefynt was stunned. But he could not help noticing that with these words the dwarf's hand had moved slightly, and it now held his ax in such a way that it could be released from its place in the dwarf's belt and brought to bear on the gnome at a moment's notice.

"What?" queried Drefynt. "Do you say that I am in the service of the enemies of Palindor?"

"It is not I who say so, it is the queen. She has spread

the word that you were imprisoned because she discovered that you can read and write the ancient scripts. She says that you inveigled your way into her court to spy on her for the Dark Lord, that you kept a secret hoard of the ancient books which survived the destruction at Perendeth, and that therein lay the secret to the destruction of Palindor." The dwarf gazed unflinchingly into Drefynt's eyes as he spoke, as if challenging the gnome to deny his words.

Drefynt considered his position for a moment.

"What say you to these allegations, gnome?" asked the dwarf, tightening his grip on his ax.

Drefynt took a deep breath. "To these allegations, honorable and good dwarf of Palindor, I say the following. I was born of Galthwain and Terendeen, two Holy Gnomes of Perendeth. I was raised in the Barrows, but was spared in the night of fires that destroyed the libraries and in which the Holy Gnomes perished. So as to your charge that I can read and write the ancient scripts, I must plead guilty, for I was trained in their usage. I have taken my vows and cannot betray my training. I am of Palindor born. More than that"—he raised himself up with dignity—"I am a Holy Gnome of Perendeth. My home is in Palindor and I forswear all other allegiances. I cannot betray my oath and raise my hand against my queen, even when I know that she is evil and has led my country astray. How much less could I be in the service of the Dark Lord, the sworn enemy of Palindor for all time?"

The dwarf relaxed and removed his hand from the ax. "Good," he said. "I and others have long suspected that you might be a Holy Gnome, and it is good to hear the words of confirmation from your own lips. But if what the queen says about you is not true, I wonder how many of her other stories are true. Know you anything about another gnome, one who left these parts suddenly and is now said to be planning the attack against Palindor? A gnome by the name of Trondwyth?"

"Trondwyth? Then he is still alive and free! May Olvensar be blessed. Trondwyth is my brother, the only other Holy Gnome to escape the carnage at Perendeth. He has taken the same oaths as I and would no more lead an army against Palindor than I would."

"And his companion? What know you of her?"

"Companion? I know nothing of any companion. When he left here, he traveled alone, and I know not what has become of him since."

"The queen informs us that he is traveling with a human. She says that the girl is most dangerous, and the two of them are to be apprehended and brought to her if they are seen within the confines of Palindor."

"This is news to me," said Drefynt. "Your words both cheer and puzzle me. I know nothing of this human or in what way she poses a danger to Queen Cerebeth. But be assured that if my brother Trondwyth is involved, the human poses no danger to Palindor itself. If anything, my brother and his companion may prove its saving."

"Aye, well, that's as may be. You should know that I volunteered from my brigade to come here and search this cottage and report back if I saw signs of life. You would do well to prepare your escape, for it is more than my life is worth to report to the queen that you have not been here. I can promise only that I will delay my report until late in the afternoon. More than that I cannot do."

Drefynt bowed. "You honor me," he said, bowing slightly in the direction of the dwarf.

Tarandron turned away and was gone.

13

INTO THE MOORTAIN MIRE

RONDWYTH AND GONDALWYN hurried toward Catherine. Trondwyth knelt by her side, raised her head, and slapped her face gently, trying to bring her back to consciousness, while Gondalwyn examined the thumb that had been penetrated by the dark blade. The cut was not deep, but already there was an unnatural gray pallor around the half-inch-long incision. Although the wound appeared to be open, no blood flowed from it.

Gondalwyn looked up and spoke to the gnome. "Wait here with her; I shall be back shortly." He stood and picked up the sword where it had fallen to the ground. There was no mark indicating where it had cut Catherine's skin. Carefully he laid the sword against a stone, blade downward, safely out of the way. Then he squeezed through the rocks that led to the dell by the track and was gone.

Trondwyth lost track of time; the night now suddenly seemed much colder as he held Catherine's head and gently rocked it backward and forward in his hands. Her face no longer felt as warm as it should have. Feeling over her exposed skin, he realized that she was growing colder as she succumbed to the curse carried by the blade. But as there was nothing he could do, he merely sat and waited, holding her head and shivering in the night air.

At length he heard a sound and looked up. By the bright moonlight he could see Gondalwyn returning through the space between the stones. In his hand the dwarf held a small bundle of leaves. He hurried over to where the High Queen lay and looked towards Trondwyth.

The gnome shook his head. "She is unchanged, except that she grows cold."

Gondalwyn knelt down beside Catherine and pressed the bundle against the skin of her left hand around the cut, tying it in place with a vine. When he had finished, he looked up at Trondwyth, who was now standing over him, watching.

"That's all I can do for now," said Gondalwyn. "I am no healer, but I have found leaves of feverfew and fennel and have cast the most powerful spell against sickness that I know. It will not make her well, but it should help for a while. There is nothing more that we can do tonight. We should get some sleep and look at her again in the morning."

Trondwyth wanted to argue, but he was cold and tired, and there was nothing they could do for Catherine now. Between the two of them they dragged her closer to the mouth of the cave where it would be a little warmer. Then the two of them settled down next to her to try to take a few hours' sleep.

In the morning they awoke to find the situation no better. Indeed, in the light of day, they found that the gray shade of Catherine's skin was not, as they had hoped, due to the color of the moonlight. Gondalwyn removed the small compress that he had applied overnight to see that the skin closest to the cut was now an unnatural white. Around the cut, perhaps an inch away, there was a narrow black ring encircling the thumb.

"That's not good, is it?" said Trondwyth, despair in his voice.

"On the contrary, my friend," said the dwarf, "it is the best that could be hoped for in the circumstances. The white color close to the cut indicates that the healing compress has halted the work of the blade. The black color merely represents the time before I could obtain the herbs and cast the spell to halt the blade's work. I have every reason to think that she will not succumb to the blade's kiríal now." Less happily, he added, "But neither will she recover without a true healer to help. I will have to stay here with her, to mind the herbs and change the compress every few hours. Trondwyth, my friend, you must go to the house of Iadron and Harsforn, place the circumstances before Harsforn, and beg for a remedy for the High Queen."

"Iadron and Harsforn? Who are they, and where do they live?"

"Iadron is an oracle, and Harsforn a healer. They live together in a house in the center of the Moortain Mire, a day's journey from this place. I have met them but once, long ago. Their manner can be aloof, but Entelred always spoke well of them. If you tell them that you come in his name, I would hope that they will treat you well."

Gondalwyn drew a crude map in the dirt, showing Trondwyth how he might reach the mire.

"I have heard that Moortain Mire is impassable," said Trondwyth. "How will I find my way through the mire to the house?"

"Oh, that's easy," replied Gondalwyn. "You can see the

house easily from the edge of the mire in fine weather. But if the weather is fine then you must not set foot in the mire, for it will be the death of you. If the women desire you to meet them, the mire will be covered in dense fog. You should simply walk straight through it. You will find their house in that way."

Trondwyth repeated this to be sure that he had heard it correctly, but was not comforted to find that he had indeed understood the first time. He retrieved his pack from inside the cave and checked the provisions and water flask given him by Entelred. With the coming of the full moon the night before, the magic of the canteen he had obtained in Smalterscairn had, as promised, ceased. After a brief breakfast and a last glance at the map drawn in the dirt, he squeezed his way out through the narrow opening between the rocks and disappeared from Gondalwyn's view.

The trek was relatively straightforward. For several thousand paces, until his stomach began to call upon him for lunch, Trondwyth followed the track along the mountainside. Then he came to a place where the track forked, one way continuing more or less straight and a second fork branching off to the right, descending steeply down the mountainside. There was a convenient rock by the side of the road, and he sat upon the rock while he satisfied his stomach's calls. After lunch he pulled his pack back on and carefully, so as not to lose his footing on the loose pebbles, followed the right-hand path steeply downward. He found that the track soon bent back to the left and began to descend more leisurely.

He continued this way until nightfall, which came as the sound of a river suddenly became very close. He rounded a corner and saw the Findell River, over which Catherine had crossed four days earlier and into which he had been deposited by the breaking of the troll's spell. He was now far downstream from the bridge which had been guarded by the unfortunate troll, and the river was wide and less fierce. It was no less intimidating to a poor gnome who did not know how to swim, however, especially as the current looked much faster than it had been further upriver. In front of him the path narrowed and crossed the river by way of a wide wooden bridge, not altogether unlike that which had been guarded by the troll. As it was beginning to get dark, he decided to camp on this side of the river and risk crossing by the bridge on the morrow. He retreated off the track into the forest and spent an uncomfortable night, waking up several times from a dream in which trolls rose up out of the ground to eat him.

But the next day arrived with a clear blue sky, and Trondwyth neither saw nor heard nor smelled any indication of trolls. So, before breakfast and with a rapidly beating heart, he walked hurriedly across the little wooden bridge, with each footstep half expecting a sudden booming command to halt.

But he crossed the bridge without incident and found a sheltered glade a little way along the path on the west side of the river where he stopped and ate his breakfast. After his meal, he continued along the path for a while as it rose up and away from the river. About midmorning, he suddenly broke free of the forest as he approached the top of a hill. He continued over lush grass until he reached the hill's ridge line and found himself looking to the southwest over a vast flat valley which appeared to be a sort of grayish green color. Away in the distance, he could see trees below and climbing the hills that ringed the valley. In the middle of the valley, too far away for him to be sure, he thought he could see a dwelling of some kind. He glanced up to the sky and saw nothing but bright blueness in which hung the glowing orb of the sun.

He descended the hillside carefully. Once at the bottom, he could immediately tell the nature of the ground in front of him. The greenish hue was caused by tufts of marsh grass sticking a few inches into the air every few feet. The gray was the color of the water that surrounded each tuft and separated them from one another. Carefully he placed one foot out across the water onto a tussock and placed a little of his weight on it. Immediately he felt as though some underwater creature had grabbed his foot as the ground itself tried to suck him down. With difficulty he pulled himself back onto the dry land and lay down on his back, resting on the firm bright green of the grass at the base of the hill.

He looked out across the mire. The dwelling place was clearer now; it was a house, right in the middle of the marsh, and completely inaccessible. Only a fool would try to reach it even in this, the best of weather. He sat and stared at the house, wondering what he should do. Once he saw somebody walking around outside. He stood up and called as loudly as he could, but there was no response. Either the figure could not hear him or it was deliberately ignoring him. He sat back down and mulled over the circumstances.

The sun was hot as it beat down on him, and Trondwyth found himself fighting off the effects of his poor sleep the previous night. For a while he tried to keep his eyes open; but he was overcome by the warm sun shining down, the drone of bees as they sought flowers for nectar, and, high up above, the singing of a songbird as it serenaded the day. He lay back and closed his eyes, drinking in the warmth and homeliness of his surroundings.

When he opened his eyes with a start, the day had turned cold and foreboding. All he could see as he looked out across the marsh were whorls of mist and gray figures dancing in and out of the swirling dampness as light currents of air moved the fog first this way, then that.

Trondwyth gulped and stood up. This was exactly what Gondalwyn had told him the situation must be if he were ever to reach his destination. He pulled on the pack that he had been using as a pillow. He could see a tuft of grass within reach, still surrounded though it was by water; he jumped and landed easily on it. Twice more he did the same thing, and then suddenly a thought struck him. He turned around, looking for the shore which he had just left but, no matter how he stared, he could no longer see any sign of the hill against which he had been so recently lying. He looked around in all directions, peering through the fog which seemed to be growing more dense with each passing moment. He had completely lost his bearings. In fright he stared down at the tufts of grass that he could just make out, now able to see only a step away through the mist. There, that one. Then that one. With a third step, he expected to be in sight of the firm grass of shore once more. But no! All around, he could see only patches of grass sticking out of gray water, all blanketed by damp, impenetrable coolness. Then he realized that the gray was not quite so light as it had been a minute ago. It would be getting dark soon.

Well, Gondalwyn had said that this was the only way to reach the house, and he was not about to fail Catherine now, no matter how frightened he became. So, clenching his teeth in determination, he concentrated merely on stepping from one tussock of grass to the next. In a surprisingly short period of time—certainly, he would have said, not long enough for him to have reached the center of the mire—he saw a dark shape looming before him, and a solid carpet of green grass. He jumped off a hillock onto the grass and found himself standing in front of the house he had seen from the hillside. A wind blew up, neither chill nor warm, and the mist began to lift. The sun was just setting in the west, over the hills on the far side of the marsh.

Trondwyth turned his attention to the house before him. He could not remember having seen such a ramshackle affair before; it almost seemed as if it would fall over under the effort of standing up. Nothing about the house was quite square and it was many years overdue for a new coat of paint. Much of the metal that was exposed was rusty; he was surprised that the windows did not appear to be broken. It did not, from the outside, look a likely place for habitation. But through the front door, which was open a crack, he could hear voices raised inside.

"Well, I don't know," said a voice that sounded as though it belonged to an old woman. "I don't see that it's our affair at all."

"Shush, dear," said another voice, similar to the first. "He'll hear. And in any case, we can't just let her die. It wouldn't be right, now would it?"

"Right? What do we care about whether something is right? Since when did we get involved in other people's fights? Oh! A rhyme! Did you hear that?"

"Yes, dear." There sounded a note of weariness in this voice. "Anyway, it's too late to argue now, because he's here."

With that the voices stopped, and Trondwyth heard the sound of footsteps coming closer to the front door. The door was opened slowly and Trondwyth was half afraid that it would fall off its one apparently usable hinge. But the hinge held and the gnome found himself confronted by two crones, each hardly taller than himself.

The two old women were dressed in old, torn garments that looked as if they had never been new, although they did at least appear to be clean.

One of them spoke. "Ah, good master gnome. We are so glad that you could visit us. My name is Iadron, and this is Harsforn. Welcome to our humble abode." She indicated that Trondwyth should enter the decrepit building and Harsforn, with a quiet "Hummph" under her breath, moved to one side to let the gnome pass.

Trondwyth passed by the two crones and into the house. There were no surprises there. Inside, the house was just as dilapidated as it had appeared on the outside, although he noticed that it had been recently swept, and things seemed to be kept tidily in their places. The front door opened into a narrow hallway, with a flight of stairs going upward on the right-hand side and a doorway into a room on the left. He could see several chairs arranged around the center of the room and a number of lighted candles in holders attached to the walls.

Iadron motioned for him to lead the way through the doorway.

"Do please be seated. I am sure that Harsforn would be glad to make you a cup of tea after your long journey." Iadron looked at Harsforn, who glared at her in return and then turned her gaze on Trondwyth.

Trondwyth did not know what to say. He certainly did not feel like putting his unwilling hostess to any trouble. But, on the other hand, she might like to feel needed. He felt the weight of the silence as it extended a little longer than was polite and then rushed out the words. "Oh, yes, please, that would be very nice. Thank you." He looked around at the chairs in front of him. "Where should I sit?" he said.

"Oh, anywhere, my dear. We have so few visitors these days, you know," Iadron said, and she and the gnome took seats as Harsforn disappeared through a doorway.

"The time was when there were always people coming to consult one or the other of us. My sister once had quite a reputation in these parts as a healer. And people were always coming to me to foretell their future and silly things like that. As if anyone would really want to know what was going to happen to him. Half the time after I told someone what was going to happen he would go out and spend the rest of his life trying to make sure that that very thing would *not* happen. Silly creatures. Anyway, it got so we never had any time for ourselves, so we built ourselves this little house here in the marshes where we could keep people away if we were so inclined. Not much need for it nowadays, though."

Trondwyth listened to this story, not sure how much of it was addressed to him and how much of it was simply the old woman reminiscing to herself. He wanted to tell her why he had come, but he felt it would be wiser to wait for Harsforn's return. She was the healer; she should be present when he told his story.

So the two sat in silence until Harsforn bustled into the room carrying an old cup and saucer, which she carried over to Trondwyth and laid on a table by his side.

"Thank you very much," he said politely, although the aroma emanating from the cup by his side was quite peculiar.

"Hope you like it," replied the other woman shortly, and looked around as if trying to decide which chair would be most comfortable. Making her decision, she sat down heavily. "Ah, that's better," she said, to no one in particular. "Having visitors does take it out of one."

The two women sat silently, neither seeming in a hurry to broach the subject of Trondwyth's arrival. Eventually, in the silence broken only by the sound of a tall clock ticking deeply in the corner, a bass counterpoint to the melody of a bird's song coming through an open window, Trondwyth felt that he must speak.

"I must thank you for permitting me to reach your house," he said.

Harsforn sat, rocking, as if she had not heard, but Iadron leaned forward slightly and said, "The enchantment will not work for much longer anyway, now that Entelred is no more. So there would have been little point in keeping you away. In any case, it seems to me that the queen. . . ." She hesitated then started again. "The queen has gone too far, killing a poor old wizard who never did anyone any harm and who was no threat to her."

"But how did you know?" Trondwyth asked in surprise.

Iadron answered his question without looking at him. "I am an oracle, you know. I may not see all things, and none of us is getting any younger, but there are some things that cannot be hidden, even from these old eyes. The queen is going too far, and it is time she was stopped."

There was another "Harrumph" from Harsforn, and the two sisters exchanged glances as if renewing an argument they had already fought.

Trondwyth suddenly realized that it would soon be dark outside. He must get a move on with his request if he was to be out of here before nightfall.

"Yes, the queen," he said, glad to have found a way to turn the conversation around to the purpose of his quest. "She sent her Dark Knights against one of our number as well. Our companion has been badly hurt"—he looked across to Harsforn, who still sat quietly rocking, eyes closed—"and Gondalwyn, another of our number, suggested that I come here to see if the great Harsforn might be able to help her."

He stopped, looking across the room hopefully. In the silence, the sound of the songbird vanished with the setting of the sun outside. In its place arose a brooding quiet broken only by the never-ending ticktock of the clock in the corner. It grew measurably darker as he waited for a response from the old woman rocking in the chair.

Eventually she opened her eyes and addressed her sister. "It is getting late. We should show your guest his room for the night."

Trondwyth wanted to protest, but the words had taken him by surprise and he was too slow.

"Yes," said Iadron. "If you have finished your tea, perhaps you would come with me."

Trondwyth was about to say that it was much too early to think of going to bed, and in any case he was in a hurry to leave—although he would have couched his objection in terms of "I mustn't put you to such trouble"—when he glanced at the clock and was amazed to see the lateness of the hour. Surely it had only been a few seconds, a minute at most, since the sun had set. Yet somewhere the better part of an evening seemed to have disappeared. He arose from his comfortable seat, a little disoriented, and found that his stomach felt full, as if he had just eaten a large meal. And no matter how he tried to convince himself otherwise, he was indubitably tired.

Iadron arose and led him out of the room into the hallway and up the rickety flight of stairs. At first he was afraid from the groans and squeaks coming from the stairs that they would not support his weight. But the stairs were more sound than they appeared, and he reached the upper floor of the house without incident. This floor seemed a little more airy and in better repair than the one below, although it was now so dark that it could just have been a trick of the half light. Without speaking, Iadron led him past two doors and then opened a third. He followed her through the doorway and saw, in the gloom, a neat little bedroom with a bed exactly the right size for a gnome.

"Sleep well. We will see you in the morning," said Iadron.

Trondwyth slept deeply and well. It had been so long since he had slept on a real bed that even without enchantment his sleep would have been undisturbed and long. The spell that Entelred had long ago placed on the bed, although now old and, with the wizard's death, losing its power, was unnecessary; the gnome awoke feeling younger and more invigorated than he had done for many a long year.

The sun streamed in through the unbroken window. He lay back in the bed, resting for several minutes before he heard sounds coming from below. He jumped out of bed and washed himself in the gnome-sized washbasin that stood in one corner of the room, then he gathered his belongings and went out into the hallway. As he had suspected the previous evening, this second story of the house was much better kept than the first. As he walked down the stairs, making a tremendous din as the stairs groaned and squealed with each step, he descended once more into a house in which everything seemed to be broken or not quite square, or both.

As he reached the foot of the stairs he was greeted by Harsforn.

"Ah, you are awake," she said. Her manner seemed considerably more friendly than it had been the previous day. "Do come join us for tea."

Tea? wondered Trondwyth. *Do these people never eat?*

But it was too late to query her, for she had ducked into the doorway of the room in which they had sat the previous afternoon, carrying a tray. He followed her and saw that the room, although there was no doubt that it was the same room, had been transformed by the morning sun. Dust danced in the slanting sunbeams that shone into the room, just enough dust to give the room a feeling of being comfortably lived in. Iadron was already seated in her chair, and Harsforn was beginning to serve the tea. He walked across to the chair that he had occupied the previous day and once more sat in it.

He was determined that he would broach the reason for his visit immediately so that he could leave and return to Catherine as early in the day as possible. He thanked Harsforn for the tea and was about to open his mouth when Iadron started speaking.

"Dear Trondwyth, I fear that we owe you a short explanation for yesterday. No, please, do not interrupt. I shall be brief and then we can set you on your way, although I fear that your comrades will be long gone before you return to where you left them.

"My sister and I have always made it a point not to become involved in the outside world. Once, a long time ago, we tried to do our best to help people. She would make people well again, and I would tell them what was going to befall them. We thought that we should serve others with the gifts that we had. But slowly we began to realize that we were being used. Never was there a moment of peace; always there would be someone coming to us with an urgent request for themselves or on someone else's behalf. And in those days there was much fighting. Always fighting. Always people wanting to be healed or to be told what would be their fortune in battle. But, you see, it is not always so easy to be a healer or an oracle. Sometimes people are supposed to be sick or to die, and it does no good to meddle unthinkingly with the fabric of our destinies. And what does one do when a young soldier comes to you and asks how he will fare in the upcoming battle? When you know that he will die in the battle, what can you say? If you tell him the truth, then it will not come about, for he will refuse to go to battle. But you cannot lie and, even if you could, it would do no good, for then others would no longer believe that you were an oracle and you would be denounced as a fraud and deceiver.

"Such problems as these came to haunt my sister and me. One day, we were visited by a young wizard, not much more than an apprentice, and we were so desperate for help that we put our plight before him. Well, the young wizard may not have lived in this land for many years as these things are reckoned, but the head on his shoulders was wise far beyond his years."

"Aye, it was that," interjected Harsforn, her sole contribution to the conversation, although Trondwyth had observed that now and then her head would nod in agreement.

"The wizard brought us to this place and showed us how to limit those who could reach us by permitting only selected ones to cross through the Moortain Mire safely. He left us with a warning. He said that yes, we had a duty to use our gifts, but they were not to be squandered on every person who might seek after us. Rather, our gifts should be used sparingly and, in particular, to protect Palindor itself when the need should arise.

"At first many tried to reach us, and for many years we denied everybody access. Several souls perished in their attempts to cross the marshes. At last, the number of those believing that they needed our help began to grow fewer. Then, occasionally, we would let one of them through if we thought that their need was especially urgent or if it in some way would help Palindor itself. Over the years, I fear that we have been forgotten now by most people in these parts, for now it is rare indeed for any soul to venture out in search of us.

"And perhaps as the years have gone by we have become a little too isolated and self-satisfied out here on our little island in the mire. Then, not three days since, Harsforn and I were sitting here drinking our evening tea when I suddenly knew that a terrible thing was happening. Not so far away, the young wizard who so many years ago helped us when we were in need was in pain, being run through by the lance of a Dark Knight. I closed my eyes and watched him die at the hands of their leader. But as he died, he looked into my eyes; he knew that I was there watching him, you see, and he gave me a message. He told me that a human by the name of Catherine must be saved at all costs, for Palindor was in danger, greater danger by far than it had ever been before, and only this human could save the land from destruction.

"Naturally, I told my sister about this immediately. We did not know what to make of it. Neither of us knew anything about any humans, and certainly we could not see how we could help in preserving the life of this one called Catherine. And Harsforn reminded me that for a long while now, we had survived by letting the world mind its own business, and there was no reason for us to become involved.

"We argued like this, off and on, until you showed up on the edge of the marsh. We could not decide whether to let you pass. I could tell that your errand here concerned Catherine, and so I felt that we had to let you come. But Harsforn was all for letting you go away again so that we could live our days in peace. Eventually, she relented. But Harsforn had to put you to a test before she would agree to become involved.

"Tea here is always a little special"—she looked across at her sister, who merely smiled in return—"and Harsforn concocted a special brew for you yesterday. And I am glad to see that you passed her test with flying colors. I am afraid that I cannot tell you what would have become of you had you not been the honest, Olvensar-fearing gnome that you are. But you are exactly that, which is the important thing, and so now Harsforn will be only too glad to help out in any way that she can. So, what exactly can we do for you?"

Trondwyth had taken all this in, wordlessly spellbound as Iadron's story unfolded. As she finished speaking he could once more hear the songbird chirping outside. The smell of fresh growing grass wafted in on a slight cooling breeze through the window. He felt lucky to be alive.

"Well, as I said, it is for Catherine's sake that I was sent," he said. "But," he said to Iadron, "you are an oracle. Surely you know my story already?"

Iadron laughed. "Being an oracle does not mean that I can read minds, nor that I know all things. It merely means that I can sometimes see shadows of what will be or of what is happening elsewhere. I cannot will myself to know things; rather, knowledge comes to me in flashes, often when I am not looking for it. Being an oracle is not a gift that one can control particularly well, especially when, in as in my case, I have had little use for it for such a long time. So pray continue, dear gnome."

"Catherine and I have been traveling together for some time, since she arrived in Palindor. What the wizard Entelred said to you in your vision is indeed true. Although Palindor does not know it, the land appears to be in great, great danger from Queen Cerebeth. A prophecy of long ago, which was recorded in the *First Book of Prophecies,* spoke of a human by the name of Catherine who would defeat the country's threat. This same Catherine and I reached the home of Entelred by separate means. We had to leave there in a hurry several days ago, along with Entelred's apprentice, a dwarf by the name of Gondalwyn, after Catherine and Entelred had visions of the oncoming Dark Knights.

"Shortly after we left, the Knights visited Entelred, searching for Catherine, and killed him. They followed our trail and discovered us that night. Catherine drove them away, but in the process she touched the blade of a Dark Knight's sword."

Here Trondwyth's narrative was interrupted by the sound of a sharply drawn breath from Harsforn.

"Immediately she fell to the ground, unconscious. Gondalwyn has some skill in the healing arts, and he suppressed the spread of the sword's power, but his knowledge was not sufficient to overcome it. For that, he said, we would need the help of a mighty healer. So he sent me here to seek the help of Harsforn while he stayed behind with Catherine, trying to keep her comfortable and to keep the power of the sword from infecting her further."

He looked across to Harsforn who, for the first time, returned his gaze.

"A Dark Sword, eh? Now that is quite a challenge. Have you ever heard of the power of kiríal, my gnome? Do they still speak of such things in the west these days?"

Trondwyth was on the point of denying any knowledge of kiríal when he saw Iadron looking at him carefully, as if much hung on the answer to this innocent question. He paused for a moment, fighting the desire to take the easy way out. Finally he blurted out, "I am a Holy Gnome."

Iadron relaxed back in her chair, seemingly pleased.

"A Holy Gnome?" said Harsforn. "We are honored indeed. I did not know that there were any such creatures left in Palindor. So you *do* know of kiríal. You must also know, then, that the Dark Knights inhabit the line between ordinary magic and kiríal. To ask a healer to heal the wound caused by the sword of a Dark Knight is to set the healer a difficult and perhaps impossible task. For a healer can combat magic, and a good healer can overcome any spell cast by wizard or necromancer. But even the best healer is powerless against the power of kiríal, for such power comes from beyond our ken, beyond this place and this time, from the depths of the all-there-is itself. And so, my good gnome, I cannot promise to undo the effects of the kiríal of the blade on your human. We can only hope that the cut was sufficiently light that the power of kiríal has had little opportunity to gain entrance to her body."

Trondwyth looked grim.

"But let us not be too sad," Harsforn continued, "for while the Dark Knights themselves are at least part kiríal, perhaps their weapons are solely of this world. I know not. So let me go and prepare a salve for your human that will take away the ills that the kiríal of the sword has placed upon her." The old woman eased herself from her chair and left the room.

Trondwyth said nothing, his mind occupied with the problem of why the Dark Knights, a product of kiríal, would obey the bidding of Queen Cerebeth. Even though she was Queen of Palindor, and even if her spirit was under Malthazzar's command, she herself was only human, and no human—indeed, no member of any mortal race—could command the forces of kiríal to do his bidding.

He looked up from his pondering to see Iadron staring at him, sadness in her eyes.

"What do you see in my future?" he asked.

The oracle shook her head. "It is not for me to tell you

nor for you to know," she said. "But this much I can see: the future of Palindor is in the hands of you and your friends, and the result will be determined at a place where the power of kirîal is great. More than that I do not know and cannot say."

Trondwyth began to speculate to himself about what the seer could mean—where was the place "where the power of kirîal is great"? where the future of the realm would be determined? But his thoughts were interrupted as Harsforn once more entered the room carrying a large leaf wrapped tightly around itself. Trondwyth stood and she offered it to him.

"An ointment is wrapped inside this leaf," she said to him. "You must keep it safe and use it as soon as you can. The leaf will keep the powers of the ointment fresh for several days, but after that it will begin to lose its power. Spread as much of the ointment as you can around the sword's cut. Within a few hours, unless kirîal is present, the human should begin to recover from the effects of the wound."

Iadron stood up and said, "Come now, good Holy Gnome. You must be going. And I can say only one thing more. You must return the way that you came, but do not be surprised if you do not complete the journey back to where you left your companions."

Trondwyth looked at Iadron, puzzled, but she merely laid her hand on his arm and pulled him slightly to indicate that he should hurry. Trondwyth thanked Harsforn for the ointment, telling her that one day all of Palindor would be grateful for her help. Iadron ushered Trondwyth out into the passageway while Harsforn looked on from the doorway.

Trondwyth carefully stowed the leaf with its precious contents into a pocket of his tunic, hitched his pack on to his back and made his way to the front door. Opening it, he was surprised to see that whereas it had been bright and cheerfully sunny outside only minutes before, now there was only a cool, clammy grayness of swirling mist. He had seen neither Iadron nor Harsforn do anything to cause the mist to fall, but he supposed that it must have arrived at their bidding. He stepped outside, onto the narrow verge of green that surrounded the sisters' tumbledown house in the middle of the mire, and turned back to face them.

"Thank you both for everything," he said.

"Good-bye," called Iadron, as her sister waved. "May Olvensar be with you."

Somehow he found the blessing comforting, as if he now could be sure whose side the two were really on. But as he stepped off the green swath into the mist, and the house was swallowed up in clouds of gray behind him, he thought he heard Harsforn speak to her sister.

"You never told him about the Hunter, did you?" were the words that he thought he heard. He turned around as the mist turned into a dense fog and all trace of his surroundings were obliterated. He took two steps back the way he had come, expecting once more to be back on the green verge, wanting to ask the two the meaning of Harsforn's words. But to his dismay he found that the green surrounding the house was not under his feet. Only two steps and, as before, he was already lost in the fog.

He stood still for several seconds and then he realized that he had no choice. He turned once more and began to walk forward into the enveloping gray.

14

DREFYNT AT SMALTERSCAIRN

REFYNT HURRIED THROUGH the woods as quickly as he could without making undue noise. He had no well-defined goal, other than to leave Carn Toldwyn far behind before the day was out. All he knew was that Trondwyth had been told to go in this direction, toward the Wastes of Kaltethorn. He was glad that, to judge from what he had been told by the dwarf Tarandron, Trondwyth was still alive and out of the clutches of Queen Cerebeth, at least for the present. Drefynt wondered who the human companion might be to which Tarandron had referred.

But speculation would not help him now. All he could do was to follow in Trondwyth's footsteps and hope that somewhere he would hear word of his brother's presence and be reunited with him.

He walked long into the night, neither wanting nor daring to rest. By now the queen must surely have been told of his presence and recent escape from Trondwyth's cottage. And surely she would have sent her soldiers on his trail. He napped uneasily that night, his short sleep disturbed by dreams of soldiers and dungeons.

He woke with the dawn, stretched himself, and without stopping for breakfast hoisted his pack on to his back and continued his walk eastward. He heard the sounds of forest animals scurrying out of the path before him, and many times he was sure that he was being watched by eyes whose owners were safely hidden amongst the trees or the dense undergrowth on either side of the path. By the end of the day, fatigue finally overcame him. That night he slept a long, dreamless sleep. The next morning, feeling much more secure, he continued his journey through the forest at a more leisurely pace.

He continued this way until, toward the middle of his third afternoon since leaving Carn Toldwyn, the trees began to be slightly less dense overhead. Suddenly he found himself standing on the bank of a narrow river. Looking to his left, he saw a bridge spanning the river and, on the opposite bank, what looked like a large clearing in which he could see small houses scattered around the edge, nestled up against the forest trees.

Smalterscairn, he thought, *home of the wood elves in this part of Palindor.*

Wood elves kept themselves to themselves, but there was not much that they missed. If Trondwyth had come this way it was unlikely that his passage would have gone unnoticed, even if he had tried to avoid the village itself.

His mind made up, Drefynt walked along the bank of the quietly flowing river until he reached the bridge. He walked across the bridge and into the wood elves' village.

Like Trondwyth before him, he passed a few elves who did not respond to his words of greeting as he entered the village. From behind the windows many unseen eyes peered at him as he passed. He walked quietly as far as the town square, where he saw the cairn of stones which had given the town its name. Across the square, Drefynt watched a couple of wood elves walking hurriedly by, but they were too distant for him to call out to them without seeming impolite. He stood on the corner, wondering what he should do next, when a wood elf walked around the corner and, with a bump, walked straight into him.

"I'm sorry," said the elf and then, as he looked up and saw that he had bumped into a gnome, a stranger, he looked embarrassed.

"That's all right," said Drefynt, eager not to lose an opportunity to talk to one of the town's inhabitants. "It was my fault for standing out of sight around the corner." Then, bowing, he made formal greeting: "Drefynt, gnome of Carn Toldwyn, at your service."

The elf was trapped into giving the appropriate response. "Caldorn, wood elf of Smalterscairn, at yours," he said hurriedly. Without a pause of any kind the elf continued, "Well, I must be on my way."

"No, wait a minute, master Caldorn," said Drefynt. "I wonder if you could help me."

The elf looked taken aback for a moment. "I? I am a mere page to the leader of the town. It is unlikely that I could help such a noble and esteemed stranger as a Holy Gnome."

It was Drefynt's turn to be surprised. "Come now," he said. "It is common knowledge that the Holy Gnomes are no more. They were all burned many years ago. I am merely a gnome in search of a friend, and I was wondering if you had seen him, that is all."

The wood elf looked at him. Drefynt looked back into the elf's face and saw, just for moment, a deep wisdom in the eyes. But then it was gone, the face before him once more the face of a subservient page, eager only to do the bidding of his master.

"Aye, well," said Caldorn the page, "be that as it may, perhaps you had best come see the new master here. It is not yet two weeks since Ederagorn the Wise finished his days here in peace, and now Jarrustin rules in his place. I will take you to him."

Drefynt tried to protest, but the elf was already walking hurriedly away across the square. Drefynt trotted after him until they came to a grand house that stood farther out from the surrounding trees than any other that Drefynt had yet seen. The door was open, and the page walked through it without knocking.

Drefynt waited outside for the call to enter. The page was gone for only a short time before he reappeared.

"Jarrustin will see you now," Caldorn said, and stood to one side to let the gnome pass.

Drefynt walked through the doorway, dropping his pack into a small cupboard on his right as he passed. He found himself in a small room that, despite its size, had about it a grandeur that seemed out of place in a village of wood elves. Drefynt had known few wood elves in his life, but those that he had known had been quiet, unassuming characters. The elf who stood now to greet him, a narrow gold chain of office hanging around his neck, had about him quite a different air. It was unsettling to Drefynt; the elf's air and manner would have sat more easily on an ill-tutored human than on a guardian of the forest.

But when the elf spoke he was polite enough. "Jarrustin, leader of the elves of Smalterscairn, at your service. Pray be seated. My page, Caldorn, tells me that you are in need of some help. What may I do for you?"

Drefynt took the proffered seat and said, "My name is Drefynt. I have come from Carn Toldwyn in search of a friend, Trondwyth by name. He is a gnome like me and would probably have passed this way journeying eastward a week or more ago. I was wondering if you or any of your good wood elves might have seen him."

"A gnome, you say? Why, yes, as a matter of fact, I think that I can be of assistance there. But you must be thirsty after your travels." His tone became more rough, commanding. "Caldorn, bring the good gnome the draft that we prepared yesterday. I am sure that he will appreciate having his thirst quenched."

From where he was seated, Drefynt could not see the page behind him, but he could see the fire in Jarrustin's eyes as he voiced the command. As the elf's eyes stayed on his page, narrowing slightly, Drefynt knew that Caldorn was challenging the command, as if it were a duty that he was reluctant to perform. Then he heard a sound as Caldorn moved, and he saw Jarrustin's eyes widen and relax. Like a good Holy Gnome, Drefynt did not challenge his host over the incident; he merely filed it away in his mind for future reference.

Jarrustin spoke once more. "It has been a long while since our little town has been visited by two gnomes in such a short space of time. But I believe that a gnome passed through here—I did not see him myself—not long ago. I was told that he entered the town through its west entrance, across the bridge, and left traveling eastward. It must have been your friend. It would be about two weeks since he was here, I think . . . yes. Ederagorn, who used to rule here, died thirteen days ago, late in the day, and it was earlier that same day that the gnome passed through."

Drefynt heard a sound behind him as Caldorn returned and placed a cup of hot, steaming liquid before him.

"Thank you," Drefynt and Jarrustin said, together. Jarrustin waved his hand, with a single motion dismissing the page and inviting Drefynt to drink, and then continued his story.

"Ederagorn was wise in his youth, but in his old age he clung too much to the ways of the old days. I have heard that he spoke with your friend as he was passing through, although of what I cannot say. Some would say that it is an ill omen to entertain strangers in Smalterscairn and that Ederagorn's death came about because of it, but I hold not with such superstitious nonsense. Come now, drink. You must be thirsty."

He paused, waiting for Drefynt. The gnome took the cup and sipped of the dark-red steaming liquid. It was surprisingly good, sweet yet tart at the same time. He drank half the liquid before placing the cup down once more before him.

"You must stay the night with us," continued the leader of the wood elves. "I must not have it be said that the wood elves of Smalterscairn have no sense of hospitality. Strangers are welcome now that I rule here. . . ."

Drefynt was finding it difficult to concentrate on Jurrustin's words. He found it oppressively hot inside the little room, and he wanted to hurry outside and take deep breaths of fresh air. He placed his arms on the chair in which he was seated and tried to raise himself, but the effort was too great. It took great strength even to keep his eyelids open. Quietly he gave up the struggle. His eyes closed, and he slept.

While the beginning of Drefynt's slumber was peaceful, its ending was anything but. When he woke it was dark, but that was not what first impacted itself on his senses. His head was in great pain, made considerably worse by the jolting which his body was undergoing. Bump, bump, bump; he was being bounced up and down, his head hitting against something with every bump. He appeared to be lying over something that kept moving, his feet dangling down on one side and his head on the other. He tried to move his hands from their position where they were digging into the small of his back, but he found that they could not be moved, nor could he roll away from whatever it was under him that was causing the continual jolting. He tried to lift his head, but could do so only with the greatest of efforts.

Slowly his mind and senses began to work through the pain, and he realized his position. He was strapped to the back of a horse or similar beast of burden, his hands tied tightly behind his back and his whole body strapped to the animal beneath so that he would not fall off. The bumping which he felt was the motion of the beast as it walked, and his head hit the flank of the animal with each step that it took.

He tried to make a noise, to shout out that he was awake, but only the faintest of cries came from his throat, which burned as if on fire. All his muscles ached; it seemed that there was not a part of his body that was not in pain; yet on and on went the bumping jostle of the ride, and there was nothing he could do about it.

Drefynt was carried in this way, unaware of his surroundings, fighting waves of pain, until shortly after dawn. Somehow he must have succeeded in going back to sleep, for one moment there had been only the semidarkness of predawn and the neverending jolting of the animal's steps; then, seemingly the very next moment, there was full light and the animal was no longer moving.

Lifting his head, he let out an involuntary groan. He could see now that his surmises about his position had been correct. He was strapped tightly to the back of a horse, which was now bending down to eat of the greenery by the side of the track. In front of his horse was a second one, head down, also eating, the two of them roped together with a stout cord. To one side of the track, where the grass verge widened out somewhat, he could see a human crouched over a makeshift fire that was sending up spirals of smoke into the still forest air.

The human was too preoccupied to have heard Drefynt's groan, so he groaned a second time, more loudly this time. The human stood and turned around to face him.

Drefynt did not recognize the face of the figure before him, but he immediately recognized the dress. The human, the tallest female that Drefynt had ever seen, was dressed all over in various shades of green. By her side hung a sword; on the left shoulder breast of her green tunic was stitched a small white cross—the emblem of the Hunters.

"So, you are awake at last, my gnomish traitor. It will not be long now before you face your queen. Prepare yourself to meet your end."

Drefynt's pain was beginning to decrease now that he was no longer being jolted along, and he found he could think reasonably clearly. He had never met a Hunter before, although like all inhabitants of Palindor, he knew stories from the past of their great and valorous deeds. They lived in the forest and owed allegiance solely to themselves and the reigning monarch of Palindor. Usually the monarch had no reason to call on the Hunters, but on more than one occasion the tide of an important battle had been turned when a Palindor king had commanded the Hunters to fight. Their skill with their broadswords was second only to their accuracy with their longbows. It was said that a Hunter could kill a rabbit at a hundred paces with a single arrow shot from his bow. Drefynt noticed that the Huntress before him was wearing her quiver, which appeared to be full, although he had not seen any sign of a longbow.

"Traitor? A traitor to whom?" he asked. "What am I supposed to have done?"

"You are Drefynt, are you not?" asked the Huntress, a slight doubt in her voice.

It was hard to summon up much dignity, strapped to the back of a horse, but Drefynt tried. "I am indeed Drefynt, last of the Holy Gnomes of Palindor, and whoever calls me a traitor shall stand before me and confront me with the evidence. To impugn the honor of a Holy Gnome who has sworn to protect Palindor and her monarch is no light matter."

The Huntress was clearly taken aback by this speech.

"Holy Gnome? Do not try your wiles on me, I warn you. The Holy Gnomes of this land are long gone. Will you tell me next that you, Drefynt gnome, were not a prisoner of Her Majesty, Queen Cerebeth of Palindor, and that you did not, by some devilish trickery, escape the confines of her dungeon deep beneath Dynas Carn Toldwyn?"

"I am he," admitted Drefynt.

"Then I care to know no more. My queen has ordered that you be brought to her, and what my queen orders, so shall it be." She turned away and began to walk determinedly back toward the fire.

"No, wait. In the name of Olvensar, I beseech you, wait!" called Drefynt.

But the Huntress did not falter in her step; the name of the High Lord had no power over her. Reaching the little fire, she kicked dirt onto it with her boot. The fire quickly died away, and the Huntress turned to Drefynt.

"Be quiet," she commanded. "No more of your lies. We return now to Dynas Carn Toldwyn. Save your traitorous lies for the queen." She stepped toward her horse, and Drefynt now saw the longbow strapped to the horse's side. In a single, fluid motion, the Huntress sat astride her horse. With a slight clicking noise and pull on the reins, she turned her horse and it began to walk slowly forwards. The rope between the two beasts grew taut, and Drefynt once more began to be jolted. Bump, bump, bump; the small procession moved again towards Carn Toldwyn.

15

DISCOVERED!

RONDWYTH CLIMBED THE hill and looked back into the valley. Already the fog had lifted, and he could see clearly the little ramshackle house of the oracle and the healer. He tapped his pocket to be sure that the ointment for Catherine was safe.

He was puzzled about Iadron's warning that he would not return to where he had left Gondalwyn and Catherine, just as he was puzzled by Harsforn's comment about a Hunter. He wished that he felt braver. It was one thing for people like Catherine to stand up to Dark Knights and to play an active part in this most serious of businesses—after all, Catherine was a High Queen, the First High Monarch of Palindor. The prophecy made it quite clear that she would defeat the power that stood against Palindor and would one day—soon, he hoped—be crowned High Queen in the throne room at Dynas Carn Toldwyn. It was quite another thing for poor little gnomes to be sucked into the maelstrom. The prophecies said nothing about Holy Gnomes, nothing about two poor creatures called Trondwyth and Drefynt or a dwarf apprentice wizard by the name of Gondalwyn. He had no prophecy to cling to to assure him that he would even be alive to see the glorious crowning of the High Queen.

His spirits sank and he wondered miserably what had become of his brother. Olvensar had said that he had an important part to play; Trondwyth wondered what Drefynt's part could be.

But, Trondwyth realized, he had better get a move on, or he might fail to play his own part the way the High Lord Olvensar desired. He had to return to Catherine and Gondalwyn and rub the ointment on Catherine's wound. Maybe, once she recovered, she would be able to offer him consolation and advice about the forces arrayed against them. Quickening his step, he walked down from the crest of the hill, toward the forest below.

It was now the morning of the third day since Catherine had succumbed to the power of the Dark Sword. The High Queen appeared to be resting comfortably in the little grassy bowl in front of the entrance to the cave. The sun shone brightly and the woods were full of bird song. Catherine slept peacefully, and the spread of the gray and black from her thumb had been well halted by Gondalwyn's attentions.

He hated leaving her, but it had to be done. He had already made five trips for herbs, and he was worried about finding them all again. Feverfew in particular was scarce in this part of the woods. Last time he had been gone nearly an hour, and it had been almost dark before he returned to make the compress that would see Catherine through the night.

This morning he had made an early start to search for the plants that she needed. Within the space of a quarter of an hour he had found all the other necessary herbs, but once more feverfew was proving particularly elusive. By now he must be nearly two thousand paces from the cave, and there was still no sign of the herb. He walked along the side of the track, his eyes casting around the verge for the telltale yellow and white. Feverfew disliked the dark of the woods and made its home here by the side of the track and in holes in walls. Farther down the mountainside the plant was plentiful, but here it was a little too high, a little too cold.

At last he spotted a plant a little way ahead. He hurried forward, glad to have found the object of his quest. He hoped that Trondwyth would not be much longer; another day or so of this and he would have to consider leaving Catherine for most of the day while he searched for feverfew to keep the evil at bay. He stooped and picked the leaves from the plant before him, leaving only the tall flowers standing by the roadside. It was a large specimen and there would be enough of the leaves on this one plant to see Catherine through the rest of the day and possibly even through the night.

He stuffed the leaves into his pouch and turned to walk back the way that he had come. The return journey went much faster, and it was only a few minutes later that he came in sight of the point where he would leave the track, go down, and then squeeze up through the stones to be safe once more in the sunlit bowl in which Catherine lay.

But as he turned the corner in the track, he saw a horse standing at the wayside, its head down, grazing on the sweet grass of the green verge. Gondalwyn hurried forward, looking around for the horse's rider. He hurried down the track to the dell and then, as quietly as he could, squeezed through the stones. As he emerged into the glade, he saw that Catherine was still lying where he had left her. But standing guard over the High Queen, broadsword drawn and glittering in the sunlight, stood a Hunter.

Gondalwyn had never seen a Hunter before. To start with, he had not known that human beings could be so big. This Hunter stood tall and straight, sword slightly raised, and he looked as if he could fell a tree with a single swipe of the weapon. His face was set firmly, as if Catherine was his property and he had no intention of letting anyone take her from him.

The two looked at one another across the grass, no more than two sword lengths separating them. Gondalwyn broke the silence.

"What are you doing here? What do you want?" he demanded, eschewing all appearances of civility.

"My name is Aramis," said the Hunter. "I am here on a quest, and I have found the object of my search." He dipped his sword and waved it slightly in the direction of Catherine. "I was sent here by Cerebeth, queen of all Palindor, to find and bring to her a human female who would be wearing a belt such as this. Having found her, I must now take her to the queen. I know not who you are, nor what enchantment you have wrought on this woman that she now sleeps too deeply to waken, but I warn you: try not to hinder my taking her away, or I will have no pity and will run you through with my sword."

Gondalwyn thought quickly and decided that it would be too dangerous to tell this unknown Hunter the truth. "Nay, nay, my good Aramis. Have no fear. I am only a poor humble dwarf, and I mean you no harm. See, I carry no battle-ax and could do you no wrong even if I intended such. But pray tell me, why does the queen enlist the help of a Hunter to find a single human female?

What has this woman done that she is such a threat?"

"That I know not," replied Aramis. "I know only that the queen sent out orders that the woman wearing this belt and a gnome traveling with her in the eastern parts of Palindor were to be found and brought to her unharmed. They plan insurrection and the death of the queen, for those who live in Reglandor are once more looking with envious eyes westward to Palindor. These two were to come to Palindor to kill the queen so that, in the confusion, the armies of Reglandor would meet with no resistance and capture Carn Toldwyn with little bloodshed."

"And the gnome, has he been caught also?" asked Gondalwyn.

"I know not, but he cannot be far from this place. Have you seen any sign of him?"

"Nay, that I have not," said Gondalwyn. "I was merely caring for this human. I live nearby and came across her yesterday laid out here just as you see her now. I could not raise her from her sleep, and I fear that she will die soon unless she be taken to a healer. I have a small gift of healing and have been preparing a compress of herbs for her wound so that it no longer is sapping her strength, but I fear that she will not live long without proper treatment from one whose gifts are greater than mine." As he spoke he dug into his pockets and withdrew a handful of the leaves which he had been gathering. "Of this I am sure: she will not survive the journey back to Carn Toldwyn without treatment from a healer."

The Hunter lowered his sword, although he kept it unsheathed. "You say that she has a wound? Where is this wound?"

Gondalwyn stepped forward and bent down over Catherine's sleeping body. Aramis sheathed his sword and knelt beside the dwarf, his frame like that of a giant next to Gondalwyn. The dwarf leaned across Catherine's body and unwrapped the compress of leaves that bound her left hand. The leaves fell away, exposing the dull gray of Catherine's hand to the sunlight. Around the small, almost invisible cut on her thumb was a white patch encircled by a dark ring.

Aramis stared at it. "Of that I have never seen the like," he said. "And it is this poison that causes her to sleep so?"

"Aye, I believe so," replied Gondalwyn. "As long as I replace the compress with fresh herbs, then the poison seems to be kept at bay. But I fear that were no new herbs to be placed on the wound, then the poison would spread and she would quickly die. If she is to live, she must be taken to a healer, but there is only one in these parts and she is a full day and a half of walking from here—perhaps a day on a horse carrying a rider and this woman."

The seed had been planted in the mind of the Hunter, and it quickly grew. "Aye, then that is what we must do. This woman would be no good to the queen were she to arrive already dead at Carn Toldwyn. You must make a new compress with the herbs that you have gathered and direct me to where the healer can be found. I will take the woman to her so that she may be healed before I take her to the queen."

Gondalwyn agreed that this was an excellent plan and quickly ground up the newly gathered leaves between two small rocks. As he did so, he kept as far away as possible from the half-hidden mouth of the cave. It required great willpower to keep his eyes from straying in that direction, to the Dark Sword that still leaned against a rock there.

He proceeded quickly, grinding the leaves and then

placing them against Catherine's wound and binding them tightly once more. That done, he quickly advised Aramis on the best route to be taken to reach the house of Iadron and Harsforn. He wondered briefly if he should explain about how the house could only be reached during times of mist. Concluding that Harsforn was truly Catherine's most likely chance for recovery, he confided in Aramis, who seemed surprised to hear that such enchantments were still to be found in Palindor.

Gondalwyn offered to help the Hunter move the sleeping Catherine to his horse but, without speaking, Aramis placed his hands under her body and lifted it high over his head. He was tall enough that he could step over the gap in the rocks without trying to squeeze his trunk through—which would have been a tight fit indeed. Minutes later, Catherine was safely strapped to Aramis's horse and to Aramis himself, in a sitting position behind the Hunter.

"I thank you, good dwarf. May Olvensar bless you," said Aramis as he turned the horse in the track.

"And may he bless you," said Gondalwyn, surprised that a Hunter would use the name of the High Lord.

Aramis lightly flicked the reins, and the horse moved forward. Gondalwyn watched as the animal with its two riders walked quickly down the track and around the corner. As soon as it was out of sight, he walked thoughtfully back to the grassy bowl in front of the cave.

Trondwyth had made good progress, but it would still be many hours' walk before he would reach the cave. He had crossed the river as late afternoon turned into the twilight of early evening, but had walked for another two hours after that. Now he was beginning to feel tired and he knew that he should rest until dawn.

He took himself off the track a short distance into the forest, sat down, and leaned against a tree. His head rapidly dropped against his chest and soon he was fast asleep.

It seemed like only a moment later that he jerked his head up suddenly, awakened by an unexpected sound. But already the sky above him was light, although still more gray than blue. Sunrise could only be minutes away, and he could hear the fluttering of wings in the woods as birds flew around, trying to find suitable perches from which to greet the arrival of the new day.

There, he heard it again. A clip-clop, as of a horse, heavily laden. He quietly made his way toward the nearby path and peered out from under a fern. Not much of the path was visible from his hiding place, but the sound of the oncoming horse was unmistakable. He waited and in due course the horse turned a corner in the path and came into sight.

Trondwyth let out a gasp as he saw astride the horse a Hunter and, behind him, Catherine, swaying from side to side. Her eyes were closed, and he could see the compress that Gondalwyn had made still attached to her left hand.

He watched as the horse with its riders passed him, moving steadily. For an instant he wondered what to do and then, almost without thought, he stepped out from the undergrowth and shouted to the retreating figures.

"Hey! Stop!" he called out. Immediately the horse was reined in and turned around. The Hunter looked at him but said nothing.

Trondwyth was nonplussed. Having succeeded in stopping the horse, he was unsure what to do next.

Finally the Hunter spoke. "A gnome, I see," he said quietly. "And for what reason, pray, does a gnome interrupt the journeying of a Hunter?"

"I beg your forgiveness," said Trondwyth a little nervously. The horse took several steps toward him before being halted soundlessly by the Hunter a mere five paces from where he stood. "I beg your forgiveness, but I could not help myself when I saw the passenger on your horse."

The Hunter smoothly and quickly untied the rope around his trunk and slid off his steed, gently letting Catherine lie across the horse's back as he did so. He stepped a pace away from his horse and then spoke once more.

"And what is my passenger to you, good gnome?"

Trondwyth did not trust the Hunter. A Hunter may not be as dangerous as a Dark Knight but he was, nonetheless, likely to be in the service of the queen. "I see that she is faint, and I have here a salve which would likely do her good," said Trondwyth. He delved into his pocket and withdrew his hand, clutching the leaf that had been given him by Harsforn.

"Are you then a healer?" asked the Hunter. "I have never before met a gnome who would claim such gifts."

"Nay," said Trondwyth. "I am no healer, but I come fresh from a visit with Harsforn, the greatest healer in these parts. I am sure that this salve with which she provided me could help your passenger."

The Hunter stepped back to the horse and placed his hands underneath Catherine's body. He lifted her effortlessly and carried her to the grass verge where he laid her down gently.

Trondwyth walked up to them and was dismayed to see the pale gray of Catherine's skin. Deftly the Hunter untied the leaf that was bound around Catherine's hand, and Trondwyth saw that the darkness had spread to cover most of the hand. Saying nothing, and fearful that he was too late, he unwrapped the leaf, exposing the small quantity of the ointment, which he began to rub into Catherine's hand.

For several minutes he worked, until all the salve was gone. Catherine seemed no different, and it was with a heavy heart that Trondwyth arose. He had been concentrating so much on rubbing the ointment into Catherine's skin that for some time he had been unaware of the Hunter's movements. But as he stood up and began to shake his legs to restore the circulation to them, he suddenly felt the Hunter throw something around his waist. In a second, he found his arms pinned to his sides by a stout cord. The Hunter said nothing as he took the other end of the cord and tied it to the saddle of his horse.

"What are you doing with me?" cried the gnome. "I have done nothing to you; all I have done is tried to help the human. Is this the way of the Hunters, to prey upon the weak and helpless?"

The Hunter paused in the act of returning Catherine's inert body to its place at the rear of the horse. "You doubt the integrity of a Hunter? You, who are a traitor to this entire land of Palindor? It will be with pleasure that I hand you over to the queen, that she might do with you as she wishes."

"Traitor? What do you mean, traitor?" asked Trondwyth. "I am no traitor. Do you not know whose body that is that you hold in your arms?"

The Hunter looked down at the sleeping Catherine and back to the gnome, but he remained silent.

"I repeat," said Trondwyth, "do you not know who that is?"

The Hunter shook his head.

"It is none other than Catherine, the First High Queen of Palindor. And I only pray that the salve that I have administered will be sufficient to return her from the land of darkness to that of the living."

The Hunter spoke, his voice like steel. "Joke not about matters of such import, gnome. Unlike many Hunters, I know of the prophecies, and Catherine will appear only when all else is lost. Your treacherous friends from Reglandor have yet to make their first move on Palindor. With the queen's help and guidance, it is likely that we who are loyal will succeed in driving them back to their own country. The time is not yet for such as Queen Catherine to be needed in Palindor, although when she does come you will tremble and quake, for she will have no mercy on such as you."

"No, wait!" called Trondwyth. "The belt—look at her belt! It contains the white stone, just as the prophecy says."

The Hunter looked down and gave the belt buckle a fleeting glance. "So, it has a white stone. Such was the sign by which I was to recognize this human and bring her to the queen. It signifies nothing. Cease your ravings, gnome. If what you say is true, then the queen will welcome you when I turn you over to her."

"You don't understand!" shouted Trondwyth, but it was no good. The Hunter tied Catherine back onto the horse and then easily launched himself into the saddle, once more tying Catherine to his midriff. With a slight motion of the Hunter's feet, the horse began to walk forward slowly. The rope tightened, and Trondwyth found himself unwillingly bringing up the rear of the sorry procession. Above, in a tree top, a bird launched itself into the air. Spreading its wings wide and flapping them lazily, it spiralled up into the air and then set out to the west, leaving the two humans and the gnome far behind.

16

AN INTERVIEW WITH
THE QUEEN

ARN TOLDWYN SEEMED unnaturally deserted as the Huntress, with Drefynt and his mount in tow, entered the town late in the afternoon. They were almost at the base of the hill on which Queen Cerebeth's castle stood before Drefynt saw any other creatures. But what he saw then chilled his blood.

The inhabitants of Carn Toldwyn were drilling like soldiers, charging at one another, clubbing, ducking, fighting. Many were dressed in battle armor, with raised battle-axes and metal breastplates glinting in the sunlight. Weapons of death that had hung unused on the walls of family homes for generations were being put to the test.

As the horses entered the gates of the castle, Drefynt recognized a gnome lounging near the entrance between practice bouts. It was one of his brother Trondwyth's neighbors from the eastern side of the town. Just as Drefynt opened his mouth in greeting, the gnome walked up and spat at him.

"Traitor," said the gnome, then turned on his heel and walked away.

The Huntress and her prisoner crossed the courtyard and came to the stables, where she slipped easily out of her saddle. She walked across to where Drefynt was strapped to his horse and quickly untied the rope. Drefynt unceremoniously slid to the ground. His muscles would not hold his weight, and he collapsed in a heap, his legs and arms tingling from being tied so long. The Huntress bent down and offered her hand, but Drefynt shook his head and rubbed his limbs to bring life back into them.

The Huntress stood to one side, hand resting on the hilt of her broadsword, awaiting Drefynt's recovery. Eventually the gnome found that he could stand, and only then did the Huntress draw her sword. Holding it out in front of her, she pointed toward Drefynt.

"Come. Now we visit the queen." She prodded Drefynt lightly, and he crossed the courtyard in the direction indicated, feeling the sword occasionally make its presence felt between his shoulders as they walked.

They entered the castle by the main portal, where the Huntress spoke to a footman. "My name is Belrea," she said. "I was sent by the queen to recover this gnome, and I am to deliver him to Her Majesty personally."

The footman showed them to a large waiting room. When he returned, he asked them to follow him upstairs, along landings, and down ever-narrowing corridors to a wooden door at the end of a small corridor. Drefynt recognized it immediately as the entranceway to the northernmost tower of the castle. They climbed the narrow stone steps until they reached a small landing about halfway up the tower. Pulling a key from a chain, the footman unlocked the door.

He looked at Drefynt. "You will await Her Majesty in here." The gnome was propelled forward by a thrust from the Huntress Belrea. He turned back toward the doorway to hear the footman say to his captor, "I will take you to the queen." The sound of further conversation was cut off as the footman closed the door and the key turned in the lock.

Drefynt looked around the room. It was unlike the dungeon in which he had languished for so many days, but was no less a prison. The room was larger and of a rather peculiar shape, a circumstance forced on it by virtue of its location up the tower. It had a single narrow slit of a window, which was shaded from the afternoon sun by the bulk of the tower. The walls were of stone, the ceiling and floor of oaken timbers. A thick layer of dust covered the floor, and with every footstep that he took, a cloud of dust rose and tickled his throat.

Drefynt walked across to the window and looked out to the south. From his location high above the town, he could see across much of the castle and its courtyards to almost the entirety of Carn Toldwyn. In the middle distance he could see the Pennyfarthing River, the southernmost boundary of Carn Toldwyn. Farther away he could see the glint of the River Findell. It curved around like a lazy snake, marking the beginning of Machrenmoor, which rose in the distance, high and bleak. He watched the shadows from the rapidly falling sun in the west lengthen.

Bored, he sat down against the wall under the window, waiting for something to happen. He was hungry and thirsty, but at least his head was no longer aching and his muscles seemed to have recovered from their confinement on the back of the Huntress's horse.

He wondered what would become of him. For reasons that he did not know, Queen Cerebeth had spread the idea that Palindor would shortly be attacked from the east by the armies of Reglandor, beyond the mountains. She had made Drefynt and Trondwyth scapegoats in this plan; to the loyal subjects of Palindor, he and his brother were traitors, spies from Reglandor. He wondered if Reglandor really did intend to attack Palindor.

His reverie was interrupted by the opening of the door to the room. He had heard no sound of a key being turned in the lock, and as he stared at the queen who walked into the room, he saw that she carried no key. Behind her, the door swung quietly closed without intervention by mortal hand. He did not move.

"You will rise," said Queen Cerebeth.

"Why?" said Drefynt, his spirit now in rebellion.

"You will rise," repeated the queen, "because if you do not, I will turn you into a worm and crush you beneath my heel."

"You have not the power," said Drefynt, rising nevertheless. "You are neither magician nor necromancer, but Queen of Palindor. But why are you doing these things?"

"You fool," said the queen. "You do not yet understand, do you? You are no threat to me. If you are the best that Olvensar can send against me, then he is even more an old fool than I thought."

"Olvensar? But surely he has not been seen in Palindor for many years. And most of the people believe that he is no more than a myth—"

"Idiot!" roared the queen. "You insult my intelligence and try my patience, Holy Gnome. I know that Olvensar has been abroad in my kingdom. He cannot come here without my knowledge. And I know that he has sent the human Catherine against me, but he cannot win."

Catherine? thought Drefynt. *Catherine?* Surely the Queen could not mean that the High Queen Catherine, the First High Monarch of Palindor, was abroad in the realm?

In a flash, he understood. Why else would Olvensar have sought their aid if there were not a serious danger threatening Palindor, a danger sufficiently grave that the High Queen had been called? But if Olvensar had sent Catherine to Palindor, and if the queen believed that Catherine was sent to do battle with her, then that could only mean that the threat to Palindor was graver than he or Trondwyth had previously realized, and the source of that threat must be the queen herself. He remembered the afternoon tea at Trondwyth's house, when Olvensar had confirmed his suspicion that the queen's spirit was no longer her own to control. But her mind and her body, surely these were still hers?

"It's the Elixir, isn't it? It's the Elixir of Life that has done this to you."

The queen laughed, a loud, long laugh of victory. "Oh, well done, good and honest gnome. You are so nearly right. And yet, in the most important detail, you are so, so wrong."

She was interrupted by a sound from outside the door. She turned and once again, without any perceptible motion or command from her, the door to the room slowly opened. Drefynt could not suppress a shiver at the sight that met his eyes. On the threshold stood a dark, shadowy shape. As it strode into the room, the gnome felt a cold and despairing aloneness fall across his spirit. The shadow came to a halt in front of the queen, but try as he might, the gnome could distinguish no features in it. It was a black creature in the shape of a warrior; it was—he felt chilled as the realization hit him—a Dark Knight.

The Knight stood before the queen and inclined its head ever so slightly.

"Yes?" said the queen. "Where is the human prisoner?"

A voice came from the shadow, deep and

commanding and yet no more than a whisper. It was unlike any voice that Drefynt had ever heard, and yet it was like all the voices that he knew. It was cold and impersonal, and yet full of hatred.

"Your Majesty," said the voice, "I must inform you that although we found the human and confronted her, she proved too powerful for us."

"Fool!" said the queen. "How could that be? There were three of you; three of the most terrifying denizens of kiríal, and yet you failed to capture one simple human?"

"Your Majesty, it was the light—the light of Olvensar that came from her. We could not approach—"

"No!" roared the queen. "She is powerless against you. Do you understand? Powerless. She will try to trick you with lights and simple magic, but she has no real power against you. You are more than a match for her. The light was only a light, nothing more. Olvensar cannot interfere; it is forbidden. She is yours for the taking. Now go, and do not return without the human, or you will feel the full force of my wrath."

The queen faced Drefynt once more, dismissing the knight. Wordlessly the knight turned and left the room, and the door closed once more on the queen and her subject.

Drefynt now understood. "That was a Dark Knight, was it not?"

"Yes, gnome, that he was. How did it feel to be in the presence of a herald of darkness?"

Drefynt ignored the question; he was thinking out loud. "It was a Dark Knight, and yet it did your bidding. But a Dark Knight is a creature of kiríal, and no human could ever command the forces of kiríal in such a way." He stared at the queen, fearing the answer to his next question: "You are not Queen Cerebeth, are you?"

The queen stared back at him, saying nothing, and a grin spread itself across her face. The grin widened and then she let out a laugh: long, loud, and terrifying. As Drefynt watched, the form of the queen flickered before him. It was hard to keep his eyes focused properly on her, for she seemed to be shimmering and at the same time growing darker and taller. Within a few seconds, the transformation was complete.

"Malthazzar!" exclaimed Drefynt. "I should have guessed long ago."

As he watched, the transformation reversed itself and he once more appeared to be in the presence of Cerebeth, Queen of Palindor. Neither spoke.

Silently the door behind the queen opened and, without a word, she turned and passed through the open doorway. The door closed noiselessly behind her.

Drefynt stood still for a moment and then ran to the door. There had been no sound of a key, but the door was locked once more. He pulled the handle as hard as he could, but the door stayed defiantly closed. Eventually he returned to the window. He stared out into the gray darkness of the evening at the few lights moving in the town down the hill and tried to absorb what he had just witnessed.

17

AN INTERVIEW

ONDALWYN WONDERED what to do next. As soon as he saw that the Hunter intended to remove Catherine, he knew that there was nothing that he could do to keep the High Queen from the Hunter's hands. He wished that he were a great wizard like Entelred, for then he could surely have prevented Catherine's removal by the Hunter. But his powers, while in some areas quite grown, were not yet ready to stand the test of person-to-person combat, especially against such a strong and athletic foe as a Hunter. So he'd felt it wiser to hide the fact from the Hunter that he was a wizard of any kind, in case they should meet again.

So now he had lost the High Queen; he could only hope that he had at least persuaded the Hunter to take his hostage to Harsforn. If Catherine were to become well once more, she might be able to find a way out of her predicament for herself.

Now Gondalwyn sat on a stone, wondering what to do next. He could try to follow the Hunter or take a shortcut down the mountainside and try to waylay him as he crossed the Findell on his way to the healer's house in the mire. But he could see little merit in those plans. Catherine needed to see the healer anyway, and even with the advantage of surprise on his side he was not sure that he would be able to defeat the Hunter in a fight.

Idly he looked around the little glade, and his eyes rested on the Dark Sword, still leaning against a stone near the entrance to the cave. A wave of anger came over him. He wanted to take the sword and strike out with it, against whom, he did not know—anyone, anything that got in his way. He pulled himself up and walked across to the sword. He looked at it long and hard, then he slowly held out his hand, grasped the hilt of the weapon, and lifted it off the ground into the air before him. He was surprised at the weight of the sword. It didn't gleam even in the full glare of the sun; it was as dark as ever, swallowing up the sunlight so completely as to seem insubstantial, a dark nothingness. Yet the weight in his hands assured him that this was far from a nothing; it was a killing weapon, a mighty sword against which few shields could hope to stand. A new emotion came over him; he suddenly desired to have nothing more to do with the sword. If it were not for the sword, Catherine would be safe now and the group would be together, making their way westward toward Dynas Carn Toldwyn and a reckoning with the queen.

He raised the sword over his head and drew back his arm, ready to fling it with all his strength into the forest. But slowly the desire left him, and his arm dropped to his side, the blade of the sword resting against the grass at his feet.

A new thought came into his mind. Just before the fight with the Dark Knights, Catherine had been changed.

She had gone to explore the darkness at the rear of the cave little more than a human child; when she returned only minutes later she had the bearing of a warrior, a High Queen. Grasping the sword more tightly and making sure to keep the blade well away from his skin, he stepped out of the sunlight into the darkness of the cave. His dwarf eyes immediately adjusted to the darkness and, without breaking his stride, he walked into the cave, past Catherine's and his packs and into the confines of the rear of the cave.

He did not know what he was looking for. He had explored the cave many times as a young dwarf and already knew its every cranny. So he was more than a little surprised to see, right up against the rear wall of the cave, a little passageway off to the left. It did not look at all new, but rather as if it had been there since the building of the mountains. And yet he knew that the passageway had not been there before. Curious now, he slowly edged his way down the passageway.

In a few steps, he found himself in a chamber. In the chamber he saw an old man dressed in dirty green gardening clothes. The man looked up, his face grave, as the dwarf entered the chamber. Gondalwyn needed no second glance at that face to know to whom it belonged. He bowed his head and brought one knee to the stone of the floor, his right hand outstretched and supporting itself on the Dark Sword.

"My lord," was all he said. He kept his head down.

"Arise, dwarf," said a voice older than time itself.

But Gondalwyn did not move. "I am not worthy," he said, still not moving. "The High Queen Catherine was entrusted to me, and I have failed to protect her." As he spoke, the sense of his failure bore down him like a great and heavy burden. He, the only dwarf ever to be chosen as a wizard's apprentice, had been unable to protect a single human from her enemies.

"Arise, Gondalwyn, if you wish to make amends. The saving of Palindor is much too important a task to be blocked by the pride of one unimportant dwarf."

Gondalwyn was stung. Even though he was truly humble and contrite, he did not like to be told that he was unimportant nor that he was prideful, even if one or both of these accusations might be true. He looked up and arose, standing as tall and straight as he could before the watchful gaze of the old man.

"Ah, there is fire in your eyes. That is good. No more self-pity, I hope?"

Gondalwyn did not know what to say, and merely shook his head slowly from side to side.

The old man continued. "Gondalwyn, do you know where you stand?"

"Nay," said the dwarf, surprised at the question. "It is a puzzle to me. I came often to this cave as a young dwarf, but I never noticed this chamber before. And yet the walls show it to be old indeed, older even than the cave itself."

"What you say is true," said the man. "This is one of the ley chambers of Palindor."

The dwarf looked puzzled, but held his tongue.

"When Palindor was created, certain places were set apart as special; places where the kiríal is particularly strong. This is one such place. Few indeed are those who have entered this chamber before."

"Catherine was here, was she not, my lord?" inquired the dwarf.

"Indeed she was," said Olvensar. "She had to find this place to prepare herself for the battle to come."

The dwarf was going to interrupt, but then thought better of it. Olvensar continued.

"But before that, it has been a long time since anyone entered this chamber. The last one to do so was an ancestor of yours, the dwarf Staubyn the Courageous. It was here that he discovered a potion that found its way into the hands of Cerebeth and that now is the cause of the black cloud that threatens all Palindor."

Now Gondalwyn did interrupt. "But, my lord, what is this cloud, and what is the battle of which you speak? Catherine, even if she regains her strength, is but one human; she cannot defeat the might of the queen's army without help. The band that was travelling with her is now scattered; and, even if were not so, what could three do against so many?"

The old man said nothing for a while, but just looked at the worried face of the dwarf. When he did speak, it was slowly, with deep conviction.

"Good dwarf, good dwarf. Do not concern yourself so. It is not in your hands alone that the fate of Palindor rests. You have a part to play, an important part, but do not be anxious about the whole affair. Be concerned only that you play your own part with honor, valor, and distinction. What more can one ask of you?"

The words bit deep into Gondalwyn's being. He hung his head, knowing that Olvensar's words were true. How many times had Entelred told him that he should not always be striving to be the greatest, to control, to understand all things, but should rather rest in the knowledge that he was fulfilling his destiny to the best of the abilities that had been given him?

"I'm sorry, my lord," he said. "I will try to perform my own tasks as they are set and worry not about the tasks of others."

"Good. If you have truly learned that lesson, then you have learned something important indeed. Now, to business. You have two remaining tasks. The first is that you deliver that sword in your hand to the High Queen."

"But how can I do that? And what good will it be? We cannot stand against an army even if the High Queen wields a Dark Sword. Greater forces than these will be arrayed against us." He stopped, aware that he was once more becoming anxious about matters that were not his concern. "I'm sorry," he said.

Olvensar ignored the dwarf's outburst. "And you must pass a message to the Holy Gnome Drefynt, brother of Trondwyth. You must tell him that you met me in a ley chamber in the Mountains of Mourn. That is all. Now begone, dwarf. You must hurry."

Gondalwyn was confused. Olvensar's commands rung in his ears, yet he wondered how he was to carry them out. He had no idea how to find Catherine and still less how he might find Trondwyth's brother. But there was no gainsaying the old man who had now turned his back on him.

He bowed slightly. "Thank you, my lord."

Olvensar sat motionless, as if the dwarf had not spoken; indeed, as if he were no longer in the chamber. Gondalwyn turned and walked the few steps up the passageway and into the cave that he remembered. He turned around as he passed into the cave, but in that instant the passageway disappeared. Now there was only the rock wall, exactly as he remembered it from his childhood.

Slowly, deep in thought, he walked to the front of the cave and out into the sunlight. He looked around and found a plant bearing large leaves. He tore off several of the leaves and bound them carefully around the blade of the sword, tying them tightly with a nearby creeper. Satisfied that the blade was now shielded so that it could do no inadvertent damage, he returned to the cave. He packed up his belongings and food and tied the sword with a creeper to the outside of his pack. With the sword dangling safely out of harm's way, he stepped out of the cave into the late morning sun.

He squeezed down through the rocks at the entrance of the bowl and then walked through the dell out onto the track. He had no chance of catching up with the Hunter if he kept to the track. But if he made his way more directly down the mountainside, he might miss the Hunter. He looked up at the sun. It was hard to tell precisely how long it had been since the Hunter had left with Catherine. In any case, he did not know in how much haste the Hunter was to return his hostage to the queen at Dynas Carn Toldwyn. But he thought that perhaps, if he hurried, he might be able to intercept the Hunter and Catherine before they reached the River Findell at the base of the mountain. What he would do if he did find them he did not know, but, remembering the words of Olvensar, he determined not to concern himself with that eventuality until it happened.

He walked across the track, into the green shade of the forest opposite and headed down the steep slope of the mountainside. It was hard going, descending the mountain so quickly. Every few minutes he would twist himself around to make sure that the sword was still hanging safely from his pack, but other than that he did not stop for rest or to catch his breath for the remainder of the day.

With the trees crowding around him, it was impossible to judge how well he was making progress. As the sun dropped low in the sky before him, he found that he could not judge the time very accurately. The exact position of the sun was hidden from his view by the trees around him; all he could do was to estimate the passage of time from the hue of the sky overhead.

Eventually, and quite suddenly, he found that he was no longer going down such a precipitous slope but was now walking between the trees almost on the level. But it was getting difficult to see where to put his feet, as it had grown so dark among the trees. And even if he had had no other clue, his stomach told him in no uncertain terms that it was well past suppertime and he should be stopping for the night.

He paused and looked around him in the gloom. Then he cocked his head to one side and listened carefully. Filtering through the trees, not far distant, was the sound of running water. Carefully he made his way forward toward the sound. His progress was now slow; even his dwarf eyes were having trouble seeing well enough in the dark.

Then without warning, the trees opened out and he stepped out onto the green grass of the bank of the Findell. Gondalwyn now had a clear view of the sky above him, and he saw that it was past gray now, nearly black. He stepped back into the shadows of the wood, unstrapped the pack from his back, and dropped to the ground. He ate heartily of the food from his pack, which he then tied up and placed under his head to act as a pillow for the night.

He fell asleep almost at once and slept deeply the night through. He awoke well after sunrise, stretched his aching limbs, and made himself a quick and hardly satisfying breakfast. The way would be easy now, but there was still no time to waste; he hoped that he would be able to reach the bridge across the river before the Hunter. He hunched the pack onto his back, checked that the sword was still tied tightly, and set off southward along the wide bank of the Findell.

The grass under his feet felt soft and pleasant, and there were no surprises as he walked along beside the river. At one point, he even found himself humming quietly to himself as if he were out for a peaceful stroll in the warm sunshine rather than on an errand on which the future of Palindor might depend.

He turned a corner where the river meandered gently and saw, a short distance ahead, the wooden bridge where the track that led down from the mountains crossed the river. More slowly, taking care to be quiet and drawing himself close to the edge of the forest so that he might dart into its dark shadows should anyone show themselves ahead of him, he made for the track.

Looking along it one way, he could see across the bridge and follow the track as it disappeared into the trees on the far side of the river. Some distance further, he knew, the track began to rise and the trees to thin as the track became a footpath along the top of the Redfyre Hills. Looking back the other way, the track immediately turned a corner and disappeared into the dark forest that clung to the slopes of the Mountains of Mourn.

Which way to go? Gondalwyn carefully examined the ground for any sign of passersby, but marks in the dirt track were indistinct; it had not rained for many days. Eventually he decided to follow the track westward. If he were behind the Hunter, he would probably meet someone who would tell him so. If not, the Hunter would probably catch up with him in due course.

Adjusting the weight of the pack on his back, he set out across the bridge with a determined expression on his face.

18

DANKENWOOD

RONDWYTH GREW MORE and more unhappy as he was pulled along, forced to walk quickly by the rope binding him to the horse in front whose strides were uncomfortably long for the poor gnome. Aramis the Hunter and Catherine the High Queen bobbed along on the horse's back, the High Queen still asleep and the Hunter seemingly oblivious to the presence of either Catherine or Trondwyth.

They trudged along in this way for the better part of the morning, crossing the bridge over the River Findell and then climbing the hills on the western side. How much harder Trondwyth found the going than when he had followed this path two days before to reach Harsforn the healer.

He watched Catherine with rising consternation as she swayed to and fro on the horse's back. Had his entire journey been for nothing? He could see no sign that her condition was changing in any way, despite his careful application of the healer's ointment.

Late in the morning they came out of the trees onto the lush green grass of the Redfyre Hills. Ahead and to Trondwyth's left, the hill which they were climbing rose some distance above them. He knew that if they continued climbing until they reached the peak, they could see over the rise into the Moortain Mire, and Iadron and Harsforn's dilapidated dwelling would be visible. To the right there was no interruption to the view, and they could see across much of Palindor. Away to the north he could make out the yellow-brown of the Wastes of Kaltethorn on which the sun was, as ever, beating. Between the hill on which they stood and the Wastes, the ground was covered with a strip of dark trees forming the closest border: Dankenwood. Ahead and to the right some considerable distance, down at the foot of the hill, the dark trees gradually disappeared so that the huge forest that covered most of Palindor crept right up to the lower reaches of the Redfyre Hills. Rising out of the carpet of greenery close to the distant coast stood, lonely and majestic, the snow-covered peak of Penmichael Brea[†], the solitary mountain in the north west corner of Palindor.

Trondwyth shivered. Looking up, he saw that the sun had been covered by an outrider from a huge bank of dark clouds that ranged from south to north across the sky and that, although most of them were still some distance to the west of the travelers, seemed to be moving rapidly eastward.

Without warning, Aramis brought his steed to a halt. He looked up at the clouds for a few seconds, gauging their distance and speed, and then glanced back past Trondwyth at the forest that they had just left.

"Time enough for food, I think, and then we must be on our way if we are to avoid the rain."

Looking up at the clouds, Trondwyth could think of no

[†] The word 'Brea' is pronounced as if it were 'Bray.'

way in which they could possibly avoid getting soaked, but he said nothing. Aramis turned his horse, and the entourage made its way back into the shelter of the forest. There the Hunter quickly dismounted and placed Catherine on the ground beside him. Trondwyth, still roped to the horse, walked across to look at the High Queen.

As he looked at her face, he could still see no change, but as he looked at her hand he could see that the healer's ointment was indeed beginning to take effect. Where there had been a small black area surrounded by gray, he could now see no trace of the darkest shadow, and the lighter gray area was considerably smaller than it had been earlier. Relieved, he let out a sigh; perhaps there was some hope after all.

The Hunter looked at him carefully but said nothing. He unpacked a saddlebag, came across to where the gnome was now seated on a small rock, and offered Trondwyth some food. Aramis sat down next to Trondwyth and offered him a canteen of water that had been filled from the waters of the Findell that morning. Trondwyth gulped down the pure, cold water to relieve his thirst.

As he handed the canteen back to his captor, they heard a deep, rolling growl from far away in the west: the storm had begun. At the same moment, much closer at hand, they heard another sound, a moan, coming from behind them. They turned and saw Catherine move first one arm and then the other. Another groan came from her throat. Aramis and Trondwyth stood and walked over to Catherine and were standing over her anxiously as her eyes flickered open and then closed once, then twice. Finally they opened for a third time, and she stared up at them from where she lay.

"Good. You are awake. The queen will be pleased," said Aramis. He walked away to finish his meal.

Catherine groaned once more and closed her eyes. Trondwyth knelt down beside her, and slowly she raised herself up on one arm. She saw that Trondwyth was bound by a rope to the nearby horse. She spoke softly so that the Hunter would not hear.

"Where are we, Trondwyth? Who is that? And why are you tied up in this way?"

Quickly Trondwyth tried to recount all that had happened while Catherine had slept. He was nearing the end of his story when Aramis arose once more, brushed off the crumbs that had settled on his clothing, and walked across to them.

"We should be moving soon," he said, indicating the sky above them.

Trondwyth looked up and saw that the clouds were now nearly overhead. Not far away to the west, he could see that rain was falling; beyond that some distance there was a wall of blackness as the rain came down in sheets over northwestern Palindor.

"Would you care for some food?" Aramis asked Catherine. "We have time for you to eat if you hurry."

Catherine merely nodded and said in a weak voice, "Yes, I'd like that very much. Thank you."

Trondwyth looked at her in surprise; this did not sound at all like the same Catherine who had stood up to the might of the Dark Knights.

Aramis walked away and returned with more bread and meat, which Catherine ate hungrily. As Aramis took the canteen back from her, he said, "And now we must hurry. The rain will be here any moment, and these trees will offer us little protection."

Then, giving no warning, Catherine in one movement slid her knees under her body and rose. Although she was shorter than the Hunter, there was suddenly a fire in her eyes that made the Hunter step back a pace.

"What mean you?" Her voice rang out, clear and cold against the background sound of thunder. "What mean you by binding a High Queen of Palindor to a beast of burden? Loose these bonds and those of my good friend and loyal companion at once."

The royal command in Catherine's voice was unmistakable. But Aramis recovered quickly from his initial shock at hearing such strength in the voice of one so recently close to death. "The queen was right to warn us of your witchery. You would command the queen's Royal Guard itself to lay down its arms with such a trick. But be aware: I serve Cerebeth, queen of all Palindor, and she has made me wise to your tricks, spy witch. You will walk behind me with your gnome friend, and let us see if you can still act the part of a High Queen after a few hours of that."

Catherine's eyes blazed at the Hunter, but he turned away. For a moment, Trondwyth feared that she would stride forward and strike him. It would be a futile gesture; the Hunter was a good foot taller than she, a man at the peak of his strength with a broadsword at his side and a full quiver on his back. Her mightiest blows would do no more than annoy him.

Catherine turned to the gnome and shrugged slightly, as if to say, "We will have to wait for a better opportunity."

Aramis clambered back into the saddle and urged his horse forward. The two ropes became taut, and the unwilling stragglers were brought into line as they marched out of the forest back onto the grass of the Redfyre Hills.

They had been walking in the open for no more than a couple of minutes when the first drops of rain reached them. And with the rain Aramis, without warning, turned sharply right in the direction of Dankenwood. For another minute they trekked steeply downhill as the rain came down harder. Trondwyth wondered where Aramis could be taking them. It would be an hour or more's journey in the open along the edge of Dankenwood before they would reach the Forest of Palindor, which might provide shelter against the storm. When they were no more than a hundred feet from the dark trees, he realized Aramis's intention: the Hunter was taking them into Dankenwood itself.

"No!" Trondwyth shouted. "You can't take us there!"

But the figure before them gave no sign of having heard; the horse continued on its way toward the trees ahead.

Catherine drew close to Trondwyth. "What is wrong? What is this place where he takes us?"

"Dankenwood is the most dangerous place in the whole realm of Palindor! No one in his right mind would enter it voluntarily. Many people have entered the borders of this wood and never been seen again."

By now they were mere steps from the dark trees, and Catherine looked properly horrified. "You mean, people just . . . disappear?"

"Not everyone who enters Dankenwood is lost; many have traveled through it without incident or cost. But many also have entered and never left."

As Trondwyth spoke, Aramis and his horse entered the shade of the dark trees of Dankenwood, followed seconds later by the two unwilling captives.

Immediately the rain stopped—the first sign that this was no ordinary wood. Although the trees were thick about them, the sky could be clearly discerned through the canopy of branches. The rain should have been able to penetrate the wood, yet none fell on the hapless travelers.

Once inside the wood, Aramis stopped his horse and turned to them. Fixing them with his eye he said,

"Dankenwood is not my favorite place either, but I have passed through it many times. Though there is undoubtedly an enchantment about this place, it has never done me any harm. So long as we confine ourselves to the path, we will pass through the wood safely. We should be out of here by nightfall if we move quickly." He turned in his saddle and they once more proceeded on their unhappy way.

Catherine turned to Trondwyth. "Well, he seems anxious but not overworried by this place."

"Aye, more fool him. Does he believe that just because he has safely passed through here before, he will do so again?" Trondwyth replied.

No one spoke for the next hour. The sky became even darker, but not a drop of rain fell in the wood around them. Several times Trondwyth tried to break a twig from a tree so that he could more carefully examine the dark leaves, but the twigs were surprisingly strong and supple and would not yield to his tugs.

For a second hour and a third they proceeded in this way. As the sky took on an even darker shade of gray, Trondwyth judged that the sun would soon be setting. Once more his fears began to grow; he hoped that the Hunter had judged the size of the wood correctly and that they would shortly be out of it. It was bad enough to be in Dankenwood during daylight; he did not want to think what might happen if they had to spend the night there. He saw Aramis look up at the sky with a concerned expression. The Hunter brought his horse to a halt and looked down at his captives; they could hear the anxiety in his voice.

"Did either of you see any tracks leading off this one?" he asked.

Both of them shook their heads.

"Then we must be on the right path, but I was sure that we'd be out of the wood by now."

The path had been uniformly narrow, no verge between where they trod and the trees of the wood themselves. The same was true of where they now stood. It was not a good place to spend the night, but there had been no sign of a widening or clearing throughout the entire afternoon.

Aramis dismounted and untied his pack, and the three of them ate a silent supper. The horse, which under other circumstances might have wandered off to look for some sweet grass, confined itself to nibbling at the few dark blades along the edge of the path. But after a couple of minutes of nuzzling the ground beside them, it gave up and stood beside its master. Aramis took pity on the animal and fed it some stale bread from his saddlebag. Immediately after supper they all tried to make themselves comfortable on the hard ground, hoping to make an early start on the morrow and get out of this fearsome place.

None of them slept well. Catherine awoke in the middle of the night and listened intently. She had expected to be disturbed by the sounds of a forest at night: an owl flapping from roost to roost, mice and other small rodents scurrying across the forest floor, perhaps the breaking of twigs as larger animals blundered through the undergrowth. Instead there was a terrifying, unbroken quiet. Nothing moved, there was no sound from anywhere about. As she tried to return to sleep, she felt something digging into her chest. She slid her hand underneath her tunic and grasped the stone which was tied to a thong about her neck. It was the Seeing Stone of Ganvestor, given to her by Olvensar, and about which she had nearly forgotten. She pulled the stone out from under her tunic and looked at it. In the gray darkness, it was hard to make out the form of the pebble which lay nestled in her hand. She sat herself up and quietly said the single word "Aramis." For a moment nothing changed, then she thought that she saw a faint gray glow coming from the stone.

As she peered into it, she saw an image of Aramis, tall and erect. Over her came a feeling that she didn't how to describe. But in that moment she knew that Aramis was an upright, trustworthy man, who would lay down his life in a moment for a righteous cause in which he believed.

The glow faded from the stone, and she hid it back where it had lain before. Lying down once more on the hard ground, she tried to make herself comfortable and gradually returned to a sleep disturbed by unhappy, confused dreams.

They awoke early, just as the first sunbeams were hitting the tops of the trees above them. Catherine noticed that the dawn was as silent as the night had been. Where there should have been a chorus of bird song to greet the early morning, there was nothing; just silence as if whatever the wood was waiting for it had not yet happened.

They ate a hurried breakfast together, exchanging few words. Aramis checked the ropes binding his prisoners to the horse and swung himself back into the saddle. Once more they were off.

"Can't be much farther now," he said as they began to move. But the minutes passed and became an hour, two hours. The path seemed to go on forever, unchanging. By now the sun was climbing high in the morning sky. Then for the first time since they had entered Dankenwood, a sound came from the undergrowth. Aramis reined in his horse. The sound continued somewhere off to their right, as if a large animal were moving noisily nearby. They waited, not moving, to catch a glimpse of the creature.

Suddenly a swath of dark ferns not ten feet away parted, and before them stood a magnificent deer. It was a beautiful creature, standing higher than any of them save perhaps the Hunter, the antlers on its head fully formed and stretching up to the trees.

Catherine counted quickly: a ten-point stag. A slight movement caught her eye and she turned slowly so as not to disturb the animal, which appeared to be watching Aramis carefully.

She drew in her breath. Aramis was oh-so-carefully leaning over, bending down, and then straightening once more, his longbow now in hand. Slowly, deliberately, he raised the bow and removed an arrow from the quiver, which never left his back. His eyes left the stag's for only a second as he checked the feathers on the arrow. Then once more his eyes locked with those of the stag as he fitted the arrow to his bow. He pulled back the bowstring, and Catherine could stand it no more.

"No!" she shouted, as the Hunter loosed the arrow. Startled, Aramis let his hand waver at the vital moment. The arrow thudded harmlessly into a tree trunk a foot from the stag's head. Aramis looked at Catherine, fury in his eyes, but said nothing.

The stag moved away, but not in urgent, fear-driven bounds. It simply resumed its slow, noisy progress through the forest. In a second the ferns closed and the animal was lost to their sight, although they could still follow its progress clearly enough by the sounds that it made.

Without a word, Aramis slipped off the saddle and landed gently on the ground. With a warning glare at Catherine, he left the path. He passed through the ferns and was, like the stag, hidden from their sight.

Trondwyth and Catherine looked at one another.

"Quick," said the gnome. "Now's our chance to get free of these ropes." The two of them worked feverishly at the knots. It was a full two minutes before the gnome's deft fingers loosed the first of his bonds, but the others quickly followed. Then he set to work on Catherine's. She gladly let the small, agile fingers of the gnome take over from her own, which seemed to have been making no progress whatsoever. In another moment the two of them were free.

"What do we do now?" asked Catherine. "He'll be back soon. The stag won't get far before he catches it." Catherine had spoken quietly so that the sound of voices would not carry, so she was doubly surprised to hear the voice behind her that answered the question.

"No. He will not return until you have long gone from this place." She swung around and saw a creature unlike any she had seen or imagined before. It was a squat man-like thing, shorter than the gnome and dwarf whom she knew, even shorter than the goblins who had captured her. The creature stood a little less than two feet high and had a dark, square face on which a broad grin exposed two rows of sharp yellow teeth that looked as if they had been built for the express purpose of devouring flesh. He was nearly as wide and deep as he was tall, giving the impression of a large cube grinning at her from the edge of the forest. The creature's dark hair was untidy and dirty, plastered down the sides of his face and over his forehead. She glanced across to Trondwyth and surmised that he did not recognize the apparition before them either.

Still, there was no reason not to be civil to it, and she opened her mouth to speak. "Good morning. I am—"

"Catherine, High Queen of Palindor," the creature interrupted. "Yes, yes, of course I know who you are. And this is a Holy Gnome, unless I miss my guess, although I thought that Cerebeth had long ago rid the world of such creatures. Still, 'tis none of my business, I suppose. And I"—here the creature suddenly bowed so low that Catherine was more than a little surprised that he did not topple forward on to the ground—"I am Fayorn, master of Dankenwood. At your service, Most High Queen." He arose and his teeth gleamed more yellow than ever in the broad smile that met Catherine's gaze.

She wondered at the incongruity that such a foul-looking creature should carry such a fair name as Fayorn, which seemed more suited to some beautiful lissome creature than the master of this dark place. These thoughts she kept to herself, instead asking, "What has become of our captor?"

"Your captor, though he may be the greatest of the Hunters, is a fool. First, he was a fool to bring you into such a place as this, where I hold sway."

"I told you so," said Trondwyth to Catherine out of the side of his mouth.

"And secondly, he was an even greater fool for leaving the path to go in search of me."

"In search of you? Then you were that magnificent stag?"

"At your service, Your High Queenship," said Fayorn. "And I should thank you for saving my life although, in truth, his arrow would not have reached me even had you not intervened. Still, it was a good gesture on your part, and did not go unnoticed."

"And what now is to become of us?" said Catherine.

"Become of you? Why, you are free to go on your way, of course. The Hunter will be coming after you, but not for many hours yet. You will find that my dominion ends not another five minutes' walk down the track."

At this point, Trondwyth spoke to Fayorn for the first

time. "Master of Dankenwood," he said, "how is it that I know not your name? It is true, as you have said, that I am a Holy Gnome, and though I have studied the books of Palindor in my youth, yet your name is not known to me. The name of Dankenwood is, of course, known throughout Palindor and as widely as it is known it is feared, except perhaps by our erstwhile captor. So who are you, and by what power do you hold Dankenwood in your sway?"

Fayorn laughed out loud, his rows of yellow teeth parting to reveal a cavernous black mouth. "I should have expected no less from a Holy Gnome. It is no wonder that your race is nearly finished, my friend. Your curiosity must lead you into trouble without end. But since you ask, and since you are a traveling companion of the High Queen, I will tell you, though only for her sake, not your own.

"I have ruled Dankenwood for many thousands of your years. I am happy here, at least most of the time. Few disturb my peace, which is how I would have it. Most of those who choose to pass through my realm are more or less honorable creatures, and so I let them pass unhindered. Sometimes those are dark of soul who try to pass through here, and they never see the outside world again. But a High Queen and her companion need not fear such a fate."

"But why did you draw the Hunter off the track and into the forest?" persisted Trondwyth.

"I could hardly permit a High Queen to pass through my realm while remaining a prisoner, could I? As the High Queen has discovered, the Hunter is well-meaning enough, only misguided, and so for that reason I will not harm him. But he could not be permitted to hold a High Queen in his power. The High Queen is needed to defeat Queen Cerebeth, who even now amasses an army in Carn

Toldwyn to do battle with you. You must hurry to defeat her, or none in Palindor will be safe from her clutches."

"So you too fear Cerebeth of Carn Toldwyn?" asked Trondwyth.

A look of anger crossed Fayorn's face. "Now you go too far, gnome. Be careful what you say; I am still the Lord and Master here." Fayorn relaxed somewhat and continued, "I fear no one. I merely state that it will be the better for all of us if the queen can be stopped soon, before her power becomes too great. Already she holds most of so-called civilized Palindor in her sway, and it will be only a matter of time before she begins to look elsewhere to extend her power. She must be stopped now, before it is too late."

"I see," said Trondwyth.

Catherine could not be sure, but she thought that she saw the faintest trace of a smile cross his face behind the gnome's flowing white beard.

"Now, you must be gone," said Fayorn. "Do not waste time. Go now, before I forget my manners." With that warning he turned and disappeared noiselessly into the dark wood.

"What do you make of that?" said Catherine.

"Time enough for discussion later. We should do as he says and be gone," replied Trondwyth. "First question: do we take the horse?"

"Really, the first question is where are we going?" asked Catherine.

"I was hoping that you would know that," said Trondwyth. "But since you ask me, I suppose the answer must be Carn Toldwyn. It is several days' walk from here, and we could proceed faster if we took the horse. On the other hand, the queen will have patrols out searching for us, and it is unlikely that we would not be captured if we followed the main tracks along which a horse could take us. I judge it to be best if we take enough food from the bags for several days and leave the horse here."

"Yes," agreed Catherine. "And if we travel on foot, then we can go where this horse cannot take the Hunter when he follows us."

So it was agreed. They unstrapped the saddlebags from the horse and found that they could be strapped to their own backs without too much difficulty. Without further ado, they left the horse and continued along the track. It was just as Fayorn had said; within a very few minutes, the dark trees were replaced by the light, airy green of the true Palindor forest. The path widened out and lush green grass appeared on both sides. Catherine wanted to stop as soon as they were out of Dankenwood, but Trondwyth urged her on.

"Firstly, we don't know that Fayorn is powerless outside of Dankenwood, and he may yet change his mind about us. And secondly, Aramis may find his way back to the horse at any time and come after us. I hope that we will come to some other paths soon and be able to lose ourselves before the Hunter finds us. There will be time enough to pause for reflection when we have distanced ourselves from Dankenwood."

Catherine saw the wisdom in the gnome's words, and the two trudged along. Weighed down though they were by the heavy leather bags and straps from the Hunter's horse, they were high in spirit as they savored the freedom from the ropes that had bound them to the animal for the past day.

19

IN THE CATACOMBS

REFYNT STAYED ALONE in the room in the northern tower of Dynas Carn Toldwyn all night. He was interrupted only once, when a guard with a gnomish look about him brought food and water. Drefynt found it hard to sleep on the wooden floor of his bare cell; at least when he was a prisoner in the castle dungeon many floors below he'd had a bed of straw to cushion his rest.

Toward dawn he must have finally drifted off, for suddenly it was night no longer and light was streaming in at the narrow slit window above his head. Almost simultaneously, there was a knock on the wooden door and a voice said, "Wake up. Breakfast!" There was the sound of metal scraping on metal, and the door swung open. Drefynt sat up as the guard from the previous evening entered with a tray of food. The guard silently deposited the tray in the middle of the room, retrieving the tray and dirty dishes of yesterday's meal. As he turned to leave the room, Drefynt spoke.

"What is to become of me? Surely I am not to stay here for long?"

The guard spoke quietly, but did not turn to face Drefynt. The gnome had to strain to hear his words.

"I know not. The queen will visit you later this morning. You shall know your fate then." Then the door was closed and locked once more.

Drefynt stood and stretched, and then walked across the boards of the bare floor to the breakfast that the guard had brought. He was surprised to see that the food was fresh and mouth-watering, better than he had seen since he had become a prisoner of the queen. Or rather, he reflected, a prisoner of Malthazzar. For it was now clear to him that Cerebeth, Queen of Palindor, was no more. In her place reined Malthazzar, Lord of Evil. Looking down at the food, he wondered how long ago Malthazzar had usurped the position of Cerebeth; how long had Palindor been ruled by Evil incarnate rather than the daughter of King Yndlarn V?

He sat down next to the tray and ate heartily of the fruit and the warm, chewy bread. He wondered what the change in fare could mean, and then it hit him. Of course: this was the breakfast of a condemned creature, his last meal. At that moment there came another scratching sound, and Drefynt stood as the door swung open. In walked two human guards carrying tall pikes. They passed through the doorway and then stood at attention on either side. Into the barren room swept Malthazzar in his guise as Queen Cerebeth.

The queen stood regally between and slightly forward of her two guards. She gazed on Drefynt, but there was no emotion that Drefynt could read in that gaze. No pity, no love, no hate, no victory. And the words that left her mouth were spoken without inflection, flat, as if they were unimportant.

"Drefynt, Gnome of Reglandor and lately of Palindor, you are found guilty of high treason against the person of Cerebeth, Queen of Palindor. For this crime you are sentenced to imprisonment in the catacombs." She turned and passed between the guards, saying, "Take him away. I never want to see him again."

The guards clicked their heels to attention as she swept out of the room.

Drefynt was silent as the enormity of his sentence hit him. Palindor had no greater punishment than that which he had just received. No one had ever been seen again after having entered the maze of passages whose entrance lay a short distance to the north of town. As the guards moved toward him, he found his tongue.

"No, you don't understand! I am not the traitor. It's your queen who is going to destroy Palindor. She's not the queen at all; it's Malthazzar in the guise of the queen."

Strong human arms grasped him and held him firmly. He was propelled forward without a word, then pushed through the doorway and out onto the small landing outside the room. One guard went before him down the stairs; the other lowered his pike and followed Drefynt, keeping the sharp point only inches from the gnome's back. The three reached the bottom of the tower and then proceeded around the northern side of Dynas Carn Toldwyn.

The entrance to the catacombs lay half an hour's march to the north of the castle. The maze of passages had been there since the beginning of time, and no one knew their original purpose. It was said that a mighty creature roamed them, perpetually hungry and looking for food, but that was just a story used to frighten misbehaving children—or so Drefynt hoped. There was only a single known entrance, and a stone was kept rolled in front of that so that no one might escape.

Drefynt was marched out of the northern gate of the castle. The path northward was rarely used, but Drefynt could see that the grass was trodden down and branches bent back or broken, as if companies of soldiers had recently passed this way. He tried to engage the guards in conversation, but they remained stubbornly silent.

Eventually they turned a corner and found themselves facing a large iron gate that was ajar, ready for their arrival. Passing through, they found themselves inside what must once have been a beautiful garden. Blooms were half hidden behind tangles of weeds and vines; plantings of flowers showed here and there through the thick, long-stemmed grass which grew everywhere. An air of sadness hung over the place.

Drefynt wondered who had created the garden and when it had been planted, but he had little time to ponder such things. He was quickly brought up before a wall, perhaps thrice his height, and he and the guards stopped. Before them, in the midst of the ivy and vines, was a gaping hole just large enough for a human to enter. The stone that usually covered the entrance had been rolled away to one side. Standing next to it were three dwarves.

Drefynt immediately recognized one of them. As he stepped forward, he spoke quietly to the dwarf whom he recognized.

"Tarandron, the queen is no more. Malthazzar has taken the likeness of the queen, and he means to hold all of Palindor in his sway. He must be stopped."

Tarandron had stared in shock as he recognized the prisoner who had been brought before him and the other dwarves. He had not heard about the gnome's recapture; he moved forward as Drefynt spoke, hearing but not comprehending the gnome's words.

"Silence!" barked one of the human guards. "Traitor

gnome and abettor of traitors dwarf, cast your eyes about you before you enter forever the dungeons of the earth."

Drefynt turned around and Tarandron stopped, sure that his ears had deceived him. Before either of them were aware of what was happening, one of the humans stepped forward and grasped Tarandron firmly. He pushed the dwarf toward the cave entrance.

The shock that had momentarily paralyzed the dwarf passed, and Tarandron saw a chance for escape. He started to run. Both humans gave chase, and in a very few steps, Tarandron was held tightly between the two of them, struggling.

Drefynt watched the scene and realized that here was a chance for his own escape. But something deep inside seemed to be bringing peace to him, telling him that he was not to run away. He looked away from the captured dwarf who was being brought back across the tangled garden. As he looked, he was certain that he saw a shape half-hidden among the leaves and flowers. He stared at it for a moment and then it was gone. But in that moment he was sure that he had seen an old man with a long gray beard, dressed in dirty green gardener's clothes. He was equally sure that the old man was the source of the peaceful feeling that had befallen him.

So Drefynt stood still, and then the guards were beside him, restraining the struggling Tarandron. Drefynt felt his arm grasped by a human hand, and together gnome and dwarf were propelled into the darkness of the cave. Tarandron began to move back toward the entrance, trying desperately to escape once more, even though one of the guards held his pike menacingly at the ready.

Drefynt pulled the dwarf's sleeve. "No, Tarandron. Let them do it."

The dwarf turned on the gnome. "What do you mean?

Are you just going to let them seal us up in here with the who-knows-what that lives in these caves?"

It began to get darker inside the cave; the stone was being rolled back into place by the remaining dwarves and one of the guards.

"No!" screamed Tarandron, "I did nothing!" He pulled away from Drefynt's weak grip and ran toward the stone, but there was nothing he could do. The entrance became smaller and smaller, the light more and more feeble until finally it was extinguished. For a few seconds he scrabbled at the stone, but he was powerless to move it. He placed his ear to it, but could hear no sound coming from the outside world.

He turned to Drefynt. "Are you so ready to die? I have a family! I must escape, or I will never see them again." The dwarf was beside himself. "You are a traitor, Drefynt—worse than a traitor. This is how you repay my kindness—by letting me be sealed up in the catacombs with a monster."

The gnome listened quietly to Tarandron's torrent of abuse. Unlike the dwarf's, his eyes were not yet accustomed to the darkness, and it was only slowly that he began to be able to see by the light of the dim glow from the walls of the cave.

Eventually the dwarf's anger subsided, and his shouts were replaced by sobs. Tarandron held his head in his hands and sobbed to himself quietly. "Why me? What did I do to deserve this? What is going to become of me?"

Still Drefynt said nothing. He found himself beginning to doubt what his eyes had told him they saw just before he was thrown into the catacombs. He had been stupid not to make an attempt at escape. Olvensar could not have been in the garden. If he had been, he would have stopped this catastrophe from happening. He should have run away, but he had let himself be tricked by the light in the garden, and now they were lost, helpless. And yet. . . .

As Tarandron's sobs subsided, Drefynt spoke at last. "Come, good dwarf, there is no need for tears. I am no traitor, surely you believe that. Come sit down with me and let me tell you my story. You will see that though all seems lost, it is not really so."

Tarandron allowed Drefynt to pull him down to the ground, and Drefynt began his tale. He told how he and his brother were the only remaining Holy Gnomes in the kingdom; how Olvensar had visited them that fateful day which seemed so long ago now; how Trondwyth had departed on a journey to the Wastes of Kaltethorn and how he, Drefynt, had remained in the service of the queen. Then he recounted the story of the book that Tarandron's son Smilthron and his friend Dargant had found, and how, reading the book, Drefynt had been trapped by the queen and his own vanity. He told of his confinement and eventual escape from the dungeon beneath the castle of Carn Toldwyn, and the last meeting between the two of them at Trondwyth's house on the edge of town. He described his travel to Smalterscairn; the discovery that Trondwyth had passed that way; the treachery of the new leader of the wood elves, Jarrustin; and his journey back to Dynas Carn Toldwyn and the queen at the hands of Belrea the Huntress. Finally, he told of the events of the preceding evening when, alone with Drefynt in the bare room high in the northern castle tower, the queen had changed her shape, becoming Malthazzar, the Lord of Evil, and then returning to the shape of the queen once more.

At first Drefynt's words were accompanied by sniffs and snivelings from the dwarf, but after a while these ceased. The story was long, but Tarandron let him tell it to its end without interruption. At the very end, Drefynt told him of what he had seen in the garden just before they had been confined to the cave. He made no mention of his doubts, stating as fact that Olvensar had been in the garden and that he had wanted them to be thrown into the catacombs.

Drefynt's story came to a close, and the two sat quietly.

Eventually Tarandron broke the weighted silence: "I'm sorry, Drefynt. I did not know. It must have been terrible for you these past days."

Drefynt said nothing. It was certainly true that performing Olvensar's task was turning out to be considerably harder and more complicated than he had expected. And he still had no idea how Malthazzar might be defeated. The only hope seemed to be the human, Catherine, whose presence had long been foretold and who now, if the queen's words were to be tursted, was present in Palindor. But he could see no way that his confinement in the catacombs would help Catherine defeat Malthazzar. He supposed, unhappily, that he had no choice now but to trust Olvensar to work things out.

"So what do we do now?" asked Tarandron.

Drefynt stood. "I don't know, good dwarf, I don't know. All I can think of is to go exploring, and see what we can find. There is no point in staying here; they will not open the cave again, and if they did, they would not let us out. All we can do is to go on and hope that Olvensar will show us a way out when it suits his plan." His words and voice carried a conviction far greater than he felt, but he had a duty to this poor dwarf who had helped him and was now paying the price.

"But what about the monster that lives in these caves?" asked the dwarf.

"Even if such a creature exists, which I doubt, can it be

worse than just sitting here until we die of starvation?" As he started to walk away, he added, "I just wish that I had some idea how Olvensar plans to defeat Malthazzar, that's all. I'd feel a lot happier if I knew that."

The tone of surprise in Tarandron's voice brought him to a halt.

"But have you not heard the rumors? The human that the queen is trying to find, the one travelling with your brother, Trondwyth—she is said to be a powerful human whose coming has long been prophesied. There is no doubt of the queen's fear of her, for she is offering a great reward for the capture of this human. There is even a rumor, though few give it credit, that the Dark Knights stalk the land in search of the human.

"The queen, of course, denies that she is afraid and insists that the girl and her companion are both, like you, spies for the land of Reglandor, whose armies are poised ready for an attack on Palindor."

This confirmation of Catherine's presence and, more importantly, the obvious fear that Malthazzar had for this human—a fear that had been absent in Malthazzar's own boasts to Drefynt—caused the gnome's spirits to rise.

"Then it is true that Catherine is in the land, and that the queen fears her," he said. "Perhaps this is the best news possible, for it means that Olvensar has not forgotten us. I should have known that it would be so." Quietly, so that his companion could barely catch the words, he recited a verse learned long ago, as a child.

"In the days after the three hundred thousand
When comes the night in the guise of light
Then shall come forth Catherine, Scalm ɣ ť in hand,
With Olvensar's might, the darkness to fight."

Tarandron spoke. "I know those words, but they are

---

† The ancient Palindoric letter 'ɣ' has no exact equivalent in the modern alphabet; its use has long since vanished except in the names of some of the most ancient objects. It is (usually) pronounced as if it were the triglyph `iyu', with each letter pronounced extremely short.

just a meaningless rhyme for children, are they not?" There were hints of both doubt and hope in his voice.

Drefynt laughed out loud and shook his head, as if amazed that he had not had sufficient faith in the High Lord before. "Of course the words mean something. They are inscribed in the *Holy Second Book Of Prophecies*. And they are part of a longer story, spread through the three books of prophecies, which foretells the coming of the first High Queen to the land of Palindor. The High Queen Catherine will come when there is none other that can save Palindor—when Palindor is at her gravest moment of danger. And, do you see, that moment is now!

"For Palindor would fight against Malthazzar were he to attack openly. The people believe that he is in Reglandor, making ready for battle, when in truth he is already here and ready to lead the troops of Palindor into Reglandor without their knowledge, bringing both realms under his sway.

"And so the human whom the queen seeks so desperately can be none other than the High Queen Catherine. She is here, somewhere in Palindor, traveling with my brother, Trondwyth. And Malthazzar, who knows only too well of the prophecy, is trying to destroy them before Catherine can defeat him in battle."

Drefynt was cheered; although he still did not understand much of Olvensar's plan, now he was at least confident that there *was* a plan, and a chance at least of defeating Malthazzar. It was with a much lighter heart that he led the way into the dim grayness of the catacombs.

20

GONDALWYN, IADRON, AND HARSFORM

ONDALWYN WAS LABORING heavily up the slope through the forest on the west side of the River Findell when the rain began to fall. At first it was just a few drops, but then it began in earnest, and Gondalwyn left the path in search of shelter from the storm. The trees were thin near the edge of the forest, offering little in the way of protection. After several minutes of wandering aimlessly in the wet, his clothes now sodden, he came across a small outcrop of rocks. One overhung a patch of ground that was still dry, and the dwarf huddled himself under and against the stones and tried to keep himself warm.

The rain came down in torrents. The dwarf shivered; the air was not cold, but the rain that had soaked him was now drying and cooling him as it did so. There was too little room under the overhanging rock to take off his wet clothes and spread them out, so he kept them on. As evening came, earlier than usual because of the black clouds overhead, he made do with a light supper of a single wafer of bread. He got wet once more as he moved around removing the bread from his pack. Then he placed the pack under his head, drew his legs up tightly around him, and tried to sleep.

It was, at best, a fitful rest, disturbed every few minutes by lightning and thunder. As the night progressed the temperature dropped and became truly cold.

Toward dawn, the rain ceased its downpour, turning into a light shower, then slowly into a pattering, then finally ceasing altogether. With aching limbs, Gondalwyn crept out from under the shielding rock. The forest floor was soaking wet, almost mud. The feeble rays from the low early-morning sun could not penetrate easily to the ground, and the dwarf shivered with cold.

He made his way back to the path, which was considerably warmer than the surrounding forest, as the sun began to rise rapidly in the sky. Wisps of mist could be seen rising from the wet earth. As best he could, and keeping to the side of the path so as not to lose his footing on the slippery mud, Gondalwyn continued his way upward. Within a few minutes he came to the edge of the forest and climbed out into the open air of a glorious midsummer day.

High above, larks were already singing to greet the day. Underfoot the grass was green, springy and sodden, although it would dry out rapidly here in the open where the sun beat down on it. He sat down and ate a hearty breakfast, grateful that there had just been enough room to keep the pack and its contents dry in the shelter of the overhanging rock.

As he had walked along the path he had continued a lookout for any evidence that someone might have passed that way, but the night's downpour had erased all trace of the passage of the Hunter and his captives.

Gondalwyn had already decided what he would do next. He was was by now close to the cottage of Iadron and Harsforn; he would visit the oracle and try to learn the whereabouts of his erstwhile companions.

The view as he climbed was breathtaking, especially to the northwest where he could see almost as far as the ocean on the other side of Palindor. But he did not stop to appreciate the vista, climbing doggedly until he was atop the hill. Looking down in front of him, he could see the Vale of Moortain. But he could not see far, for here there was a thick fog from the swampy ground that had absorbed the rain from the previous day's downpour and was now drying in the warmth of the new day. He hurried down the slope, being careful not to slide as the ground turned to mud under his feet. Within seconds he was in a cold, wet cloud, though he was far from the base of the hill. He kept going downhill as best he could, then found himself traveling squishily along the flat. Much sooner than he had expected, he saw before him a darkening to the gray of the fog, and suddenly he was standing in front of the house which he sought.

The mist seemed a little thinner here. He stepped forward and onto the landing of the front porch. The house looked deserted, but he knocked loudly on the wooden door.

A few seconds passed, then a voice called out, "Wait a minute."

A moment more and the door swung open, and before him stood Iadron the oracle.

"Ah, Master Gondalwyn, it is so good to see you again after so long. I am only sorry that the time for the High Queen has finally come to Palindor. But where are my manners? Do come in, won't you?"

"I thank you kindly, mistress Iadron," said the dwarf. "I

too am sorry that we must meet in such circumstances. I imagine that you know already that Entelred is no more."

"Aye, that I do. His spell that protects us is already weakening. Harsforn and I are preparing to leave this house before the end of the day, or we will be trapped here by the swamp. But we had to wait for your arrival, good dwarf."

"You knew that I was coming, then? Ah, I should have realized . . . you probably knew of it before I did myself," said Gondalwyn with a trace of a smile as he entered the front room.

"Aye, I have known of your arrival since the last time I saw Entelred, which was many, many years ago. Did you not know that we have something here for the High Queen?"

"Nay," said Gondalwyn, surprised at this. "Did Entelred also know all this was to happen?"

"Nay, good Gondalwyn. Even seers see only dimly, and Entelred was no seer, only a wizard with great ability. But Olvensar spoke to him many years ago and gave him the gift for safe keeping. He passed it on to us when he first cast the spell over the mire, believing that it would be safer here with us. And I fear, from what I saw of the Dark Knights' work at Entelred's abode, that he was correct. But wait here while I fetch it."

Gondalwyn wished that he commanded the magic that would continue Entelred's spell over the mire, so that Iadron and Harsforn would have no need to leave their house, decrepit though it was. But he knew that such powerful enchantments were still beyond him; now, with Entelred's death, they would likely be beyond him for the rest of his life.

The oracle returned, carrying a small bundle. Behind her, Harsforn entered the room.

"Good day, good Harsforn," said the dwarf, but he received only a nod in reply. He held out his hands, and into them Iadron placed the bundle. It was a dirty gray cloth that might once have been white, although it was now impossible to tell. The bundle was surprisingly light.

"Do you know what this is?" he asked, looking carefully at Iadron.

The oracle shook her head. Gondalwyn slowly, carefully unwrapped it. He was not sure what it was until the last fold was uncovered; then all three of them, even Harsforn, could not help but gasp in amazement. Before them was a scabbard, the like of which none of them had ever seen, although each of them immediately knew its name.

Gondalwyn lifted it and turned it around in his hands. It was hard to say what was so special about it. The leather was fine white, and the tip and mouth were protected by bands of pure gold. A gold bar ran down the length of one side, and fixed in the middle of the bar was a single muddy white gemstone, the twin of the one in Catherine's belt buckle. Attached to the scabbard was a strap of leather, which Gondalwyn saw to be covered with runic writing that he could not decipher. He looked up at Iadron.

"It is none other than Scelberon, which holds the High Queen's sword, Scalm ɣ t. Do you have the sword also?"

The oracle shook her head again. "Nay, that we have not. Perchance the scabbard would make a good resting place for the Dark Knight's sword which you carry with such care," she ventured.

Now it was the dwarf's turn to shake his head. "Nay. This scabbard was built to protect and empower one sword alone, the legendary Scalm ɣ t,. I trust that we shall find the sword in Olvensar's good time. In the meantime, I will place the scabbard with the few belongings in my pack where it should be safe from prying eyes."

So saying, he carefully wrapped the scabbard once more and thrust it deep down to the bottom of his pack. When he had done this, he turned once more to the oracle. He saw that Harsforn had already left them.

"Good Iadron, I pray thee one more favor, the request that I came here to make. I am in search of the High Queen and the Holy Gnome Trondwyth. Do you know where they might be found? I fear that I will not find them without your help."

"Aye, noble dwarf, I may be of help, although my words may bring you little comfort. The Holy Gnome was here but two days since, and my sister provided him with a salve to heal the wounds of the High Queen. As we speak, the two of them are traveling together and are about to pass through the northern boundary of Dankenwood."

"Dankenwood? Why would they enter that dread place?" asked Gondalwyn, visibly shaken.

"Good dwarf, you misunderstand me. They pass through Dankenwood even now. They will soon pass *out* of the wood into the forest of Palindor that lies to the north of Dankenwood."

"Then where are they bound?" asked the dwarf.

"I know not. Possibly to Smalterscairn, but I see only dimly and could be mistaken."

"Then I must myself pass through Dankenwood to reach my friends?"

"I cannot say. Certainly it would be the quickest way, if you could be sure of passing through safely. That I cannot promise."

"I understand, and I thank you for your words. I trust that we shall meet again in more pleasant circumstances."

"That also I can neither see nor say, good dwarf. I can only wish you the blessings of Olvensar in your quest for the High Queen."

Gondalwyn bowed low and, with Iadron close behind, let himself out the front door. He was surprised to see Harsforn standing outside, a small cloth bag held over her shoulders and a second one at her feet. In answer to his querying look, Iadron spoke.

"We must leave now. As you see, the mist is thinning, and we no longer have any power to bring it back. Go, good dwarf, and may your journeying be fruitful." Iadron lifted the bag to her shoulder, and without another word the two strange humans, if such indeed they were, stepped as one into the mist. The swirling grayness took them from Gondalwyn's sight.

He stepped off the landing himself and was startled to hear a loud cracking noise behind him. He turned in time to see the roof of the old house caving in. He watched, transfixed, as the walls sagged inward and then slowly gave way with a grinding sound. Suddenly he felt dampness on his feet and, looking down, saw that the swamp was advancing rapidly into the green ring that surrounded the house. Turning away from the house, he saw that the mist was beginning to lift.

Hurriedly he ran from the house. With each step, the swamp seemed to be trying to slow him, to suck him downward into its watery grasp. But he struggled on and, finally, out of breath, found himself on solid ground once more. Turning back to look the way that he had come, he saw that he had not been a moment too soon. The mist had now lifted and in the middle of the swamp, where a house should have been visible, there were only a few sticks showing above the swamp grass. Even as he watched, these were sucked down until they were no more.

21

FOREST FORGE

EITHER THE GNOME Drefynt nor the dwarf Tarandron had any idea where they were nor how long they had been making their way through the dim grayness of the catacombs. They had walked continually since their long discussion, stopping only for occasional rest and, twice, long periods of sleep. Their feet were sore and aching, and by now Drefynt was sure that had they been walking in a straight line on the surface they would have been perhaps as far away as Smalterscairn.

But their progress deep under the ground was anything but straight. The tunnels wound around and around, branched, climbed up, then down, then doubled back on themselves. For only two things were they thankful: the tunnels rarely came to a dead end, which meant that they had at least the illusion of progress, and there had been neither sight nor sound of any other occupants of the tunnels. This especially pleased Tarandron, who had heard many stories at his mother's knee of the monster who lived in the catacombs and ate anyone who wandered into them.

No living citizen of Palindor knew the origin or meaning of the catacombs—nor did anyone know exactly how large the maze of underground tunnels truly was. After all, no one had ever been known to leave them having once entered. These thoughts were not comforting to the two companions, but they plodded on. Whoever was in front arbitrarily decided which way to turn whenever the tunnels branched. Some of the time they talked, discussing their lives or the purpose behind Olvensar's plan, reminding themselves that surely it was not a part of that plan that they remain trapped in the catacombs forever.

Drefynt had just finished telling his companion about some of the Holy Writings he had read as a young gnome, and both were trying to keep their minds off the soreness of their feet and the gnawing tightness of their stomachs, when they stopped, sure that there had been a noise somewhere in the darkness off to the right. They stood still, hardly breathing, waiting for the noise to repeat itself, but it did not do so. They started moving again, Tarandron in the lead, and Drefynt noticed without comment that at the next branch the dwarf led them determinedly to the left, away from the noise which they both hoped they had imagined. Twice more they thought that they heard something, both times agreeing that it came from behind them somewhere.

Eventually Drefynt became too exhausted to continue and whispered to Tarandron, who was a few paces in front of him, "I cannot go on. I must rest and sleep for a while. Olvensar must show us a way out of here soon, but right now I need to sleep."

Tarandron stopped beside his companion, and the two of them nervously lay down on the hard rock. Drefynt fell asleep almost immediately, but Tarandron lay awake for a considerable time, listening intently. Eventually his eyes too closed, and the sound of deep, heavy, regular breathing could be heard for some distance through the tunnels.

Drefynt was the first to wake. The hardness of the stone floor was digging into his ribs. He sat up and rubbed his limbs to encourage circulation, and found himself looking straight into a pair of dark eyes. Involuntarily he let out a shriek, bringing Tarandron to his feet in a single motion.

Eyeing them carefully was a strange creature crouching close to the ground. In the grayness of the passages it was hard to see it properly, but it looked somewhat like a giant dormouse with golden-brown fur. Its dark black eyes seemed to see perfectly well in the darkness, judging from the way that its gaze switched rapidly between the two prisoners of the catacombs.

"Hello, my friends," said the creature before either dwarf or gnome could speak. Its accent was that of the eastern parts of Palindor. "You certainly make enough noise. You can be heard for thousands of paces, you know."

Drefynt bowed low. "Forgive us," he said, "but we are unaccustomed to travel in such passageways. My name is Drefynt; I am a gnome of Carn Toldwyn. This is my good friend, the dwarf Tarandron of the same town." Drefynt was almost sure that he had seen surprise cross the creature's face when he had given his own name, but it was gone so quickly that he began to doubt himself.

"And I am the dablik," said the creature, leaning forward and peering closely at Drefynt. "Tell me," it continued. "If you are truly Drefynt of Carn Toldwyn, then you must know something of Trondwyth the gnome."

Drefynt, already elated at having found a creature that

seemed alone (and reasonably friendly) in these oppressive tunnels, became almost joyful at the sound of his brother's name.

"Why? What do you know of Trondwyth?" he asked, adding, "He is my brother."

"I was with Trondwyth not long since, in the home of Entelred the Wise. Alas, Entelred was killed by Dark Knights sent by the queen in her mad search for Trondwyth's companion, Catherine. The two of them escaped with Gondalwyn, Entelred's apprentice wizard, and I know not what has become of them. I was making my way toward Carn Toldwyn to discover what I could about the queen and her plans, for surely there will shortly be a meeting between Queen Cerebeth and the High Queen Catherine, and I wish to witness it. But what are you doing wandering around these tunnels? This is hardly the place for gnomes and dwarves."

Drefynt told the dablik how they came to be in the tunnels, leaving out only that he was a Holy Gnome, for he did not yet fully trust the creature before him. As he brought his story to a close, he said: "So you see, we are lost in these tunnels and have no hope of escaping by ourselves. We are hungry and thirsty and were beginning to lose hope that we might ever escape. We beg you to show us a way out if you know of one."

The dablik gave a twittering laugh. "Oh, that's easy, my friend Drefynt. There are hundreds of exits; even I do not know them all." The dablik stopped speaking and seemed to sniff the air around him for a moment, then he held out a paw and ran it over the stonework of the tunnel. He seemed satisfied. "Come," he said, "we are only a few minutes from an exit that will bring us out near the forge of Samuel Ironhand. He will be good to you." Then he turned and set off rapidly back the way that Drefynt and Tarandron had come.

They had to trot to keep up with the dablik and were both nearly out of breath when, a few minutes later, they turned a corner and nearly fell over themselves in surprise. They had run straight into what seemed like a green curtain, and the dablik was nowhere to be seen. They pushed through, Drefynt in the lead, and found themselves greeted by the sight of a smiling dablik, standing alone in the center of a small clearing in the forest. The ferns through which they had come swung back into place behind them, completely hiding the opening through which they had left the catacombs.

The clearing was surrounded by tall bushes with large deep-red berries hanging from their branches. The dablik ran to a bush and pulled off a berry.

"Come, make a hearty breakfast," he said.

The others needed no second exhortation. Together they fell on the bushes and ate the sweet, juicy berries, easing both their hunger and their thirst.

By the time that they had finished eating, Drefynt noticed that the sun, which had been hidden behind the tops of the trees when they had first emerged, was now in full view above the top of the clearing. All three sat down, and Drefynt pressed the dablik for some of his story. He and Tarandron were amazed to hear that the catacombs, which they had thought were a self-contained maze of twisting passages a little to the north of Carn Toldwyn, were actually just a small part of a vast network of underground passages that ranged across the entire realm of Palindor and—so the dablik thought, although he could not personally verify it—even beyond.

But they could gain little more than this from the furry creature whose golden hair-fur shone in the sun. As they fell silent, the quiet of the forest glade in which they basked was broken by a distant, insistent *clink, clink,* as if someone were hammering metal on metal. The dablik stood and motioned the others to do the same.

"That is Samuel Ironhand, hard at work." He pointed through the wood in the direction of the sound. "Go toward the sound and you will soon find him. I take my leave now. May Olvensar be with you until we meet again." Without another word, the dablik plunged into the green curtain that covered the tunnel entrance and, with a final flash of yellow sunlight on golden fur and a flick of his tail, he was gone.

The gnome and the dwarf looked at one another.

"Well, I suppose that there's nothing else for it," said Drefynt. "We will have to go and find this Samuel Ironhand. I seem to remember that name from the old books, but I cannot remember the stories that go with it."

Tarandron looked surprised. "You do not know the story of Samuel Ironhand?" he asked. "Why, the Samuel Ironhand whose hammer we now hear is only one of the most famous dwarves yet living in Palindor. He is a direct descendant of *the* Samuel Ironhand who received his name for the weapons that he made for the great King Yndlarn I and, so it is said, before that for Toldwyn himself. His forge is deep in the forest, north of the elvish town of Smalterscairn. We have traveled far indeed in the tunnels. Come; it will be an honor to meet a dwarf of such distinguished family."

He led the way out of the forest glade in the direction of the hammering sound. Drefynt followed a couple of steps behind. The forest floor was slightly springy underfoot and, kneeling to touch it, Drefynt found that it was covered by a thick layer of needles, dry on the surface but damp underneath, as if it had rained hard a few days earlier and had not yet thoroughly dried. They came across an occasional shadowed puddle where the rainwater still sat, but such puddles were small and few and created no difficulty in their travel toward the rhythmic *clang! clang! clang!*

After traveling in this way for nearly half an hour, they stepped out of the forest into a large clearing. Along one side of it was a horse track that, judging from the length of the plant stems that intruded into it, was used infrequently. Closer to them, across the grass of the clearing, stood a tall metal archway with what appeared to be writing across the top. From this distance Drefynt could not make out the words. Beyond the archway, the two could see small buildings grouped together in a compound; it was from inside the compound that the noise of the hammering was coming.

Tarandron stepped out onto the grass without hesitation and walked across it toward the archway. Drefynt held back for a moment, then scurried out to catch up with the dwarf. As they reached the archway, Drefynt stopped to make out the words across the archway's top: ⋏⋏ꟼ⊢⋊ᴄ ⋈⁼ ᴒ⁻⋊ ⁻⋏ᴑꟼ ⋈⁼ ᴒ⌐⋈ᴑ ꟼ⋏⋌⋊⋀ ⋈⁼ ⥾⋊⋏ꟼ⋈ᴑ⋏ (SAMUEL OF THE HAND OF IRON MAKER OF WEAPONS).

The noise of the hammering had stopped, but only Tarandron noticed, for Drefynt was concentrating on the ancient script above his head. He recollected seeing something similar long ago in some of the oldest Holy Books, but he could not be sure that it was exactly the same writing. He could make out the word *forge* clearly enough, and signs that probably meant *iron* and *hand*, but more than that he could not understand.

He looked down from the archway and into the compound, which housed two small buildings. Off to the right appeared a homely cottage, freshly painted and maintained with loving care; to the left there was a lower, open building in the center of which was a brick structure—presumably an enclosed fire grate, for smoke curled from the chimney—next to which was standing a dwarf in dirty overalls. As he looked, the dwarf raised both hands in greeting. Drefynt could see that the brick must indeed contain a fire, for the dwarf held a hammer in one hand and a glowing length of metal in the other.

Drefynt and Tarandron walked slowly across the muddy ground of the compound toward the cheery-looking dwarf.

"Good mornin' to 'ee," said the dwarf. "I'll be right with 'ee, but you'll just 'ave to excuse me while I finish my work." So saying, he stuck the metal, which was held by a pair of black tongs, into the white heat of the fire. The travelers watched as the dwarf withdrew the metal from the fire and then hammered it down flat so that it was twice as wide as it had been when it had been placed into the heat; then the dwarf heated it once more and folded it over upon itself so that it once more regained its original shape. The dwarf looked up at them. "Only two more to go. I'll be another 'alf 'our 'ere yet. Do go 'ee over to the 'ouse. The missus'll see to 'ee and I'll be over to see 'ee jest as soon as I be finished 'ere."

Drefynt and Tarandron looked at one another, then Tarandron thanked the dwarf and the two of them once more crossed the compound, this time toward the house. They stood outside the beautifully finished wooden front door—elven work, Drefynt was sure—when a movement off to one side caught their eyes. Drefynt looked across the porch to see an ancient dwarf sitting quietly in a chair, smoke curling upward from his pipe and a cheery glint in his eyes.

"Excuse me," said Drefynt.

The dwarf removed the pipe from his mouth, slowly, and said, "Ar, that be all right. We don't often get strangers in these parts. We're glad to see 'ee. Sam's wife be not in jest at the moment; she be out picking berries, but she'll be back soon. Why don't 'ee jest take the weight off of yourn feet until Sam be finished with his work? He do 'ave another two folds to go, I reckon, afore that sword be ready for shaping, unless I be missing my count. So set yeselves down, and wait 'ere with Old Sam till Young Sam be finished."

The dwarf gestured toward a long bench that ran along one side of the porch, and Drefynt and Tarandron gladly sat on it. The two waited for the old dwarf to speak once more, but he merely placed the pipe in his mouth, looked at them curiously for a moment, and then closed his eyes. They would have thought that he had gone to sleep in the warmth of the sun, save that when there was a pause in the hammering, he said "fourteen" to himself and then again, a few minutes later when the same happened once more, his eyes opened wide. "Fifteen," he said. "A good, old-fashioned fifteenfold sword. A weapon worthy of a King's Knight, I reckon. 'Appen that Young Sam will be over to see 'ee now."

And, indeed, the old dwarf was correct. In only a few moments, the dwarf who had been working at the forge stepped out and crossed the compound toward them.

"We 'ave visitors, Young Sam," said the old dwarf as the younger one drew near.

"Aye, so I see, Old Sam," said the other. "I bid 'ee good day and welcome to the forge of Samuel Iron'and," he greeted the visitors cheerily. "Please do excuse our manners; we be not used to visitors in these 'ere parts."

Drefynt thought the younger dwarf was eyeing them with some suspicion, as if trying to decide something about them.

Tarandron rose and bowed low. "Tarandron the Bold, house builder of Carn Toldwyn, greets thee in the name of the High Lord Olvensar."

Drefynt and Young Sam both waited for the closing portion of the formal greeting. But the words "and Queen Cerebeth of Palindor" remained unspoken. Young Sam responded in like manner and in a voice quite unlike the uncultured brogue he had used before: "Samuel Ironhand, son of Samuel Ironhand and WeaponsMaster of Palindor, greets thee, Tarandron the Bold, in the name of the High Lord Olvensar." The two bowed low to one another, and Tarandron introduced his companion to the eminent dwarves. Then Young Sam bid the visitors resume their seats while he sat in a chair next to his father.

When next Young Sam spoke, he continued in the voice of an educated creature. "So, a Holy Gnome wanders into my compound accompanied by a dwarf from a family well known for its deeds of heroism in battles past. Strange things are indeed afoot these days in the land of Palindor. It was a gnome in the presence of a human that we were asked to report, so I think we need not trouble the queen with news of your presence here. Yet, a Holy Gnome! It is long since my family has seen such in Palindor, is it not?" he asked his father.

"Aye, Sam, that it is. Not in my lifetime has there been a Holy Gnome in these parts."

Drefynt felt bound to interrupt. "But you are mistaken. The Holy Gnomes were destroyed long ago."

"But by whom?" snapped Old Sam, with surprising vigor.

"What do you mean?" Drefynt tried to read the eyes of the old dwarf, whose twinkle had become subdued. "There was a fire in the Barrows at Perendeth. All the Holy Gnomes, along with their books, perished in the flames."

"Aye, aye. But who set the fire? Would you not say that perhaps the queen herself had a hand in it?"

"Sam, Sam," said Young Sam. "There is no need to try to trap the poor gnome." He looked at Drefynt. "We saw you reading the writing, you see."

Drefynt realized how he had given himself away. Few in Palindor would have realized that the marks above the archway at the entrance to the compound were writing, they were of such an ancient script. And none but a Holy Gnome would have had the knowledge to begin to read the words. He bowed his head. "I admit it," he said, and then, standing: "Drefynt, Holy Gnome of Palindor, bids thee greeting in the name of the High Lord Olvensar." He took his seat once more.

"But not Queen Cerebeth?" queried Old Sam.

Tarandron looked at Drefynt, who kept his lips tightly shut and said nothing.

"You should tell them, Sam," said the old dwarf to the younger.

"That I will," replied Young Sam. "Some ten days ago we had other visitors here. Less welcome ones. They were Dark Knights here at the bidding, so they said, of the queen.

"We have lived here quietly since the dawn of history in Palindor. Each generation had its Samuel Ironhand, and each generation has passed on its knowledge of weapons making to the next. The first Samuel Ironhand, it is said, served none other than Toldwyn, King of Palindor, before there were kings in Palindor. His skill at making weapons has never been surpassed in the land even to this day. It is said that he was taught deep secrets by Olvensar himself and his mightiest swords and shields were imbued with magic. Alas, over the years, these secrets have been lost to us. While the Ironhand family still makes the best weapons in the whole of Palindor, they rely for their use on the skill of the maker and no longer on enchantments.

"But the mightiest weapon forged by the first Samuel Ironhand, and in this very place, was made in the presence of Olvensar and was imbued by the High Lord with powers of kiríal. Olvensar left strict instructions with the first Samuel Ironhand that this weapon, a sword, should never be spoken of to others, nor should it ever leave this place. This Samuel Ironhand promised, and thus it has been from that day onward. For generations the sword has lain untouched in a chest inside our cottage. None but we two knew that it even existed, although rumors of it have surfaced occasionally. Even we know not the secret of its power.

"Then the Dark Knights came. They rode in here knowing exactly what they were looking for, and we were powerless to defend ourselves against such creatures. They arrived in the late evening with no warning. There were three of them and, even though we have weapons here aplenty, it would have been futile to use them against the kiríal of such creatures. They herded us outside the house. One of them kept watch over the three of us—Old Sam; my wife, the good dwarf Merren; and me—while the others went into the house. In a short time they reappeared, mounted their horses, and were gone. We saw no sign that they had taken anything, but Old Sam and I went straight away to the chest buried under the floorboards in the kitchen. We knew immediately that the boards had been disturbed, so it was no great surprise to find the chest empty. Until this time, no Ironhand has ever spoken of this sword outside of the family; you are the first to be told about it. Where it is now, I do not know for, as I say, there was no sign of it when the Dark Knights left."

"But why are you telling us these things?" Drefynt asked.

"Because the servants of the queen stole what does not belong to them, and it is clear that you owe no allegiance to the queen. I was in Smalterscairn yesterday, passing time with the elves there, who are divided in their allegiance. Talk is that the queen is setting herself up against Olvensar himself and that the time for the arrival of the First High Queen is nigh. Indeed, some say that she already walks in Palindor, accompanied by a Holy Gnome."

Drefynt carefully watched Young Sam. "And what think you of such stories?"

"I know not. The queen has spread the word that Malthazzar is now powerful in Reglandor, and the gnome and human whom she seeks follow him. According to her, they intend to weaken Palindor from within so that Malthazzar will have an easy victory when he attacks Palindor. Jarrustin, the leader of the wood elves, believes this to be true, and so do many of his subjects.

"All I know is that the Dark Knights were here in the name of Queen Cerebeth. They knew of the existence of a sword we believed to be a secret, and they stole it against Olvensar's express wishes. Therefore I am not inclined to trust the words of the Queen of Palindor until such time as I am given a reason to trust them."

Drefynt glanced at his companion and then spoke to the two Sams.

"We must not detain you any longer; we should be about our business and let you be about yours. But this I feel I can tell you; Cerebeth, Queen of Palindor is no more. In her place stands Malthazzar, Lord of Evil, and it is he who now, in the form of Queen Cerebeth, rules over our land. You have seen for yourself the forces that Malthazzar controls. If what you say is true and the High Queen Catherine walks in Palindor, then she is our only hope. My companion and I search for the High Queen and my brother, Trondwyth, who like me is a Holy Gnome. Should Malthazzar find them, they will have need of every hand that is raised to their assistance. I am sure that they would not deny the hand of another dwarf, should it be offered," he continued.

But Young Sam shook his head. "I thank you for your offer. It is not from fear, I assure you, that I decline. But Old Sam here is getting on in years, and he needs my help. Further, I have no claim to skill at fighting. I can, however, offer assistance of a different and possibly more useful kind. Come with me, Tarandron the Bold."

He led the way inside the house; Old Sam stayed rocking in his chair on the porch, his head nodding once more as if asleep. Young Sam led the others into a small room in which stood an old wooden chest. He opened it noiselessly and withdrew a battle-ax that caused Tarandron to let out a gasp of admiration. Sam held it out, and Tarandron grasped it firmly. When Sam let go of the weapon, Tarandron's arm dropped involuntarily as the full weight of the axe made itself felt. He turned it around in his hands, marveling at the craftsmanship.

"The ax was made by my grandfather's grandfather," said Young Sam, "the last dwarf to bear the name 'Ironhand' who knew the deep secrets." He shook his head sadly. "It is indeed unfortunate, but there no longer lives in Palindor the creature who could form such an axe today. But take it outside and take its measure."

Holding the ax in front of him, Tarandron carried the weapon outside, followed by Young Sam and Drefynt. He hesitated on the porch, looking around.

"Take it out back where you cannot be seen," said Old Sam in a low voice, without opening his eyes.

"Aye, take it to the back of the house; there is room

there for you to test its mettle," agreed Young Sam.

The three trooped around to the rear of the house to a clearing covered by lush grass. As they came to a halt, Tarandron looked more carefully at the weapon in his hand. The haft of the weapon, carefully shaped to conform to a dwarf's battle stance, was of the finest cherry wood and varnished to perfection so that it shone brightly in the light of the sun. But the blade was the weapon's crowning glory. There was no blemish to be seen on its surface, even after all the years in which it had lain unused in the chest inside Sam's cottage. The two edges appeared to be as sharp as if they had been honed yesterday.

"Throw it and see how it performs," said Young Sam.

Tarandron looked up and saw a tree perhaps twenty-five paces distant on which one limb hung down towards the ground. It would make a good target; not an impossible shot, but certainly not one for a dwarf out of practice and with an untried blade. If he could only hit the tree he would be well satisfied. He spread his legs and dropped his hands to his side, releasing the ax with his left hand as he did so. The weight of the ax in his right hand dragged his arm downward and then up in an arc; the strength in his muscles helped the ax swing upward behind him and then up over his head. Near the top of the arc, he released the blade to go on its way. He was stunned to see the ax, leaving his hand slightly askew, right itself as soon as it was free of his control and head, blade first, for the target. It flew through the air as if it knew exactly where Tarandron desired it to land and struck the limb of the tree right where it met the trunk. It sliced cleanly through the wood and then, its energy spent, dropped to the ground where it buried its blade deep into the soft, damp earth. The severed limb dropped to the ground by its side.

Tarandron looked at Young Sam in amazement; Sam merely returned the gaze with a smile. Then, before they could say anything, all three heard the sound of hoofbeats coming from the front of the cottage. Sam hurried off to see who was visiting his remote cottage while Tarandron ran across the clearing and pulled the ax from the ground with a single mighty pull. He checked the blade to make sure that it was clean and undamaged, and then stuck the ax in his belt.

He and Drefynt walked around to the front of the cottage to bid the Sams good-bye once again and begin the journey to Smalterscairn where, perhaps, they would hear more rumors concerning the travels of Trondwyth and the High Queen.

As they reached the front of the cottage, they saw Young Sam standing next to his father in earnest conversation with a forest Hunter seated astride his horse, which was standing on the grass next to the cottage's porch. As they approached, they heard the words of the conversation.

"A human and a gnome, traveling through the forest alone? Nay, I think not," they heard Old Sam say.

As they drew up, Drefynt spoke to the two dwarves on the porch. "We bid you good day and thank you for your hospitality."

"Aye, you be right welcome," said Young Sam, his speech once more the thick brogue with which he had first greeted them.

Drefynt and Tarandron walked back toward the track, leaving the two dwarves conversing with the Hunter. But they had not gone far before they once more heard the sound of hoofbeats, this time not far behind them and coming rapidly closer. The Hunter rode into sight behind them and, a few seconds later, reined in his horse by their side. He slipped out of his saddle in an easy motion and began to walk with them along the track.

"You are bound for Smalterscairn?" he enquired of them.

Drefynt answered for the pair, while Tarandron idly fingered the haft of his new weapon, ready to use it against this stranger if events should require it.

"Aye. We are travelers, and the dwarves back there informed us that it is the closest village where we might purchase some provisions."

"'Tis a wood elf village, so you may be unlucky in your aims," said the Hunter. "But it is also my destination, so perhaps we might travel together." Neither Drefynt nor Tarandron spoke, and the Hunter continued. "I beg your pardon—Aramis the Hunter at your service." He bowed low.

"And Drefynt, gnome of Carn Toldwyn, at yours; and this is my traveling companion Tarandron, dwarf of Carn Toldwyn."

"I was traveling with two companions," said the Hunter. "A human girl and a gnome much like yourself. But our path took us through Dankenwood where we became separated some three days since, and I fear for their safety. I have been searching the forest to no avail. You have not seen my companions in your travels?"

"Nay. We are only recently from Carn Toldwyn and have traveled not near Dankenwood. But perhaps you could describe your companions and give us their names, so that we might know them should our paths cross."

Aramis looked doubtful and walked silently as he pondered Drefynt's request. When he spoke once more, he changed the subject.

"If you are recently come from Carn Toldwyn, then

how go things there? Does the queen still prepare for war?"

"Aye," replied Tarandron, "that she does."

"But can Palindor win a battle against the armies of Reglandor? Especially if Malthazzar himself leads them, as some say? I wonder how Palindor can hope to prevail against such a foe."

Drefynt and Tarandron exchanged glances. The Hunter continued. "Indeed, I remember a story I heard in my youth that a High Queen would be raised up in the hour of Palindor's greatest need, to lead the realm to victory. I cannot but wonder if such a time is not now at hand."

Now it was Drefynt's turn to be troubled and full of doubt. It was obvious that the Hunter knew about Catherine, but was he searching for her to offer his aid or—as seemed more likely—was he working for Cerebeth and hence, unknowingly, for Malthazzar? Sadly Drefynt concluded that it would be prudent to remain silent about Catherine until he was more sure of this Hunter.

"We know not of such things," he said. "We are merely travelers, exploring the land in these troubled times. But walk with us to Smalterscairn, pray, and tell us more of yourself."

The three travelers continued on their way, sharing stories but not mentioning the High Queen until, at last, the path widened, and they stopped before the entrance to the village of Smalterscairn.

22

A Meeting of Friends

CATHERINE'S STRENGTH HAD still not fully returned, so her travel through the forest with Trondwyth was slower than it should have been. Their way was further hindered by the lack of paths in this part of the forest. Instead, they had to make their own way through the trees. Sometimes they would come across a stand of dense undergrowth and have to either force their way through it or find their way around it, which was easier but slower.

Trondwyth had hoped that they might reach Smalterscairn in a single day's travel, but as the evening sky began to turn dark he knew that his expectations had been considerably off the mark. Though he was not sure of their exact location, he thought that it would be at least another full day's journeying before they would reach their destination.

As to what they would actually do when they reached Smalterscairn, he was uncertain, although he tried not to show his concern to Catherine. Although he had been treated courteously by Ederagorn when he passed through before, he remembered how weak and frail the leader of the wood elves had looked on that occasion. A new leader might not welcome him in the same way. The note from Olvensar had made it clear that not all the wood elves were to be trusted; he hoped he was not leading the two of them into a trap.

For Catherine's part, she was fighting to keep her strength. They had stopped only once during the day to pick berries from the bushes along their path. She knew that though she had tried her hardest she had slowed them considerably with her slow pace. Now, as the day wore to a close, she found herself hungry and thirsty and exhausted. All she wanted to do was to curl up on the ground where they walked and go to sleep. As they made their way around a small patch of brambles, heavily laden with luscious-looking blackberries, she saw an especially inviting bed of thick, soft pine needles. She walked over to it and dropped down on it.

"I must sleep," she said, tucking her arms underneath her head.

Trondwyth did not argue. He looked around and decided that this was as good a place as any to stop for the night. It looked safe and sheltered, so he left Catherine sleeping peacefully while he returned to the brambles and ate his fill of the fruit hanging from their branches.

Both felt well rested when they awoke the following morning. Catherine was ravenous, and she hungrily consumed blackberries from the bushes nearby while Trondwyth stretched himself and made ready for another day's journeying.

As they set off, Trondwyth judged from the speed of Catherine's step that she was now fully recovered from the effects of the Dark Sword, so at last he felt that he could ask her some of the questions which had long been on his mind.

"What will we do once we reach Smalterscairn?" he asked.

"I know not for sure," answered the High Queen, "but it lies between us and Carn Toldwyn, where we must eventually fight. Perhaps we can gain news of our enemy there."

"And when we reach Carn Toldwyn, what then? The two of us are no match for the might of the armies of Palindor. While it is true that not everyone will fight in the queen's name, still there will be more than enough to be a match for us. We will be captured and brought to the queen, and she will have no pity on us."

"Ah, good Trondwyth, do you not see? It matters not how the queen and I come face-to-face, but only that we do so. Only then will the true battle for Palindor take place. That is the battle that must not be lost, although I confess that I do not yet know how she will be defeated. I must leave that in Olvensar's hands."

As they spoke they came to a small clearing and quickly made their way across the green grass. As they did so, a movement overhead caught Catherine's eye and she looked upward into the deep-blue sky. Trondwyth stopped beside her and followed her gaze upward. High overhead, he saw a bird of prey wheeling, apparently in search of food. As they watched, the bird stopped its circling and headed off in a straight line to the west.

"We are seen," said Trondwyth nervously. "Come, we must hurry."

Catherine set off at such a pace that it was as much as the gnome could do to keep up with her. They journeyed this way all day, and as the sky began to darken in the east, it was Trondwyth who was glad that the day was drawing to a close. But he knew that they could not be far from Smalterscairn now, and if they would only press on a little longer they might well reach their destination before nightfall.

Among the evergreens surrounding them began to appear other, deciduous, trees. Trondwyth recognized these as a sign that they must be nearing the Pennyfarthing River. The two quickened their pace further, and in a few minutes found themselves standing on the bank of the slow-moving river.

Trondwyth looked about him, unsure in which direction Smalterscairn lay. Downstream, he decided, although without any great conviction, and so the two set off walking quickly along the riverbank, their steps just keeping pace with the water flowing beside them.

They had been walking for about a quarter of an hour, and Trondwyth was just beginning to wonder if perhaps they should turn around and try walking upstream instead, when they saw ahead of them a bridge. Trondwyth recognized it immediately as the bridge that he had crossed, so long ago now it seemed, on his journey eastward from Carn Toldwyn into the Wastes of Kaltethorn. Of Smalterscairn itself there was no sign, even though they must be close to it and on the same side of the river.

They paused for a moment while Catherine searched the ground for a pebble. Finding one, she dropped it into a pocket. The two pressed forward and shortly they reached the track which crossed the bridge. Trondwyth indicated the way that they should go. They walked together up the narrow track, Trondwyth now in the lead, and soon found themselves passing by the small wooden cottages that marked the outskirts of the wood-elf village.

Trondwyth had told Catherine about the ways of the

wood elves, so she was not surprised at the lack of welcome that they found. The gnome had also warned the High Queen about the contents of Olvensar's note, so it was with some caution that they entered the square of Smalterscairn just as the sky turned gray with early twilight.

The cairn of stones was as Trondwyth had last seen it and as Catherine had imagined it. Unhesitating, she strode forward while Trondwyth hung back in the shadows, surprised at her boldness. She walked up to the cairn, felt in a pocket of her tunic, withdrew a small round pebble from it and thoughtfully added it to the pile. Then she looked around, as if waiting for someone. In a matter of seconds a door across the square opened and Trondwyth saw Ederagorn's young elf page hurry out to greet his companion. He noticed that the page had sprung from the grandest residence facing the square rather than the meanest one, which had been Ederagorn's abode.

Trondwyth stepped forward out of the shadows and unhurriedly walked across the square to where Catherine was now exchanging words with the page. As he reached them, Catherine turned to him and spoke.

"This is Caldorn, page to the wise elf Jarrustin. He tells me that Ederagorn, who ruled the wood elves so well for so many years and whose counsel you shared when you visited Smalterscairn, died late in the evening of the very day in which you were here. Jarrustin now rules in his place and has invited us to sup with him this evening." Turning to Caldorn, she continued. "Lead onward, good Caldorn."

A feeling of unease gripped Trondwyth, and he wished that he could tell Catherine of it. But she was walking forward, following Caldorn toward the home of the elf leader, seemingly unconcerned about the possibility of danger.

They entered the doorway and stood in a room which Trondwyth immediately saw was a good deal more grand than the one in which Ederagorn had received him. But he had no time to form more than that fleeting impression before a youngish elf, a gold chain around his neck, arose from behind a desk and greeted them.

"Jarrustin, ruler of the wood elves of Smalterscairn, at your service. Pray be seated, and my page will provide you with refreshment."

Catherine remained silent, but Trondwyth knew that it would be rude not to identify themselves to the leader of the elves.

"Trondwyth, gnome of Carn Toldwyn, at *your* service, as is his companion, the human Catherine. Please accept our sympathies that the wise elf Ederagorn has passed from this place and our wishes that you will be known as a ruler as wise and just as he."

As he spoke the word "Catherine," he thought that he detected a narrowing of Jarrustin's eyes. Behind him, he heard Caldorn suck in his breath.

Jarrustin indicated seats before him and repeated his command to Caldorn that refreshment should be brought for the visitors. The page seemed unwilling to obey the command, but after a threatening look from his master left to do his bidding.

"Now, my friends, what brings you to Smalterscairn?" asked Jarrustin. He flung a wide smile at Catherine. "It is so rare for a human to honor us with a visit, especially one so knowledgeable about the cairn and our customs."

Trondwyth was stunned by Catherine's reply, which was delivered in a voice of iron.

"I am Catherine, High Queen of Palindor, and I demand to know whether you stand with me or against me, Jarrustin of Smalterscairn."

The directness of her speech took Jarrustin by surprise as well; he leaned back in his chair, confusion on his face. It was several seconds before the elf's smile returned.

"The rumors are true, then. Catherine, the First High Queen, does indeed walk abroad in Palindor. And so the reign of Queen Cerebeth draws to an end?"

Catherine did not answer immediately and when she did open her mouth she was interrupted by the sound of Caldorn returning with a tray. He placed it on the desk where they could all reach it. On it were two cups of tea and several slices of fruitcake. The page withdrew to a corner of the room.

"Help yourself," said Jarrustin, picking up a slice of cake. "I have only recently taken tea myself, but I am sure that you will find it refreshing after your long journey."

Catherine and Trondwyth raised their cups and drank. The warm liquid reminded them how thirsty they were and, one after the other, they drained their cups in long draughts.

Replacing her cup on the tray, Catherine opened her mouth to speak once more. But before she could say anything, she found her eyelids drooping. Fighting hard to keep awake, she looked across to her companion and saw Trondwyth fall forward, headfirst, on to the desk before them, and a deep snore came from his throat. Then it was too much effort to stay awake, and her own head began to drop. Her arms cushioned her fall but she did not know it, for she was asleep even before her head rested on the table next to Trondwyth's.

Aramis, Tarandron, and Drefynt paused for a moment at the edge of the village. Together they moved forward, the Hunter in the lead, past a smattering of wood-elf residences, until they stood at one corner of the village square.

They strode forward into the square, where Aramis

took his leave of the others. Gently holding the reins of his horse, he made straight for the largest of the cottages that lined the western side of the square. While he was yet a few steps from the cottage, its door was flung open and an elf wearing a gold chain about his neck strode out. He stepped forward and stopped in front of the Hunter.

Watching from a distance, Drefynt thought that the elf looked faintly ridiculous, looking so grand and carrying himself as if he were the master of all, yet standing little more than a third as tall as the mighty Hunter who could kill the elf with a single blow should he feel so inclined.

The sounds of their greeting could clearly be heard across the village square, but Drefynt's eavesdropping was interrupted by a young elf who suddenly dashed out of the shadows and tugged on the gnome's sleeve.

"Master gnome, you must hurry away from here. It is not safe." The elf ran away as suddenly as he had come.

But before Drefynt or Tarandron could move, they heard the Hunter's voice ring across the square.

"Do not toy with me, Jarrustin. I come in the name of the High Queen Catherine, and if you do not tell me instantly where you are keeping her prisoner, I will strike you dead where you stand."

Gnome and the dwarf looked at one another and, without a moment's hesitation, ran forward to where the elf and the Hunter were standing. Jarrustin took a step backward as they drew up. He opened his mouth and emitted a single wordless call. Before the three travelers could move a muscle, an arrow thudded into the ground not an inch from the Hunter's right foot.

"Hold!" commanded Jarrustin. "If you move, my elves will take your lives without further consideration."

Streaming out of doorways, there appeared an army of wood elves. Some were armed with bows and arrows, others with slingshots primed with rocks, and others with small daggers or knives. In seconds the travelers found themselves surrounded.

"Make sure that they are unarmed, then put them with the others. The queen will be here shortly and she will be right pleased to see our newest arrivals."

Aramis, Tarandron, and Drefynt were searched roughly. Tarandron's battle-ax, which was in plain view in his belt, was immediately removed. The elves took the Hunter's quiver and broadsword, then found and removed a dagger from his right boot.

The three were roughly marched from the square along a small alleyway. After a brief walk, they were commanded to stop in front of a building that was shorter than Aramis and appeared to be windowless. At the doorway stood a lone elf carrying a spear who snapped to attention as soon as he saw the oncoming party.

The building was small, but it appeared to be remarkably sturdy. The door in particular looked to be of heavy oak and was barred by an enormous plank. Two elves stepped forward and, straining, lifted the plank. The guard with some difficulty pulled open the door and Aramis, Tarandron, and Drefynt were pushed forward into the darkness. Immediately the doorway was closed behind them, and they heard the sound of the bar being lowered into place on the outside.

They were in a room dimly lit with stray light that filtered its way through the many branches of dead wood that constituted the roof of the building. But the light didn't affect Drefynt's hearing, and as he was pushed into the hut he heard a sound which was as welcome as it was unexpected. It was unmistakably Trondwyth saying his name: "Drefynt." The brothers embraced, tears of joy on both their faces.

As his eyes grew accustomed to the dim light, Drefynt saw Trondwyth's human companion at last. She could be none other than Queen Catherine, although she certainly had little of the look of a queen about her at the moment,.

But Catherine was looking past the two brothers to the Hunter who, too tall to stand in the tiny hut, had seated himself on the ground.

"So, Hunter, you too are now a captive. Are you betrayed by your friends?" she asked.

The Hunter lowered his head in submission. "High Queen, please forgive me. I knew not that you spoke the truth. I learned the truth in Dankenwood from Fayorn, master of that place, and I now beg your forgiveness."

"You are forgiven, fair Hunter. We are glad to count you amongst our number."

Aramis continued. "I came to Smalterscairn and was told by Jarrustin, the elf who now rules in the village, that you were nearby and his prisoner. When I demanded to be taken to you he did, as you can plainly see, comply with my request, although not in the manner in which I had hoped. And to you, innocent travelers," he said, nodding in the direction of Drefynt and Tarandron, "I must also apologize for involving you in matters in which you have no part."

"On the contrary . . ." began Drefynt and explained to the Hunter how he and Tarandron had been searching for Trondwyth and Catherine. One by one, each captive told some of the story of how he had come to be in the hut. Most shocking was Drefynt's revelation that Queen Cerebeth was no more, but Malthazzar now ruled in her stead. By late evening all were firm friends, united in the cause of Catherine against Malthazzar.

"We should sleep tonight. They will bring food in the morning, and then perhaps we can think of a way to escape," said Catherine.

"Aye," agreed the Hunter. "We should conserve our strength, for we shall be needing it soon. That traitor Jarrustin said that Queen Cerebeth would be here soon. We must be prepared for her when she arrives."

Catherine looked thoughtful, but she said nothing further. Gradually, one by one, the prisoners nodded off to sleep, awaiting the coming of a new day.

Gondalwyn's journeying was not hard. After crossing the mire and finding himself once more on firm ground, the apprentice wizard dwarf stayed only a short while, searching for a trace of the path taken by Iadron and Harsforn. Seeing no sign of their passage, he began to make his way northwestward, going up the side of a hill at a glancing angle so that his climb, though less steep than the most direct route would have been, was both longer and easier.

He stopped briefly at the brow of the hill and looked around. The view was magnificent. Behind him, the grassy hill dropped down into the Moortain Mire, on the other side of which the Redfyre Hills that encircled the mire once more rose, blocking the view beyond. In front of him the grass sloped down to the southern edge of Dankenwood. He could see over the tops of the trees across much of Palindor as far as Penmichael Brea in the distance. Bringing his eyes back to the forest before him, he could see that the dark trees that marked Dankenwood were only a narrow band. To his left, they became even narrower and eventually disappeared completely, so that the trees of the true Forest of Palindor met the grass at the foot of the hills some distance to his left. He hastened forward along the top of hill. Above him, high in the clear blue sky, he saw a hawk circling, searching for food.

After the better part of an hour of rapid walking, he

observed that now the dark trees of Dankenwood no longer stood between himself and the forest. He made his way down the slope, setting himself as best he could in the direction of northwest, for in that direction lay his destination, Smalterscairn. As he reached the bottom of the hill and entered the forest he did not look up. Had he done so, he would have seen a hawk cease its circling and, with a twist of its body but no flapping of wings, set out for Carn Toldwyn.

Gondalwyn's progress was hardly slowed as he came into the forest. The Forest of Palindor, which covered the greater part of the realm, was populated for the most part by tall evergreens, well spaced, so that a creature such as dwarf or gnome might move easily between them. Only near rivers and on the damper western side of the forest did passage become difficult, for there the evergreens, joined by deciduous trees, grew closer together, and the undergrowth became sufficiently dense to impede travel. Gondalwyn's greatest difficulty was to maintain a reasonably straight course, and in this he tried to guide himself by aid of the sun, whose golden rays shone easily through the airy branches above.

Even so, the march from the Redfyre Hills to the village of the wood elves was long. It was not until the morning of his fourth day of travel that Gondalwyn awoke from his night's sleep with the expectation of reaching his destination soon. Though hungry, he began on his way without pausing for breakfast. About midmorning he stopped briefly to eat a late breakfast of red berries. Then, setting his direction once more by the sun, he continued on his way.

In a few minutes he saw first an oak tree and then a willow, a sure sign of water not far distant. Another ten minutes of rapid walking and he saw in front of him a small elf house, the first habitation on the outskirts of Smalterscairn.

For the first time since he began his trek, he stopped and pondered what he would do next. He could march boldly into Smalterscairn, but to do so seemed foolhardy. He did not know for sure whether his friends had yet arrived there; further, he had no way of knowing whether the town was inclined toward Catherine's cause or against it. On the other hand, if he tried to enter unnoticed he was not likely to be successful. Wood elves being who they were, he would be discovered and made to explain himself. Neither eventuality pleased him, and he considered his problem for several minutes. Eventually he thought that he saw a solution.

He removed the pack from his back and hid it behind a tree out of sight of the cottage ahead. Then he carefully untied the Dark Sword from the pack and took a firm grasp of its hilt. Holding the sword so that it pointed upwards, he waved his hand over it, being careful not to touch the dark weapon. As he waved his hand, he muttered an incantation. The sword began to shimmer in his hand, then slowly it faded from sight.

Holding his hand carefully to keep the point of the now-invisible sword from touching anything, he moved forward toward the village. He passed three small houses, sure that he was being watched. He saw no sign of the watchers, but as he drew in front of a small, windowless hut, he heard the scurrying sound of elvish feet at a run through the trees nearby, as if some creature were hurrying into the village for help. For a second, he paused, unsure what to do. The hut before him had a single doorway which was barred by a plank and guarded by a serious-looking wood elf carrying a spear taller than himself.

He stepped forward until he was standing in front of the elf guard, who lowered his spear and pointed it threateningly toward the dwarf. Gondalwyn heard the sound of more scurrying feet behind him, but he did not turn. He tightened his grip on the invisible sword.

The elf before him said nothing, but his stance made it clear that Gondalwyn was not to approach any closer.

"Good morning to you," said Gondalwyn. "Gondalwyn, dwarf of Mourn, at your service."

"Tretenar, wood elf of Smalterscairn at yours," replied the elf, bowing his head ever so slightly.

"I am surprised to see a wood elf guarding a hut in such a manner. Tell me, what is inside?"

"You will find out soon enough," said a stern voice behind him. Gondalwyn swiveled and found himself confronted by a group of wood elves numbering at least twenty, all save one armed. The single unarmed elf, who wore a narrow gold chain about his neck and appeared to be the leader, commanded two of his companions to raise the plank barring the doorway to the hut. Gondalwyn was unceremoniously pushed inside, and the door closed and barred behind him.

For a second there was silence and then the hut, which was by now becoming quite full, erupted with joyful greetings and stories quickly retold.

Eventually Catherine asked, "Gondalwyn, why did they let you in here when you are armed?"

Gondalwyn glanced at his hand, but the sword was still invisible. He smiled inwardly at this further confirmation that Catherine was indeed the High Queen whose arrival had been prophesied many years ago. "Armed, my lady? Tell me, what weapon do you see?"

"Why, you are holding that terrible Dark Sword on which I cut myself. I repeat my question: why did they let you in here with such a fearsome weapon?"

The dwarf carefully extended his arm towards Catherine. "Catherine, High Queen, the sword is invisible to all eyes except yours. They knew not that I carried a weapon. And now I gladly offer you the sword, so that you may use it as you see fit."

Catherine held out her hand and grasped the hilt firmly. As before when she had held the dread weapon, she felt a strange tingling in her hand. But this time the tingling was stronger and spread rapidly up her arm and through her entire body. As the companions watched, her face seemed to glow in the dim half light which filtered through the roof of the hut.

Then the sword slowly began to appear in her hand. At first there was just a shimmering shadow, a hint of what might be there, then the sword in all its awesome blackness stood clearly in her hand.

Gondalwyn watched carefully as his spell was undone by powers far greater than the meager learning that he possessed. Then he was doubly surprised to see a sudden glint come from the sword, as if a hint of fires hidden deep within. The glint disappeared as quickly as it had come, but the dwarf knew then that there was more to this sword than met the eye.

Catherine looked around the hut and spoke in a voice of authority. "Come, we must not tarry. The queen's servants will soon be here, and this is neither the time nor the place for such a meeting. We must leave here immediately. Gondalwyn, remove the plank that bars our way."

Gondalwyn turned to face the door. Catherine crouched on the ground beside him, ready to spring out as soon as the door was open. Closing his eyes with concentration, the apprentice wizard moved his hands slowly in front of him. Words came from his lips as sweat formed on his brow.

All in the hut were tense; there was no sound other than the quiet incantations coming from Gondalwyn. Then there was a thud from outside, and the dwarf turned to the High Queen. Bowing slightly, he said, "It is done. The way is no longer barred." With a slight movement of his hand the door opened, seemingly of its own volition, and the dwarf found himself staring into the eyes of Tretenar, the elf guarding the hut.

But Tretenar's eyes did not return the gaze. Instead they were fixed on those of the human next to Gondalwyn, who was now moving out through the open doorway and bringing herself to her full height as she did so. Tretenar took a step backward as Catherine stepped into the open. As the sunlight touched the sword in her hands, it became transformed. No longer was it a dull, dark shadow; instead, a light poured forth from the blade and Catherine lifted it high in front of her. Tretenar turned from the sight of the High Queen and, his legs carrying him as quickly as ever they had before, he fled from that place.

Behind her, Catherine's companions streamed out of the hut. One glance at the weapon which Catherine held in her hand was sufficient for Gondalwyn.

"*Scalm y t*, the sword of the High Queen!" he exclaimed.

And indeed there could be no mistaking the sword that Catherine carried. It glistened in the sunlight, not so much reflecting the rays as adding to them its own light.

"Weapons," said Aramis. "We must have weapons. *Scalm y t*, for all its power, is but one sword. We must have more."

"But where did they put them?" asked Tarandron.

They were startled to hear a voice from behind them. They turned and saw Caldorn, Jarrustin's page.

"Hurry!" the elf said. "They are all meeting in the square, waiting for the queen's guard to arrive and take you away. Tretenar, who was guarding you, will bring them here at any moment, and they must not find me here. Be gone into the forest, down the path by which the dwarf entered the village. Wait for me, and I will return with what weapons I can carry."

Catherine bowed to the page and then led her companions along the path into the forest. They traveled only a short way before halting near Gondalwyn's pack.

He scrabbled around inside and withdrew Iadron's gift, which he offered to Catherine. "Scelberon, the sword's scabbard," he said.

She tied it around her own waist and then sheathed the sword effortlessly. The white gemstone embedded in the scabbard flared brightly.

They had but a short while to wait before Caldorn reappeared, carrying the Hunter's bow and quiver of arrows and, with difficulty, for the weight was great, Tarandron's battle-ax.

The wood elf dropped the weapons at the feet of the group and turned reluctantly to return to his village.

"Hold, master elf," commanded Catherine. "Your place is surely by our side."

Caldorn looked up gratefully. "Thank you, Your Majesty. I would be honored to be counted among your companions." He stepped back into the circle.

"Come, we must hurry from this place before it is overrun by the elven army or, worse yet, the queen's soldiers," said Catherine. So saying, she began to move once more along the path.

They traveled for perhaps two hours before stopping

deep in the forest to take stock of their position. All agreed that Catherine should lead them, but she was undecided herself what they should do next. Alone of all of them she was a stranger to Palindor, and so had the least understanding of the geography of that land. She knew that she must face Malthazzar and was about to order them forward to Carn Toldwyn when Gondalwyn remembered his conversation with Olvensar in the chamber in the Mountains of Mourn.

"He told me that I must pass this on to Drefynt," said the dwarf. "My meeting with Olvensar took place in a ley chamber in the Mountains of Mourn. Does this mean anything to you, good gnome?"

Drefynt thought deeply for a moment. What message was Olvensar trying to give him? He was about to shake his head, when suddenly an idea came to him. The ley chambers were places renowned as being specially connected with the kirial that undergirded Palindor; but there was one other such place, a place of supreme kirial, not a chamber underground, but a monument standing high on a windswept moor.

"Of course! That's it!" Turning to the High Queen, he said, "We must not go to Carn Toldwyn. Olvensar intends the meeting with Malthazzar to happen in a place of great kirial. And that surely means that we should make for Toldwyn's Quoit, on the moor to the south of Carn Toldwyn. It is there that the battle is to take place."

23

CATHERINE
AND MALTHAZZAR

ALTHAZZAR WAS FURIOUS. So many times one or another of Olvensar's pawns had been in his grasp, but each time they had escaped. Only hours ago a messenger elf had arrived from Smalterscairn to inform his queen that the human for whom she had been scouring the land had been found and was prisoner in a guarded hut in the town. And now this.

Malthazzar, still with the outward appearance of Queen Cerebeth, tried to take the news calmly, but the hawk's message—that Catherine's entire party had escaped from Smalterscairn—enraged him. The bird, fearing his master's wrath, flew away, leaving Malthazzar alone with his anger.

Slowly the shape of the queen dissolved, and Malthazzar took his true black, shadowless form. The Lord of Evil paced the floor, thinking furiously. How could a mere human, little more than a child, pose a threat to his plans? Yet he knew that with Olvensar's hand guiding her anything was possible. And though he had not felt

Olvensar's presence in Palindor for some time—and that in the far-off Mountains of Mourn—Malthazzar was sure that somehow Olvensar must have had more than a passing involvement in the events of recent days.

Malthazzar's hawks had done their job well, reporting to him the movements of all those that he had determined were aiding the human. He had seen how all their paths had taken them to Smalterscairn, and had been hopeful that once there they could be captured and brought before him. It would have been just a moment's work to strike the girl-woman dead, thus ending all fear that the age-old prophecy might indeed come true.

Now fear was rekindled in Malthazzar's dark breast. Catherine had escaped and was on the move once more. The sword *Scalm y t*, the only weapon in the whole of Palindor that could stand against his power, had been recovered from Samuel Ironhand by his Dark Knights only to be lost once more, and now it could be anywhere in the realm. He could see Olvensar's hand in all this; surely it was only a matter of time before the human and the sword came together. Indeed, perhaps they had already done so. And of *Scalm y t* scabbard, Scelberon, without which the sword's power was severely weakened, there had been no trace. Perhaps that too would soon be in the enemy's hand. The dark shape shivered.

Alone in his room in the high north tower of the castle that overlooked the capital of Palindor, the spirit of Malthazzar became a black shadow. The shadow spread itself around the room and drifted out of the window. It grew and grew, rising high in the air as it did so. It covered the castle's grounds and grew further, until it covered the whole town of Carn Toldwyn. Some of the residents looked up toward the sun, unsure why they suddenly felt chilled, but they could see nothing to cause the sensation of cold. The invisible grayness grew further as Malthazzar searched his realm for traces of kiríal.

There, there, there . . . the spirit of Malthazzar could feel the pull of AND coming from the ley chambers around the kingdom: rooms, underground holes over which he had no control and about which he had not a little fear. His spirit did not approach these places, but spread itself wider over the land. The shadow reached Smalterscairn and, for the first time, ceased its growing.

Down there, near that hut, there had been recent kiríal, Malthazzar was sure of it. The cloud dropped closer to the ground, becoming darker as it did so, until it hovered just outside the hut where, only hours before, Catherine had wielded the sword *Scalm ɣ t*.

Yes, he was sure of it now. Catherine had *Scalm ɣ t* in her possession. The cloud was about to rise and depart when it halted. There was more. The cloud became a shade darker and colder as, far away in the tower in the castle, Malthazzar concentrated his thoughts, distilling them into the black cloud a third of a kingdom away. There was more here, more kiríal beyond the appearance of *Scalm ɣ t*. What was it? What was it?

Then suddenly Malthazzar knew. The dark cloud faded into nothingness and a suddenly tired Malthazzar moved once more in the castle tower. The time was truly upon him, for Catherine had not only the sword *Scalm ɣ t* in her possession, but also the scabbard Scelberon. Against the combined might of sword and scabbard he knew that his own powers would fail. If Catherine could strike him with the sword, he must flee this land, powerless to return for many years, his hopes for revenge against Olvensar dashed.

The darkness that was Malthazzar shrank, and once more he assumed the form of Queen Cerebeth. The door behind him silently unlocked itself and swung open, and the queen stormed out of the room to issue a proclamation.

The word went out quickly. Queen Cerebeth now had proof that the armies of Reglandor were poised, ready to invade Palindor. They were to be led by none other than the Lord of Evil, Malthazzar himself, and all they were waiting for was word from his spies that it was safe to move forward into Palindor. The young human woman was still somewhere in Palindor and must be stopped at all costs. The queen's command now was that she must be killed; the woman was a witch, with special powers granted her by Malthazzar, and she would kill any who tried to impede her if given the chance. She was traveling with a band of renegades that she had brought to her cause: a dwarf, two gnomes, a Hunter, and possibly a wood elf. If anyone saw this party, he was to report it immediately; the queen's Royal Guard was standing ready to ride anywhere in Palindor at a moment's notice to meet and kill the traitors. The queen herself would ride with her guard, for if the traitors and their human leader were not stopped, it would mean the end of Palindor as everyone knew it.

The word spread. Birds of the air flew from place to place, carrying the proclamation to all the dwellings in the land. Malthazzar knew that it could not be long before Catherine and her band were spotted and, as soon as they were, he was ready to ride forth to meet them.

It was two days of forced marching before Catherine's small band reached the easternmost edge of Machrenmoor. The little party traveled purposefully through the thickest parts of the forest, knowing that their chance of reaching their destination depended on their remaining unseen.

Around noon on the third day of traveling,

Machrenmoor suddenly lay exposed before them. For some time the land had been rising, and suddenly the thinning forest disappeared completely, its place taken by heather-strewn ground from which the occasional outcrop of granite sprang. The wind whipped around them as they stepped out from the shelter of the trees, and they drew their clothes tightly around them as protection. The sudden cold challenged the bright sunshine that poured down out of a nearly cloudless sky.

The companions climbed the first hill of the moor, and Trondwyth pointed out their destination atop the next one. Catherine shielded her eyes against the glare of the sun, but all she could see was what looked like a small group of stones standing atop the hill. Wordlessly, they began to move downwards into the shallow valley which separated the two hills.

Their emergence from the forest had not gone unnoticed. High above, a hawk saw the small group walking out into the open. It descended to take a closer look, to be sure of the message to take to his master in the castle not far away on the northern edge of Carn Toldwyn.

He swooped down toward the bedraggled party. As he flew no more than a few feet from their heads, satisfied that they were the ones whom his master sought, his eyes caught a sudden movement on the part of the tall human dressed in green.

Aramis let loose the arrow and it traveled straight and true. The bird dropped like a stone and was dead before it hit the ground.

Tarandron looked questioningly at the Hunter.

"A spying bird, my friend. It would have reported our presence to the Evil One," said Aramis.

Caldorn interrupted. "Then we must hurry, for look! There is another."

All eyes followed the direction of the elf's outstretched arm. There, high in the sky, they saw another hawk, already making its way northward toward the town.

"It will be there in minutes; we must hurry if we are to reach the quoit first," said Drefynt. "The way from the town is easier, and Malthazzar will be after us as soon as he hears of our presence. He will want to keep us away from the quoit at all costs."

They hurried down into the valley. The stones of their destination were no longer visible, hidden by the mass of the moor rising above them as they began the arduous climb up the other side.

All except Aramis were puffing heavily, short of breath, when once more they saw the stones. The ground below them became level once again as they reached the top, high plateau of the moor. The stones were no more than two thousand paces distant.

Far off to the north, they could see the northern part of Carn Toldwyn as it rose up the slopes of the hill on which the royal castle stood. The southern parts of the town and the path that led from the town to the moor were hidden by the intervening bulk of the moor itself. They could see no sign of movement.

Then Drefynt said, "Look!" He pointed toward the castle.

The others could see nothing.

"What is it, Drefynt?" asked Catherine. "I see nothing."

"What flag is flying from the castle?" asked Drefynt.

"I see no flag and, even if there were one, it would be too far to see its design."

"But a flag always flies when the queen is in her castle. If there is no flag she must have left, and I can think of only one reason for the queen to leave."

"We must hurry," said Catherine, and their weary legs

began to stride out across the final stretch between their party and the granite rocks. They did not stop until they were in the very shadows of the stones which made up the quoit.

Catherine had never seen anything like them before. There were only four stones here on the very highest point of bleak Machrenmoor. Three of them stood tall, taller even than the Hunter Aramis; great blocks of granite, one end buried in the ground, the other reaching high above them all. And across these three upright stones lay a fourth: a massive slab, perhaps a foot deep, but fifteen or more feet across. The quoit looked like a giant milking stool, or an enormous three-legged table.

"What is it?" asked Catherine.

Drefynt looked at her in surprise. "Why, it is the burial place of Toldwyn, First Warrior of Palindor. Come, we must enter."

Catherine was uncomfortable about walking between the stones. Though the lichen covering them made it obvious that the quoit had stood for many centuries, the moment that the sun was blocked out by the huge slab stone lying across the top of the other three stones, she felt a fear that the rocks would topple inward on her and she would be crushed to death. She closed her eyes and swallowed. Forcing herself to ignore her surroundings, she stepped further into the quoit.

In the very center of the stones was a fifth one, smaller and flatter than the one above her head, sunk into the ground beneath their feet. She wondered if it were beneath this stone that the warrior Toldwyn was buried. But she had no time for speculation, for now Aramis spoke, quietly and without fear, but in a voice which could not be ignored.

"They come," he said.

Catherine looked up, following his gaze, and drew in her breath. Coming across the flat moor from the north was an army ready for battle. She could not count the numbers accurately, but as she watched she saw the head of the army come to a halt and the sides spread out. The companions walked out from between the standing stones, so that they would be seen by the warriors.

The part of the army that they had first seen remained stationary, but from behind them more and more soldiers came, some astride horses, some walking. There were humans, gnomes, dwarves, elves, fauns, centaurs, even a smattering of goblins. Many of the creatures Catherine could put no name to. And still they came, spreading out, quietly forming a circle around the quoit.

The companions looked at one another but said nothing. All simply watched as the soldiers of Queen Cerebeth's army continued encircling the stones. At last it was done; no matter which way they faced, Catherine and her companions stared into the eyes of the army not a hundred paces distant. Still no one asked Catherine what they were to do.

Then, at the northernmost part of the circle, a small gap suddenly formed. The gap became wider and they saw a gnomish standard bearer astride a small pony make his way through the gap. Once inside the circle, the pony took a few paces and then the bearer moved his mount to one side.

Then the queen's carriage came into view. Pulled by a set of six magnificent steeds, the royal carriage passed through the circle which closed up behind it. The carriage stopped opposite the standard bearer. The carriage door opened, and out stepped Queen Cerebeth.

Drefynt could not help noticing how much less frail she looked than the last time he had seen her. Surely her courtiers had noticed the change in her? But no, he reflected, she had been seen so rarely that they probably had noticed nothing.

As for Catherine, she merely gazed at the old woman who stepped down from the coach before them. At first, she could hardly believe that this was the person against whom Olvensar had sent her to fight. But as Queen Cerebeth turned and faced the quoit, the eyes of the two queens met, and each saw in the other more than anyone else present had seen.

Malthazzar saw in Catherine the form of the hated High Lord Olvensar, the one who had banished him from his own kingdom, the one who was now threatening to destroy his plans to rule the Three Lands of Abuscan: Palindor, Reglandor, and Soltarwyn.

Catherine looked into the eyes of Queen Cerebeth and saw blue steel and a flaring hatred for her. She knew that one of the two of them would not leave this place alive.

Catherine heard a sound from one of her companions and turned to see Aramis nocking an arrow to his bow. Tarandron lifted his battle-ax from his belt. Catherine looked towards Drefynt, a query in her eyes.

The Holy Gnome shook his head. "No, Your Majesty. It is your fight, and you must not permit it."

The young High Queen, in a tired voice, said, "No, my friends. This is between Malthazzar and me. You must under no circumstances come to my aid. Do you understand?"

The Hunter and the dwarf gazed at the High Queen. Slowly, Tarandron let go the battle-ax, and it fell to the ground.

"Is that a command?" asked the Hunter, challenge in his eyes.

"It is. Replace your arrow; it is not necessary."

Aramis unhappily removed the arrow from the string and returned it to his quiver.

Catherine turned to face Malthazzar once more and, without thinking, took a pace forward, then another and then another. Queen Cerebeth also stepped forward, until the distance between them was little more than a sword's length. Neither the companions nor the encircling army moved. The two queens looked into each other's eyes. Slowly, Catherine's arm moved across the front of her body until her hand lay on the hilt of *Scalm y t*. But as she tried to withdraw the mighty sword from the scabbard, she found that her arm felt weak, as if all strength had suddenly flowed out of it. She tried to tear her gaze away from Queen Cerebeth, but the eyes before her would not let her turn away. She tried to close her eyelids, to shut out the gaze which was upon her, and she found that she was unable to do even that.

Then she noticed for the first time that a short scabbard was hanging from Cerebeth's side. The Queen of Palindor stepped closer, and slowly her hand withdrew the blade and held it upright before Catherine's eyes. The blade seemed to glow a dark gray, as if imbued with a deadly life of its own.

Catherine was aware of a circle of watching eyes as the queen's army looked on at the battle of wills. Looking into the eyes of her opponent, she felt hope ebbing away.

Under her breath, so that only Catherine could hear the words, Cerebeth spoke. "So, you foolish human, you thought that Olvensar's power would protect you here, did you? You should not have trusted him. Here my power is great, and here you will prove it by dying at my hand."

The queen twisted her wrist so that the dagger hung, point downward, over Catherine. It began to fall.

In that moment, a scream of horror came from the

direction of the quoit as the companions realized that their High Queen was about to meet her death. Malthazzar's eyes glanced away toward the quoit, and the spell was broken. Catherine jumped to one side, and the dagger slashed a hole in the side of her tunic and bit deep into the leather of her belt before Malthazzar pulled it free.

Catherine tried desperately to draw *Scalm y t* but found that she still could not pull the sword from the scabbard. Her strength was returning, but not quickly enough. The blade began to move free as Malthazzar prepared his dagger for another slash, this time sideways. The dagger's blade glittered darkly as it swept from left to right in front of Catherine.

She tried to dodge backward, but the blade once more ripped through her tunic just below the throat, and now the tip of the blade broke through Catherine's skin and she saw the blade finish its swath with drops of red on its tip. As she moved backwards, *Scalm y t* at last came free in her hand. For a brief moment the blade shone with a deep power before her eyes, but the effort of freeing the sword from its scabbard caused her to lose her footing on the stunted, slippery grass. She slipped sideways down to the ground.

Looking upward, the scene burnt itself into her mind. All around was a ring of creatures, each leaning forward to see the end of the enemy. Above her stood Malthazzar, only the dark eyes—black now, no longer blue—betraying the fact that this was indeed Malthazzar, not Cerebeth. Malthazzar brought the dagger up high above his head, point downward, ready for the single, final thrust which would put an end to Catherine.

Catherine looked downward, casting her eyes away from the sight of the sword momentarily hanging over her, and her eyes came to the grass in front of her. There they saw, smeared with drops of blood, the pebble which she had worn for so long around her neck. The slashing of the dagger had ripped through the stone's thong, and both pebble and thong had spilled out to lie on the grass in front of her.

As she looked at the stone only inches from her eyes, time seemed to stand still.

"Malthazzar, Malthazzar." The words sprang from her lips as she gazed at the pebble. The moment seemed to last for ever. Vaguely, she wondered why the death blow had not yet fallen, but still she kept her eyes on the stone. As she watched, the stone turned from gray to black. A dark cloud seemed to fly out of the stone and attach itself to the form standing over her which now staggered back and dropped the dagger it had been holding.

Around her, the circle that had been pressing toward her fell back with a communal indrawing of breath as the onlookers watched a transformation come over the one who had led them to this place. Before their eyes, their queen became taller and darker. Suddenly a feeling of fear, of the knowledge that evil incarnate was nearby, gripped each creature in the circle.

Catherine continued to stare into the Seeing Stone of Ganvestor; she saw black shadows fighting, surrounded by a yet deeper black. She saw black blood dripping from black weapons held in black hands. Malthazzar took another step backward, his eyes covered by his hands. Those in the ring nearest him backed farther away, for there was now no doubting who it was before them.

The dark, shadowy cloud that had emanated from the stone became even darker and swirled around the figure that it enveloped so that it became harder to distinguish cloud from creature. Then across the breadth of the moor and beyond was heard a scream. It was not loud, yet it carried to the very ends of the Three Lands. And each creature who heard it knew that the sound could only have come from Malthazzar, the Lord of Evil.

As Catherine watched the stone, she too heard the scream. Her blood chilled at the hatred contained in the sound, hatred directed at her and the ancient power she represented. An image of the old gardener as she had last seen him in the ley chamber in the Mountains of Mourn came to her. He looked so real, as if he were present in the flesh, his inscrutable eyes looking at her, into her, through her with an incomprehensible depth, power, and assurance. A wave of peacefulness swept over her as the man's name formed itself on her lips. Quietly she spoke the name: "Olvensar."

The quiet word was swallowed by the sound emanating from the black cloud; yet, as she spoke the name, her fear of the dark sound was completely gone, even as that sound took on a new, tormented quality. There was a twisting in her hand and *Scalm y t* flew out of her hand, flinging itself toward the form of Malthazzar, now several steps distant.

Catherine watched as the sword reached the cloud around Malthazzar. The cloud flickered for a moment and then became the darkest black that she had ever seen, swallowing the very light that surrounded it. There was a tremendous crack, like a thunderclap, and then the cloud began slowly to turn lighter and thinner. As it dissipated, she could see that there was no longer anyone inside it. A wind sprang up from the sea, and quickly the cloud turned from black to gray to white. In a few moments, it could be seen no more.

A sudden exhaustion overtook Catherine. Her head fell to the ground, and she slept.

24

THE CHOICE

ER FRIENDS HAD remained in the shadow of the quoit during Catherine's battle with Malthazzar. Each one of them had wanted to do something to help the High Queen, but Catherine's command as well as the certainty that this was Catherine's battle had stayed their hands.

But the moment they saw Catherine's head fall to the ground, they all ran forward to help as quickly as they could. As Aramis, the fleetest of them, knelt down by her side, some of those in the encircling army moved forward to offer assistance.

Catherine was carried back to the castle in the royal carriage while word of who she was spread. By the time that they arrived in the courtyard of the castle there were few in Carn Toldwyn who did not know that the prophesied High Queen was now in the town.

Gondalwyn rode in the carriage with Catherine. When he had first seen the bloodstained tunic, he had been concerned that she had been cut by a dark blade just as had happened in the Mountains of Mourn. He watched the cut anxiously for signs of darkening of the skin, but was relieved to see that there was no such change.

Catherine opened her eyes wearily as the carriage drew to a halt at the castle.

"It's over," said Gondalwyn. "How do you feel?"

"Tired. So tired," replied Catherine and then closed her eyes once more.

The High Queen was carried into the castle and laid upon a bed. She slept for nearly two full days, a watch being kept over her every moment of that time. Then she awoke, lifted her head, and looked around with a sparkle in her eyes that showed Drefynt, who was looking over her, that it truly was over at last. The High Queen was ready to take her place on the throne.

The inhabitants of Palindor wanted Catherine to become their queen, just as Cerebeth had been before her, but Drefynt explained that a High Queen, while entitled to sit on the throne, was not permitted to rule in the usual sense. Normally the son or daughter of the previous king or queen would accede to the throne, but Queen Cerebeth had died childless.

Much debate followed as to who would rule the land, and eventually a solution was found. In place of a single monarch, a council of ministers was chosen by the people. This council would have five members, and by common consent the first council comprised Gondalwyn, Tarandron, Drefynt, Trondwyth, and Aramis.

Aramis soon found that he had no taste for life in the town and left to return to the forest that he knew so well. His place was taken by Caldorn, the young wood elf.

A full year passed in Palindor. Learning was reintroduced to the schools. Drefynt and Trondwyth were kept busy trying to remember as much as they could of the Holy Books that they had once read, in order to try to record at least some portion of their wisdom for the benefit of others.

Catherine recovered fully from her battle with Malthazzar and was greeted with joy and thankfulness wherever she went in the kingdom. She traveled widely, visiting almost all the realm, excepting only the northwest corner near Penmichael Brea and the Sunset Islands which lay over the horizon to the west. She and Gondalwyn were preparing a visit to the latter toward the end of the summer, when one afternoon she felt the desire to be alone.

She slipped out of the castle and wandered the streets of Carn Toldwyn. Eventually she found herself heading northward outside the town. After a while, she entered the gardens that housed the entrance to the catacombs.

In the past year the gardens, in accordance with Drefynt's wishes, had been attacked by a team of gardeners, and they were now one of the greatest sources of pride in the land. The grass almost glowed green as the High Queen walked over it, drinking in the feast of color around her. She passed the entrance to the catacombs, where the stone was still rolled in front of the cave.

Suddenly she stopped in front of a small pool. From the center of the water grew a tree, still young but with a single yellow-orange fruit hanging from one of the branches. She halted, abruptly transfixed by the sight. Somewhere in the back of her mind she was sure that she had seen such a sight before, strange though it was. She looked at the tree and the lone fruit carefully, her eyes narrowing. Then from behind her came a voice.

"Katrin."

She spun around, not so much startled by the sound as

frightened by the word. Where had she heard that word before?

Turning, she saw the unmistakable figure of Olvensar clad, as ever, in the dirty overalls that may once, long, long ago, have been green, and carrying in one hand an ancient wooden staff. Olvensar, his eyes meeting the High Queen's, stepped closer, until she could have touched him had she so wished.

But she was still trying to place the word that he had uttered. Somewhere, in a dark, distant corner of her mind, she seemed to recognize that word.

"Look, Katrin," Olvensar said, his arm pointing down towards the pool at their feet.

She turned back to the pool and peered into its depths. At first all she could see was the reflection of the tree with its single fruit mirrored in the still waters. But as she looked further, another scene began to come into focus. She saw that it was a room: a white room with three occupants, all human. One was lying on a bed covered with white sheets that almost glistened, they were so clean. The other two were standing near the bed, looking down at the person on the bed.

Gradually the scene became clearer, and she could see the faces of the two who were standing: a man and a woman. They wore an expression that she had not seen before, a mixture of worry and of hope long since turned to despair. She saw a tear running down the cheek of the woman. As she looked into that face, once more the High Queen became puzzled. She knew she had seen that face before: long ago, it seemed now, as if in a dream. Desperately she tried to remember.

She followed the direction of the tear-filled gaze toward the bed, looking at the figure lying there. It seemed to be a girl, asleep, but in a way that she had not seen before. Tubes of some sort were going to the girl's nose, mouth, arm and under the bedclothes. She studied the face of the girl. And then she recognized the face and remembered it all.

She drew in her breath sharply and looked away from the pool toward the old man standing next to her.

His eyes met hers, unblinkingly. "It is your choice," he said. "I cannot make you choose one way or the other. Do you stay here, or do you return whence you came?"

The High Queen looked back at the scene in the pool. It was like a still photograph that was now perfectly in focus. Nothing moved, the one moment of decision trapped inside the pool, waiting to be released, its future to be decided by a word from the High Queen.

"What happens if I don't go back?" she asked.

"Then you will remain here and die in that world," came the answer.

"And if I do go back, will I ever return here?"

"That is not for you to know."

The girl looked back into the pool. She looked first into her father's face as he tried to be brave, then into her own, unreadable, as cold as death itself, and then, finally, into her mother's.

Unblinking and without looking away from that third face, she made her decision. "I must go back."

"You are indeed a High Queen, for few would have had the strength so to decide," said Olvensar.

Out of the corner of her eye, she saw him raise his staff and tap it lightly on the ground. Still she kept her eyes on the face of her mother. The face seemed to grow larger, coming closer, as if she were falling into the pool. Then the picture began to dissolve, becoming more and more blurred. She felt dizzy, confused, and closed her eyes to try to maintain her balance.

Katrin suddenly realized that she was no longer standing; that, instead, she was lying down on what felt like a hard bed, and she seemed to be encased in a cocoon of some kind. Then the pain hit her, great waves of pain in her head and left arm especially. Vaguely, she realized that one of the tubes in the scene in the pool had led to the girl's left arm.

She felt weak, weaker than she ever had done before. Summoning every ounce of her strength, she struggled to open her eyes. They flickered open once, twice, and then the third time she found that she could keep them open. Two faces hovered over her, and gradually they came into focus.

She tried to smile and then weakly she spoke.

"Hello, Mom and Dad. I'm back."

The body of this text was created in twelve point Garamond type with fourteen point leading. The initial caps are from volume 5 "Paris Book of Hours," by BBL Typographic and the font used is Tiffany. *Palindor* was printed on 35# Mandobrite paper.